SO SAY THE FALLEN

Stuart Neville

SO SAY THE FALLEN

Harvill *Secker*

LONDON

1 3 5 7 9 10 8 6 4 2

Harvill Secker, an imprint of Vintage,
20 Vauxhall Bridge Road,
London SW1V 2SA

Harvill Secker is part of the Penguin Random House group of companies
whose addresses can be found at global.penguinrandomhouse.com

Penguin
Random House
UK

Copyright © Stuart Neville 2016

Stuart Neville has asserted his right to be identified as the author of this
Work in accordance with the Copyright, Designs and Patents Act 1988

First published by Harvill Secker in 2016

www.vintage-books.co.uk

A CIP catalogue record for this book is available from the British Library

ISBN 9781910701515 (hardback)
9781910701522 (trade paperback)
9781473524460 (paperback)

Typeset in India by Thomson Digital Pvt Ltd, Noida, Delhi

Printed and bound in Great Britain by Clays Ltd, St Ives plc

Penguin Random House is committed to a sustainable future
for our business, our readers and our planet. This book is made
from Forest Stewardship Council® certified paper.

MIX
Paper from
responsible sources
FSC
www.fsc.org   FSC® C018179

For Jo, who has given me so much.

'I can't just live for the other world. I need to live in this one now.
So say the fallen. So they've said since time began.'

The Drop, Dennis Lehane

I

Detective Chief Inspector Serena Flanagan focused on the box of tissues that sat on the coffee table between her and Dr Brady. A leaf of soft paper bursting up and out, ready for her tears. Just like when she'd been diagnosed with cancer. A box like this one had sat close to hand on the desk. She didn't need one then, and she didn't need one now.

Dr Brady had no interest in abnormal cells, growths, tumours. Flanagan's mind was his concern. He sat cross-legged in the chair on the other side of the table, chewing the end of a biro. It clicked and scratched against his teeth, a persistent noise that triggered memories of exam halls and waiting rooms, and made Flanagan dig at her palms with her nails.

The counsellor pursed his lips and inhaled through his nose in a way that Flanagan found even more irritating than the click-scratch of the pen. Irritating because she knew it preceded another question that she had no desire to answer.

'Do you feel you owe anything to Colin Tandy's family?' he asked.

'No,' Flanagan said. 'Nothing.'

'You're quite emphatic about that.'

'He made his choice,' she said. 'He set out to kill me that morning. He failed. So I killed him.'

Dr Brady paused, his gaze fixed on hers, a small smile on his lips that might have appeared kindly to anyone but Flanagan.

'But you didn't kill him,' he said. 'You killed the other one, the gunman. Colin Tandy rode away on the motorbike. You had nothing to do with him winding up under a bus.'

Flanagan saw herself outside the small terraced house on the outskirts of Lisburn where she'd taken a statement from an assault victim. She remembered the street, the graffiti painted white on red brick. She saw the bike, the two men, the semi-automatic pistol aimed at her, felt the Glock 17's grip in her hand. Something hot splitting the air close to her ear. Then the pillion passenger's helmet cracked open, the jammed pistol useless in his hand. She felt the empty cartridge, sent spinning from the chamber of the Glock, bounce off her cheek. In her mind she heard the brass hit the pavement, a sound like a Christmas bauble falling from the tree, but she knew she couldn't possibly have heard it over the noise of the traffic and the screaming.

She saw the passenger – Peter Hanratty, she later learned – lean back on the motorcycle's pillion seat. Then she put one in his chest. This time the cartridge spun into her hair before falling away, falling like the passenger – except he didn't. His torso hung over the motorcycle's back wheel, his arms suspended at his sides, feet caught on the rests.

Flanagan moved her aim to the rider, saw the fear in his eyes as she aligned the forward and rear sights of her pistol.

Not armed.

The thought pushed through the terrible stillness of her mind. She couldn't shoot him. He wasn't armed. But still she kept pressure on the trigger; a fraction more and the next round would discharge, sending the bullet through the visor of his helmet to pierce him somewhere between his left eye and the bridge of his nose.

They stayed there, both of them, frozen for a second that felt like a day. He knew he was going to die. She knew she was going to kill him.

But she couldn't. He wasn't armed.

Flanagan eased her finger from the trigger, released the pressure. He saw the movement of her knuckle, and the bike launched away, spilling the dead passenger to the ground.

She wouldn't find out until later that bike and rider wound up under a bus only two streets away.

Tandy didn't die. Not then. He lived on, if it could be called living, for another five years before what remained of him slipped away. Detective Superintendent Purdy had told her in the canteen at Lisburn station during lunch a few weeks ago. Perhaps he could have chosen a better time and place, but how was he to know? Flanagan herself wouldn't have dreamed the news would tear her in two.

She broke down there in the canteen, in front of everybody – constables, sergeants, inspectors, detectives, cooks, cleaners. They all saw her collapse, levelled by a desperate grief for a man that deserved none from her.

Six sessions she'd had, now. At the end of the first, as Dr Brady glanced once again at the clock on the wall behind Flanagan, he told her what she'd already figured out for herself: every possible emotion she had about that morning more than five years ago had been wrapped up, tied down, stowed away while Tandy lived the non-life he had condemned himself to. Only when his body followed his brain into death did the memory rupture and every distorted feeling spill out where she could no longer deny it. Guilt at the men's deaths, fear at almost meeting her own, elation at surviving, sorrow for their families. These things had grown there in the dark, swelling and bloating like the rogue cells in her breast, until the whole of it flooded her at once, drowning her, more emotion than she could hold within.

Flanagan didn't remember much about the incident now, the initial breakdown, only how frightened DSI Purdy had looked, the shock on his face. Looking back now, weeks later, it seemed as if she had watched herself from across the room, seeing some other woman splinter into jagged pieces. And if she could, she would have told that woman to pull herself together, not to make a spectacle of herself.

A week of leave and three months of counselling had been prescribed. As if that would fix everything, as if this smug doctor could plaster over the fissures in Flanagan's mind by simply talking about the incident.

She and Alistair used the unexpected break to book a last-minute holiday in Portstewart on the north coast. An apartment near the old golf course, overlooking the sea. It was a good week. Days spent at the Strand, the long sandy beach at the other end of the town, even if the weather didn't justify it. They ate at the new restaurant between the dunes, a converted National Trust building, little more than a shack on the beach. Glorious breakfasts and lunches devoured before returning to the sand and the water.

Almost a week of peace, as near to happiness as they'd come in the last year.

One night, as sea spray whispered on the bedroom window, they talked about the proposed counselling. 'What harm could it do?' Alistair asked.

More than you can imagine, Flanagan had thought. But she said, 'All right, I'll give it a go.'

And Alistair had put his arms around her and they had made love for the first time in months. He had no nightmares that night, had barely any during the week by the sea. But after, when they returned to their house outside Moira, the terrors came back. There had been little intimacy between Flanagan and her husband since.

'Time,' Dr Brady said, smiling that fake smile of his.

Flanagan looked over her shoulder and saw that the session was done. She quietly thanked God and left the room with the most cursory farewell she could get away with.

2

Roberta Garrick walked him along the hall to the rear sitting room of her beautiful house. The room that had been converted to a hospital ward. Reverend Peter McKay followed her, feeling as if she dragged him by a piece of string. Conflicting desires battled within him: the desire for her body, the fear of the room beyond, the need to run. But he walked on regardless, as much by Roberta's volition as by his own.

Mrs Garrick. After all that had happened, he had only recently stopped thinking of her by that name. Even when he had bitten her neck at the force of his climax, her thighs tight around his waist, she had still been Mrs Garrick to him. She was Roberta now, and the intimacy of using her first name frightened him.

She stopped at the door, snug in its frame, and took the handle in her palm. For the hundredth time, McKay noted the length of her fingers, the smooth near-perfection of her skin, the nails just long enough to scratch. She turned the handle and pushed the door.

Her husband, still Mr Garrick to him in spite of all the hours McKay had spent at this bedside, lay where he'd left him last night. But dead now. Even from the doorway, from the other side of the room, it was obvious a corpse lay there. McKay imagined if he touched Mr Garrick's forearm the skin would be cold against his fingertips. Like a side of meat.

Bile lurched up into McKay's throat at the thought, and he swallowed it. Now was not the time to be squeamish. He had been a rector for two decades, presided over more funerals than he could remember, seen hundreds of cadavers lying in a waxy illusion of sleep. This was no different.

Keep hold of yourself, he thought. Whatever happens, keep hold of yourself.

Roberta took slow, measured steps from the threshold to her husband's side. McKay followed, keeping back from the bedside. What had once been a spacious sitting room was now cramped, with a wardrobe and a chest of drawers, a bedside locker, a television on the wall and, facing that, the electric care bed.

A care bed. Not a hospital bed. Mr Garrick had been quite clear about the distinction, though McKay could see little difference between this and the beds that populated every hospital ward he'd ever visited. Cost thousands, Mr Garrick had said. It lay positioned so that he could see through the patio doors, out onto the beautifully tended garden and the trees beyond. Now the curtains were drawn, and the sun would never shine on Henry Garrick again.

McKay put a hand on Roberta's firm, still shoulder and felt the warmth of her through the fabric of her light dressing gown. Warm skin, not cold, like her husband's would surely be. McKay swallowed bile once more. He squeezed gently, but if she felt the tightening of his fingers she did not let it show.

Her husband lay like a man in sound sleep, his mouth open, his eyes closed. A snore should have rattled out of him.

What devastation, McKay thought. How Mr Garrick had lived this long was mystery enough. A little less than six months ago he had been driving his favourite car, an early seventies Aston Martin V8 Vantage, through the country lanes that surrounded the village. The investigators had estimated his speed at the time of the accident as approximately fifty-five miles per hour. Charging around the bend, he had managed to swerve past all but one of the cluster of cyclists he had come upon. One of them, a young father of two, had died within moments of being struck, his helmet doing him little good against the force of the impact with the Aston's bonnet.

Mr Garrick had not been so lucky. As the car swerved then spun, it swept through a hedgerow before barrel-rolling across a ditch and into a tree. The car's front end buckled, forcing the engine back into the cabin, taking Mr Garrick's legs.

The fire had started soon after. The cyclists who had such a narrow escape did all they could, one of them suffering severe burns as he dragged what remained of Mr Garrick from the wreck. Another was a nurse, well experienced in trauma surgery. They kept him alive, whether or not it was a merciful act.

Regardless, now he lay dead, drool crusting on his scarred chin. Pale pink yogurt clinging to the wispy strands of his moustache. The same yogurt his nightly sachet of morphine granules was mixed with. Ten empty sachets lay scattered on the table over his bed, behind the row of framed photographs. One of Mr Garrick's parents, long gone, one of him and Roberta on their wedding day, another of his wife, tanned and glowing, smiling up from a beach towel. Then finally a small oval picture of Erin, the child they had lost before her second birthday.

Reverend Peter McKay had presided over that funeral too. One of the hardest he'd ever done. Grief so raw it had charged the air in the church, made it thick and heavy. McKay had heard every sob trapped inside the walls, felt each one as if it had been torn from his own chest.

Roberta reached out to the picture of the smiling child, touched her fingertips to the face. McKay moved his hand from her shoulder, down her arm, until his fingers circled her slender wrist.

'It's maybe best you don't touch anything,' he said. 'For when the police come.'

Then Roberta's legs buckled and she collapsed to her knees beside the bed. She reached for her husband's still hand, buried her face in the blanket, close to where his legs should have been. McKay watched as her shoulders juddered, listened as her keening was smothered by the bedclothes. The display of grief quietly horrified him, even though his rational mind knew hers was a natural and inevitable reaction. But his irrational mind, that wild part of him, clamoured, asking, what about me? What about me? What about us?

McKay kept his silence for a time before touching her shoulder once more and saying, 'I'll make the phone calls.'

He left her to her wailing and exited into the hall.

Such a grand place. Mr Garrick had built it for his new wife when they first married seven years ago. Six bedrooms, half of them with bathrooms, three receptions, a large garage that held Mr Garrick's modest collection of classic cars. An acre of sweeping lawns and flower beds. Enough money to pay for a gardener and cleaner to look after it all.

They should have had a long and happy life together. But that was not God's will, Mr Garrick had once said after he and Reverend McKay had prayed together.

God had no part in it, McKay had almost said. But he held his tongue.

McKay seldom thought of God any more, unless he was writing a sermon or taking a service. Reverend Peter McKay had ceased to believe in God some months ago. Everything since had been play-acting, as much out of pity for the parishioners as a desire to keep his job.

No God. No sin. No heaven. No hell.

Reverend Peter McKay knew these things as certainly as he knew his own name.

He went to the telephone on the hall table, picked up the handset, and dialled.

3

Flanagan stood at the kitchen sink, a mug of coffee in one hand, looking out over the garden. Rain dotted the window, a lacklustre shower that had darkened the sky as she watched. Behind her, Alistair sat at the table with Ruth and Eli, telling them to eat their breakfast, they'd be late. Flanagan had showered and dressed an hour ago; she had her holster attached to her belt, the Glock 17 snug inside, hidden beneath her jacket, her bag packed and ready for the day. Still half an hour before she needed to go.

Mornings had been like this for months now. She rising early, still tired, her night's sleep fractured by Alistair's gasping and clutching. A year had passed since the Devine brothers had invaded their home, since one of them had plunged a blade into her husband's flank. A year since she had pressed wadded-up bedding against the wound, begging him not to die.

He blamed her. She brought this upon their family. He hadn't said so after that first night in the hospital, but she was certain he still believed it. Once, he had asked her to think about getting out of the force. Or at least leaving the front line, taking an admin role. Her reaction had been angry enough that he had never asked again.

Last night had been bad. Flanagan had lain silent, pretending to sleep as Alistair wept in the darkness. Choked, frightened sobs. Eventually, he had got up and left the room. She had heard the faint babble of the television from downstairs. At some point she had fallen asleep, only to be disturbed by the bed rocking as he got back in. He lay with his back to her. She rolled over and brought her body to his, her chest against his shoulders. He stiffened as she reached over and her hand sought his.

'You don't have to,' he said, his voice shocking her in the quiet.

'Have to what?' she asked.

'Pretend,' he said. 'With the children, maybe. But not with me.'

'I don't . . .'

Words hung beyond the reach of her tongue. Anger rose in her, but the root of his bitterness remained so veiled that she could form no argument against it. Instead, she rolled over and crept to her cold edge of the bed. She did not sleep again, rose with the sun, and set about preparing for another weary day.

So now she stood apart from them, as she did more often every day. Her husband and children at the table, she at the window, no longer even trying to make conversation with her family. An intruder in her own home, just as those boys had been.

Alistair's voice cracked her isolation. She turned her head and said, 'What?'

'Your phone,' he said, a tired sigh carrying the words.

Her mobile vibrated on the table, the screen lighting up.

She crossed from the sink and lifted it. Detective Superintendent Purdy, the display said.

Purdy had only a fortnight left on the job, retirement bearing down on him like a tidal wave. He had confided in Flanagan that although it had seemed like a good idea a year ago when he'd first started making plans, the reality of it, the long smear of years ahead, now terrified him.

Flanagan thumbed the touchscreen. 'Yes?'

'Ah, good,' Purdy said. 'I wanted to catch you before you left for the station. There's been a sudden death in Morganstown. The sergeant at the scene reckons suicide, so—'

'So you thought of me,' Flanagan said. 'Thanks a million.'

Flanagan hated suicides. In most cases, the minimum of investigation was needed, but the family would be devastated. Few grieve harder than the loved ones of someone who has taken their own life. They'd be coming at her with questions she could never answer.

'You're closer to Morganstown than you are to Lisburn,' Purdy said, 'so you can go straight there.'

'I'll leave now,' she said.

'Take your time. From what the sergeant said, it looks pretty straightforward. You remember that road accident about six months ago? The car dealer?'

Yes, Flanagan remembered. The owner of Garrick Motors, a large used car dealership that occupied a sprawling site on the far side of Morganstown. He had been badly burned, lost both of his legs, if Flanagan recalled correctly. A popular churchgoing couple, good Christians both. Close friends with one of the local unionist politicians. The community had rallied around them. After all, Mr Garrick had contributed much to the area over the years.

'The wife found him this morning,' Purdy continued. 'She phoned the minister at her church first. He went to the house, then he called it in. The FMO's on scene already.'

Flanagan knew the steps by heart. When a sudden death was reported, a sergeant had to attend to make an initial assessment. Was it natural? Had the deceased been ill? Was it suspicious? If the latter, including a suicide, the scene would be locked down, the Forensic Medical Officer summoned, and an Investigating Officer appointed.

Today, it was Flanagan's turn.

'What's the address?' she asked, pulling the notebook from her bag. She held the phone between her ear and shoulder as she uncapped the pen and scribbled it down.

Alistair looked up at her from his plate of buttered toast. Ruth and Eli kicked each other under the table, giggling.

'I can be there in ten minutes.' Flanagan stuffed the notebook back into her bag, then hoisted the bag over her shoulder. 'I'll call DS Murray on the way.'

She was halfway to Morganstown, trees whipping past her Volkswagen Golf, when she realised she hadn't said goodbye to her husband or children.

A uniformed constable opened the door to Flanagan. A beautiful house, inside and out, at the end of a sweeping drive. Not long built, by the look of it, and finished with enough taste to prevent its grandeur straying into vulgarity.

'Ma'am,' the constable said when Flanagan showed her warrant card. 'In the back.'

He looked pale. Flanagan wondered if it was his first sudden death. At least the next of kin had found the body, and the constable had been spared delivering the death notice. Flanagan remembered the first time she'd been given that duty, calling at the home of a middle-aged couple whose son had lost control of his new car. Everyone has to do it some time, the senior officer had said, might as well get it out of the way. Even thinking about it now soured Flanagan's stomach, and she had done dozens more since then.

She stepped into the hall, past the young officer. 'Where's the sergeant?' she asked.

Wooden floors. A staircase with polished banisters rose up to a gallery on the first floor, cutting the hallway in two. Art on the walls, mostly originals, a few prints. Framed scripture verses. A large bible ostentatiously open on the hall table.

Serious money, here, Flanagan thought. So much money there was no need for another penny, but still you couldn't help but make more. And yet it didn't save Mr Garrick in the end.

'In the living room,' the constable said, 'with the deceased's wife.'

Flanagan looked to her right, through open double doors into a large living room. A stone fireplace built to look centuries old. No television in this room, but a top end hi-fi separates system was stacked in a cabinet, high quality speakers at either end of the far wall. A suite of luxurious couches and armchairs at the centre, all arranged to face each other. The widow, Mrs Garrick, red-eyed and slack-faced sitting with a man whom Flanagan assumed to be the clergyman, even though he wore no collar. Her hands were clasped in his. The other uniformed officer sat opposite them: a female sergeant she recognised but whose name Flanagan could not recall.

She got up from the couch, and said, 'Ma'am.' She carried a clipboard, held it out to Flanagan.

'Are you my Log Officer?' Flanagan asked, keeping her voice respectfully low.

'Yes, ma'am.'

'Have you done this before, Sergeant . . .?'

'Carson,' the sergeant said. 'A few times. I know the drill.'

'Good,' Flanagan said, taking the offered pen. She saw Dr Phelan Barr's signature already scrawled on the 38/15 form. She signed beneath and handed the pen back. 'DS Murray's on the way. When he arrives, send him back, and I'll come and speak with Mrs Garrick. Then I want you on the door to the room, understood?'

'Yes, ma'am.'

'Is there a clear path from the door to the body?'

'Yes, ma'am.'

'Okay, make sure anyone you let in knows to stick to that.'

Flanagan looked over Sergeant Carson's shoulder to see Mrs Garrick and the rector watching from their place on the opposite couch. Flanagan nodded to them each in turn. 'I'll be with you in a few minutes,' she said.

She walked along the hallway to the right of the staircase. On the other side, she saw the dining room with its twelve-seater table, and the kitchen, all white gloss and black granite. And here what had once been another reception room but now was a makeshift care unit.

The Forensic Medical Officer, Dr Barr, stood over the corpse, writing on a notepad. Flanagan looked from him to the bed and the scarred ruin of a man beneath the sheets. She let a little air out of her lungs as she always did at the sight of a body. A tic she had borrowed from DSI Purdy.

Barr heard and turned to her. A small man in his late fifties who always managed to look dishevelled no matter how smartly he dressed. He was known to have a drink problem, had lost his marriage over it, yet Flanagan had never so much as caught a whiff of it on him, he kept it so well hidden.

'Ah, DCI Flanagan,' Barr said. 'Never a pleasure.'

'Likewise,' Flanagan said.

A small joke they always shared over a body. Neither of them enjoyed the company of the dead, but it was when they most frequently met. Flanagan took a step inside the room, smelled the hospital smell, and the death.

'Well?' she asked.

'I'll call it suicide,' Barr said, 'unless something remark-able turns up. I expect the post-mortem to confirm an over-dose of morphine granules.' He waved his pen at the wheeled overbed table that had been pushed aside, presumably to give Barr access to the body. 'I count ten sachets of granules. One mixed in with a carton of yogurt would be enough to give him a good night's sleep. I expect he dumped the lot in and chewed them up. He just swallowed and went to sleep. Simple as that.'

Flanagan saw the pot on the table, and the spoon in Mr Garrick's hand. And the framed photographs lined up on the table. She couldn't see them from here, but she assumed they were of loved ones, living and dead. Hadn't she heard something about the couple losing a child? A wisp of a memory, a conversa-tion overheard in the supermarket in Moira, did you hear about the Garricks? The wee girl drowned when they were on holiday, isn't it terrible?

Tragedy clustered around some families. Most lived their lives untouched by the kind of sorrow that plagued a few. One child lost, then another years later. Or illness of one kind or another taking a mother while her children were tiny, then a sibling, an uncle, or a cousin. Some families drew such misfortune to them like the pull of gravity.

Flanagan went to ask a question, but something stopped the words on her tongue. She looked again at the table pushed close to the patio door, one end pressed into the drawn curtain.

'What?' Barr asked, shaking her loose from her thoughts.

'Nothing,' she said. 'Any note?'

'No,' Barr said, 'but I don't think we need to wonder too hard about his motivation.'

Flanagan could not begin to imagine what the last six months had been like for this man, or for his wife. What kind of life could this be? Then she scolded herself. She knew plenty of police officers left mutilated by bombs who had fought back, fought hard, and made new lives for themselves. Painful lives, maybe, but meaningful nonetheless.

From the doorway, a voice said, 'Ma'am.'

Detective Sergeant Craig Murray, still nervous around her despite being her right-hand man for almost nine months. He had worked out well so far. Conscientious, reliable, smart enough to know when to shut his mouth. She'd keep him as long as she could. Good assistants were hard to come by; her last, DS Ballantine, hadn't worked out, even as capable as the young woman had been. The trust between them had broken down – it couldn't have done otherwise – and without trust, the relationship would not work. Ballantine would be all right.

Flanagan wouldn't be surprised if she made Detective Inspector within the next few years.

'What do you need me to do?' Murray asked.

'Stay here,' Flanagan said. 'Help Dr Barr with anything he needs. I'll be speaking with Mrs Garrick.'

She left them, walked along the hall to the double doors leading into the living room. Flanagan paused there and watched.

Mrs Garrick and the rector, hands still clasped together, staring at some far-off memory. Each looked as battered as the other, as if the rector grieved as hard as the widow. The police-woman noticed Flanagan, stood, and said, 'Ma'am.'

Flanagan entered the room and said, 'Thank you, Sergeant Carson, I can take it from here. You know what to do.'

Carson left them, and Flanagan walked to the centre of the room, stood in front of the minister and the widow. 'Mrs Garrick,' she said, 'I'm very sorry for your loss. I'm Detective Chief Inspector Serena Flanagan. Can we have a quick chat?'

The minister stood, releasing Mrs Garrick's hand, and reached for Flanagan's. A small and slender man, narrow-shouldered, salt-and-pepper hair, a neatness about him that bordered on prissy. As they shook, he said, 'I'm Peter McKay, the rector at St Mark's. Do you have to do this now, or could it wait for another time?'

'It's usually best to have an initial conversation as soon as possible,' Flanagan said. 'Mrs Garrick isn't obliged to talk to me, of course, but the sooner we get it out of the way, the better.'

McKay looked down at Mrs Garrick, who remained seated, worrying a tissue between her fingers. She still wore her silk dressing gown over her nightdress, red hair spilling across her shoulders. A good-looking woman, mid thirties. If not beautiful, then at least the kind to make men look twice. The kind teenage boys whispered to each other about, tinder for their adolescent fires.

'It's all right,' Mrs Garrick said, her voice firm despite the tears. 'Let's get it out of the way.'

'Thank you,' Flanagan said, sitting on the couch opposite. 'I'll be as quick as I can.'

McKay took his place once more beside Mrs Garrick, slipped his fingers between hers. He squeezed, Flanagan noticed, but Mrs Garrick did not return the gesture. Flanagan took her notepad and pen from her bag, readied them.

'Mrs Garrick,' she said, 'can you please tell me, as simply as you can, what happened last night and this morning.'

Mrs Garrick took a breath, held it as she closed her eyes, then exhaled. Her eyelids fluttered, releasing another tear from each. She wiped at her cheeks, sniffed, and then spoke.

'Everything was normal,' she said. 'Or as normal as it can be, I suppose. I made dinner for us both, cottage pie, easy for Harry to eat with a spoon, you see. I ate with him, with the tray on my lap. We do that every evening. Then Harry always has his yogurt for dessert. That's what he mixes the morphine granules with.'

'You didn't do that for him?' Flanagan asked.

'No. I did at first, but Harry insisted on doing it for himself a few days after he came home from the hospital. He hates being waited on. He wants to do as much for himself as he can, whether he's fit to or not.' Mrs Garrick's eyes went distant for a moment. 'He wanted to, I should say. Everything's past tense now. It'll take a while to get used to that, like when –'

She froze there, mouth open, words that would never leave her tongue. Flanagan remembered the photograph of the child and kept her silence.

After a while, Mrs Garrick blinked, inhaled, and continued.

'We kept the box of little morphine packets by the bed, where he could reach them. One sachet to get him through the night. The doctor told us he's not to chew the granules. They're supposed to be swallowed whole so they dissolve in his stomach as he sleeps. Best way to take them is to mix a packet with yogurt and just eat it with a spoon. So he ate his dinner as normal, then I helped him do his toilet. Then the doorbell rang, and it was Reverend Peter.'

The rector spoke up. 'I sometimes call by to see Mr Garrick. Just to chat, see how he's doing. We pray together.'

'I gave Peter the yogurt to take to Harry,' Mrs Garrick said.

'He didn't eat it, though. He said he'd keep it for later.'

Mrs Garrick turned to McKay. 'You were with him for, what, half an hour?'

'Something like that.'

'You didn't look in on him after Reverend McKay had left?' Flanagan asked.

'Reverend Peter,' McKay said. 'Or Reverend Mr McKay. But not . . .'

The rector's voice faded as his gaze dropped, his cheeks reddening.

Mrs Garrick cleared her throat and said, 'Just to kiss him goodnight. The yogurt was still there, and I told him to eat it up and get some sleep. I didn't go in after that. Some nights I do, some I don't. Depends how tired I am. I just cleared up, did the dishes, and went to bed myself.'

'And this morning?'

'I woke up before five, before the alarm went off. I usually wake Harry around six-thirty, and I like to have an hour or so to myself. When it's quiet.'

'I know the feeling,' Flanagan said, offering Mrs Garrick a hint of a smile.

'Anyway, this morning, I don't know why, but I decided to look in on him earlier than usual. Funny, that, isn't it? This morning of all mornings. I went to his door and I knew straight away something was wrong. He always snores when he's on the morphine. You can hear him on the other side of the house.'

Mrs Garrick's eyes brightened. 'Maybe that's why I went in to him, do you think? Maybe I wasn't conscious of it, but I didn't hear him snoring when I came downstairs, so that's why I went to his room. Is that why?'

She looked to Flanagan for an answer, as if being right would make everything better.

'Possibly,' Flanagan said, giving another kind smile.

This time, Mrs Garrick returned the gesture, but only for a moment before the smile fell away. 'So I opened the door,' she said, 'and I just knew. He hadn't turned his light off, the one by the bed. He was just lying there, all quiet and still, and I knew he was dead. My first thought was his heart, it'd just given up. Then I saw he'd moved the pictures from the locker, put them in front of him, and I wondered why he did that. And then I saw the spoon, and the box of sachets beside him on the bedclothes. So I knew then what he'd done.'

'But you didn't call an ambulance or the police,' Flanagan said.

'No,' Mrs Garrick said, now squeezing McKay's fingers between hers. 'Maybe I should have, but I suppose I wasn't thinking straight. Peter's been with us since the accident, every step of the way – before that, even. He's always been such a rock for us. Him and the Lord Jesus. So Peter was the first person I thought of.'

The rector spoke up. 'I came over as soon as Mrs Garrick called. And when I saw Mr Garrick, I called the emergency services.'

'Then we came in here and prayed,' Mrs Garrick said.

Flanagan pictured them both, kneeling, eyes closed, mouths moving, talking to nothing but air. Stop it, she told herself. They need their belief now. Don't belittle it.

'How about Mr Garrick's mood in recent days?' she asked. 'Had you noticed any change?'

'No,' Mrs Garrick said. 'His mood was up and down, it has been – had been – since the accident. Good days and bad days, like you'd expect. But he always had God with him. He always clung to that. Didn't he, Peter?'

McKay nodded. 'Harry always said God must have let him live for a reason. He wouldn't leave him to suffer like that if there wasn't a purpose behind it.'

'And what did you say?' Flanagan asked. The question rang more curtly than she'd intended and the clergyman flinched a little, before his expression hardened.

'I agreed,' he said. 'I could never say otherwise. It's what I believe.'

'Of course,' Flanagan said. 'But what changed?'

McKay's shoulders slumped. 'Who knows? Sometimes faith isn't enough, I suppose, no matter how much I'd like it to be. Sometimes faith lets us down.'

Flanagan saw something in his eyes in the moment before he looked away. An image flashed in her mind: a man falling. The image lingered long after her questions were done.

4

When it came to matters of faith, Reverend Peter McKay had lied so long and so often that he sometimes couldn't tell the difference himself. And no matter what he believed, or rather didn't, Mr Garrick had survived this long purely on the certainty that there was some greater reason for his agonised existence. McKay would never have told him otherwise.

This policewoman terrified him.

He wore his mask with such practised skill, he didn't think she could see through it, but still, the fear swamped him like cold water. She can't see, he told himself. She is blind to my sin.

If she knew what he had done, if she knew where his hands had been, what wicked sweetness he had tasted, her questions would not be so cordial. Her tone would not be so sympathetic.

'I think that's all for now,' she said. What did she say her name was? Flanagan, wasn't it? Yes, Flanagan. 'I will have more questions for you both once the coroner's report is done. And I'll need to get formal statements, but there's no immediate rush.'

She leaned forward, spoke softy.

'Mrs Garrick, there are things we need to do here. For your husband. Things you might not want to see. Things you might not want to hear. Is there somewhere you can go, maybe? Just for the next few hours?'

'My house,' McKay said. Perhaps too quick, too eager. As he watched Flanagan's face for a sign that she'd noticed, Roberta twitched her fingertips against his palm.

A warning. Careful. She'll know.

She'll know the things we did together.

But Flanagan's expression did not change from one of warm sympathy.

'That sounds like a good idea,' she said. 'And I'll know where to reach you if I need to. If that's all right with you, Mrs Garrick?'

Roberta hesitated, then nodded, and said, 'Of course.'

'Good,' Flanagan said. 'Perhaps you want to go to him. We can give you a few minutes alone, if you like. I'd just ask you not to touch anything.'

'Yes,' Roberta said. 'Please.'

She stood, and Flanagan and McKay did the same.

Flanagan took Roberta's hands in hers, saying, 'And once again, I'm truly sorry for your loss.'

McKay went to follow Roberta, but she turned, put a hand to his forearm, telling him, no, just me. Alone. He watched her leave, a feeling he could not identify biting at the edge of his consciousness.

'St Mark's, you said?'

Startled, he turned back to Flanagan. 'Yes,' he said. 'Morganstown. At the end of the main street.'

'I know it,' she said, scribbling on her pad. 'I think I've been to a couple of funerals there. You probably conducted the ceremonies.'

'Probably,' he said, walking away, towards the doorway. He stopped there, one hand against the frame. He watched the medical officer leave the rear room, stand respectfully outside it with his hands folded in front of him, next to the sergeant with her clipboard. Beyond them, Roberta, standing over her dead husband.

Don't weep, McKay thought. Don't weep. At least give me that.

But she wept, and for a moment so fleeting he couldn't be sure it had ever been at all, he hated her.

5

The photographer had finished his work long ago. Now the coroner-appointed undertakers wheeled the trolley into the room, the black body bag upon it open and ready to receive Mr Garrick. The empty morphine sachets, the yogurt pot, the spoon, had all been bagged up and taken away.

The undertakers rolled back the bedclothes, exposing what remained of the lower portion of Mr Garrick's body. One of the undertakers, a young man showing his inexperience, hissed through his teeth. A buttoned pyjama top covered Mr Garrick's torso, an adult nappy enclosed his groin. And the stumps of his legs beneath. Still wrapped in bandage and gauze, still stained brown and yellow with serous fluid. He rested on a layer of medical absorption pads, the kind Flanagan remembered from having her children, one of the indignities of childbirth no one mentions in polite conversation.

'Can't blame him, really, can you?'

The same undertaker who'd hissed a moment before. Flanagan looked up at him, but did not reply. He couldn't hold her gaze, though she hadn't meant it as a challenge. But what he'd said . . .

Can't blame him.

Blame him for what?

The older man said, 'I apologise for my colleague.'

The younger man's face flushed red as he whispered an apology of his own.

They counted off, then hoisted the corpse onto the trolley. They folded the body bag around Mr Garrick and zipped it closed, an ugly sound in this quiet room, then wheeled the trolley out to the hall. Dr Barr entered as they left.

'You still here?' Flanagan asked.

'I was going to ask you the same thing,' he said, walking to the patio doors. 'Are you going to close the scene now?'

'I suppose so,' she said. 'Everything useful has been packed up. DS Murray's gathering up any other medication in the house. I don't think there's anything more to do here, do you?'

Barr shook his head and pulled aside the curtain, showing the room in natural light for the first time since Flanagan had arrived. Flanagan moved the table back towards the bed, gave him room. As she did so, one of the framed photographs toppled forwards, almost fell to the floor, but Flanagan caught it. She put it back in its place, a picture of a child, in the row of loved ones who'd kept watch over Mr Garrick's last peaceful breaths.

Except they hadn't.

A strange thought. Flanagan tried to connect it to whatever had started to tug at her mind shortly after Mrs Garrick and the minister had left. Like an itch she couldn't reach.

Barr said something, but Flanagan didn't hear.

The photographs.

She studied them, one after the other. The itch deepened.

Barr spoke again. 'I said, he'd have had a nice view from here.'

Flanagan turned her head, followed his gaze. A well-kept garden, an expanse of healthy green lawn, an assortment of shrubs, a few rock and water features, all bordered by a small wood, leaves beginning to brown, late afternoon sunshine spearing through the branches.

'A nice view,' Flanagan said, returning her attention to the photos. 'But not much of a life.'

Dr Barr buried his hands in his pockets. 'It would have got better, though. He still had a lot of healing to do. A lot of pain to suffer. I spoke to his doctor earlier. Mr Garrick had lost too much muscle tissue for it to be wrapped over the bone, so healing was slower than below-the-knee amputations. That and a couple of infections had made it an even harder road for him. But given time, he'd have got there. He could've been mobile again. He wasn't going to be locked in here for ever.'

'Then why did he do it?'

'With a journey that tough, that painful, maybe he couldn't see the end of it.'

Flanagan hesitated, then asked: 'Are you definitely citing suicide?'

Dr Barr turned to her, his eyebrows drawing together. 'I haven't seen anything here that suggests otherwise. Have you?'

'No,' Flanagan said. 'Not really. Just . . .'

'Just what?'

She indicated the photographs, put words to what had bothered her. 'We've both attended suicides before. We've both seen something like this. The pictures of family. When people take that step, they often want to see their loved ones.'

'Yes,' Dr Barr said. 'And?'

'He couldn't see them,' Flanagan said. 'They were facing away from him. I didn't realise when I first came in, the way the table was sitting by the patio doors. But when I moved it back . . .'

Dr Barr looked down at the table, from one framed photograph to the next, a frown on his lips. 'Maybe he wanted them close, but he couldn't stand to see them. Or let them see what he was about to do. Who knows? When a person is about to take their own life, rationality doesn't come into it. Anyway, it's in the coroner's hands now. Hope not to see you again too soon.'

'Likewise,' Flanagan said as Dr Barr exited.

Alone, now.

She stared at the table and the photographs for a few seconds longer before blinking and shaking her head, chasing the notion away. Another question she could never answer, one of a long list that spanned her career. This was a suicide, and no photograph would change it into something else.

Flanagan turned in a circle, surveying the place where Henry Garrick had spent the last miserable months of his existence. The bible on the nightstand to one side of the bed, the selection of motoring magazines on the other. Above the bed, another framed verse of scripture, like those in the hall. Flanagan whispered the words.

Isaiah 41: 10: Fear thou not; for I am with thee: be not dismayed; for I am thy God: I will strengthen thee; yea, I will help thee; yea, I will uphold thee with the right hand of my righteousness.

She stared at the verse, suddenly aware of the currents of air around her, warm and cool. The sound of other people in the house. Birdsong outside.

'Ma'am.'

She stifled a gasp as she spun on her heel to see DS Murray in the doorway, a plastic bag full of medicines and pills hanging from his hand, Sergeant Carson behind him.

'Shit,' she said, catching her breath.

'Sorry, ma'am,' Murray said. 'Is there anything more you need us to do? We're all kind of twiddling our thumbs here.'

Flanagan walked to the doorway. 'Close the scene, Sergeant Carson.'

Carson scribbled on the scene log as she bit her lower lip in concentration, then handed the clipboard to Flanagan. With her signature, Flanagan authorised the closure.

'You did good work today,' she said to Carson.

A faint bloom flushed on Carson's cheeks. 'Thank you, ma'am.'

As the sergeant walked away, Flanagan spoke to Murray. 'I'll lock up here. Send the uniforms on their way, and you head back to Lisburn. Make a start on the paperwork. The FMO's going to report suicide, to be confirmed by the coroner. You know what to do.'

'Yes, ma'am,' Murray said. 'Keys are on the hall table. Two sets, so I'm not sure Mrs Garrick took hers with her.'

'All right, I'll see to it. Get going.'

Flanagan listened to their muted voices and the scuffing of their boots as they left, the front door closing, two engines igniting, tyres on driveway. Then silence, even the birds outside seeming to have hushed.

This rarely happened, that she was left alone at the scene. Normally, she would come and go from the site of a murder, the body lying *in situ* for as long as it took to explore every inch of its surroundings. But not today. This is simply a house of the bereaved, Flanagan thought, as if Henry Garrick had died of some illness on a hospital ward.

What, then, do we do for the dead?

It had been years since she or Alistair had lost a family member. Before the children, in fact, when Alistair's father had died. She remembered his going around their home, closing blinds, shutting out the light. She had wanted to open them again, saying no one would see their isolated house. But Alistair had insisted. It's what you do, he'd said. A mark of respect.

So now Flanagan went back to the patio doors and pulled across the curtain that Dr Barr had opened. Then she walked from room to room, doing the same, the darkness deepening as each window was blotted out. She noted the objects, the artwork, the furniture, the ornaments, the electronics. Wealth she would never know in her lifetime. If the Garricks weren't millionaires, they must have been close.

Flanagan walked through the kitchen, again pulling down blinds, so the granite worktops changed from glistening sheets of black to dark pools. Through to the utility room, top of the range washing machine and tumble dryer amid more cupboards and a sink. A door leading to the rear of the property; she checked it was locked. Another door, open, a small bathroom. A third door, a key in the lock. She tried the handle, then turned the key, snick-click.

The door opened outward. A step down into a large dim garage. Flanagan felt around the door frame for a light switch, found it, and fluorescent tubes flickered into life.

Glistening metal from one side of the garage to the other. Space for five cars, but only four were lined up here. For a moment Flanagan wondered where the fifth could be. She hadn't seen anything other than the modest cars of the visitors when she pulled up, but then she remembered: the car Mr Garrick had been driving when he crashed.

She looked at the rest, marvelling at the money invested in these machines. She recognised a Porsche 911 by its profile, and a vintage MG, and a Mercedes convertible, the long boxy kind she remembered seeing on television as a child. Closest of all, a Mini Cooper, no more than a year or two old. The far wall was lined with racks of alloy wheels and tyres, and a large red tool chest. All of it appeared too clean to have seen much use. The cleanliness of the cars, however, suggested Mrs Garrick had continued to enjoy them, even if her husband could not.

Flanagan turned off the lights and locked the door behind her, leaving the key where she'd found it. Back through the kitchen, out to the hall and its wide central staircase. She climbed up to the gallery landing above. From up here, the hall looked all the more impressive. Facing the top of the stairs, a set of double doors. The master bedroom, Flanagan assumed. For no reason she could grasp, she went to the other rooms first, all blandly decorated spaces for guests, all neutral colours and beech veneers. Once all of them were darkened, Flanagan returned to the master bedroom and opened the double doors.

This room was not like the others. Her eyes were drawn first to the cherrywood four-poster bed and its silk canopy. Flanagan guessed it cost more than her car. Everywhere else, furniture that at least appeared to be antique. She stepped inside, felt the depth of the carpet underfoot. A scent of perfume hung in the air. On the dressing table beneath the window, a selection of bottles, Chanel, Dior, Yves Saint Laurent, and more that she guessed were too expensive to be familiar to her.

Flanagan looked to the other side of the room, and the two doors at either end of it. One stood ajar, showing the bathroom beyond. She guessed where the other led to, and opening it proved her right: a dressing room. A light flickered on automatically and she saw rows of dresses in cellophane shrouds, drawers of jewellery, racks of shoes. She lifted one of the dresses down from its rail, checked the label. Not only could Flanagan never afford such a thing, she'd also never fit into it. Not now, anyway.

Something turned inside her, a hard, ugly thing. An emotion she felt so rarely that it took a few moments to recognise it.

Envy.

I covet these things. I covet this life.

No you don't, Flanagan thought, as she felt a ridiculous blush heat her cheeks. She returned the dress to its rail, backed out of the dressing room, and closed the door. Why had she even entered? She had no business in there. What had begun as a courtesy to the dead man and his widow had turned into a sordid exploration. A familiar sense of intrusion crept into her, the same as she felt when she searched any victim's home, a house full of secrets revealed to a stranger. Except this time, she was indeed an intruder.

Time to go, she thought. She went to turn towards the window and its open blind, but something caught her attention on the wall. What? She let her eyes defocus and refocus until they found what had snagged her: a picture hook on the wall, centred over a tall chest of drawers. The dusty shadow of a frame that had once hung there.

Flanagan's gaze moved to the chest's top drawer, and the single brass knob at its front.

I have no reason to look in there, she thought.

'I have no reason,' she said aloud.

Even so, she reached for the knob and pulled. The drawer slid open with no resistance. She took one step closer so she could better see inside. Bundles of papers, brown envelopes, a scattering of hairbands and clips.

And a large framed photograph of the child, perhaps a year old, held in masculine arms. Bright-eyed, smiling, two small teeth in the lower gum. A wisp of hair on her head.

Dead and gone, Flanagan thought. And I envied this life.

She pushed the drawer closed, held her fingertips against the wood as she pictured her own children, at school now. The Garrick child would have been close to six, a year younger than Eli. They might have been in the same playground, chasing and teasing each other.

The chime of the doorbell made her cry out.

6

Roberta hadn't spoken on the short drive to McKay's house. Her gaze had remained fixed ahead, her face cut from flint. When they arrived at St Mark's and the adjoining rectory, she waited in the passenger seat for him to open the door. He had offered her his hand to help her out, but she ignored it, climbed out by herself. She walked to the door of the house where he had lived alone for a decade and stopped there, not looking back as he approached.

The house had been built at the same time as the church, a century and a half ago, from the sandstone quarried near Armagh. Like all rectories, it was large, with four bedrooms and three receptions. Had he and Maggie ever had children, then they might have made good use of the space. But there were no children, Maggie was ten years in her grave, and McKay couldn't remember the last time some of those rooms had been opened. Cold and damp, draughts slipped through every closed window and door. He sometimes imagined himself a ghost haunting the dark hallways.

The church grounds stood behind an iron fence at the south-western end of Morganstown's main street, the last buildings before the countryside. The Morgan family had paid for the building of the church in order to serve the community that earned its living in its linen mill. The mill had died with the linen industry, but the rows of red-brick two-bedroom houses remained, as did Morgan Demesne, the mansion seated in acres of woodland at the other end of the village, now owned by the National Trust.

These days, the village was mostly populated by young professionals who took advantage of easy access to the motorway that served Belfast, but few of them ever saw the inside of McKay's church. His congregation was drawn from the older generations who had stubbornly refused to be bought out of their homes, and the dozens of farms that sprawled across the surrounding countryside.

Main Street – in truth, Morganstown's only real street – stretched to just a few hundred yards, a filling station with a small shop at the north-eastern end. Clusters of modern houses, built during the property boom, branched away from Main Street, SUVs and executive saloons parked on their driveways. Apart from a handful of band parades every summer, it was as uneventful a place as could be imagined. Sometimes McKay enjoyed the peace here; sometimes the quiet made him want to scream.

He unlocked the door and stood aside to let Roberta enter. Still she did not speak, not even to thank him. He followed her into the hallway, watched as she paused at the bottom of the stairs, looked up, then back at him. Then she walked into his living room. He remained in the hall, looking at the stairs. No, not at them, but at the memory of them. That Sunday four months ago.

She had smiled at him from the second to last pew as all others around her bowed their heads in prayer. He had stood in the pulpit, his stare fixed on her as he recited the words, just shapes in his mouth, no meaning to them whatsoever.

Roberta sat there, glowing like an ember among the sad, grey, slack faces. Farmers, most of them, scrubbed-up for their weekly duty. Broad-backed wives, thick-fingered children. Boys who could drive tractors before the age of seven; girls who longed for the monthly socials and the chance to spin around in the arms of some pimply lad.

He'd been dreading this service, just as he dreaded every one. He felt certain they would see the sin on his face, know what he'd done. And they would point and hiss, and call him hypocrite, how dare he preach to them after he'd taken her into his bed, after his weakness had betrayed them all.

He watched as Roberta stood, sly and silent as a cat, and made her way to the door. She gave him a glance over her shoulder, her eyes meeting his, and he could not help but stumble over the prayer. The door closed silently, and a few seconds later, as he found his place again, he felt the cold wash of displaced air.

After the service, after he had shaken hands with the departing congregation, after he had listened and laughed and consoled and thanked, he let himself into his cold and lonely house. With a fluttering in his stomach, and a heavy heat beneath that, he went straight to the living room, knowing she waited for him.

But she did not.

'Not here,' he said to himself. A mix of relief and disappointment flooded him. He let the air out of his lungs, feeling himself deflate.

McKay backed out of the room, intending to go upstairs to change. It wasn't until he put his right foot on the bottom step that he saw the pair of shoes there, two steps above. Two steps higher, her coat. Halfway up, her blouse, slung over the banister.

He swallowed and began to climb.

At the top of this flight, at the turn, her skirt. Then tights, underwear, leading to his bedroom, the door open for him like an eager mouth.

Roberta lay in his bed, the duvet pulled up to her chest, the flame of her hair lying across her bare shoulders. He knew he should tell her to get out, tell her this had gone far enough, tell her this madness had to end.

But she threw aside the duvet, offered herself to him, and he pulled the white collar from his black shirt and claimed the madness for his own.

Now, two hours after McKay had driven her away from her home and her dead husband, Roberta stood at the centre of his small living room, glowering where she had once glimmered. He had left her there earlier while he went to the kitchen, where he had remained until now, unable to face the question he needed to ask. He waited in the doorway to the living room, afraid to cross his own threshold. He cleared his throat. She turned her head to him, her eyes still red and brimming.

'What now?' he asked.

She stared at him, as if she expected him to answer his own question.

He cleared his throat again and said, 'Maybe we should talk.'

'About what?' she asked.

McKay opened his mouth and found no words there. He opened his arms, showed her his palms, tried to speak once more, but fear closed his lips.

Say it now, he thought. Say it now or say it never.

'About us.'

Roberta held his gaze for a moment, then looked away. She said, 'I'd like to be alone for a while. If you don't mind.'

He wanted to protest, but tightened his jaw to trap the words in his throat. He brought his hands together, balled them into one fist, felt his nails dig at his palm. Somehow, he wrestled a smile onto his lips that at least felt kindly, even if it might have looked more like a grimace. Not that she could see it anyway. She stared at the fireplace, her arms folded across her breasts.

'All right,' he said. 'Of course. I'll be upstairs if you need me.'

McKay closed the door behind him and climbed the stairs. No trail of clothes to follow now. No sweet insanity waiting for him in his bedroom. Only the cold loneliness that had slept with him for the last ten years. He sat on the edge of his bed, trying not to remember the scent of her there, how, every time she left, he had smelled her on the pillows and the sheets, how he had brought them to his face and breathed deep.

He covered his eyes with his hands, rested his elbows on his knees.

Now he recognised the feeling that had crept in on him as he had watched Roberta go to her husband's corpse: the sensation of the thing he desired slipping through his fingers.

'Dear God,' he whispered. 'Please don't take this from me. Not now. Please don't.'

Then he remembered he didn't believe, hadn't believed in months, and he despaired.

7

Flanagan went to the bedroom threshold, saw the front door open and a slender middle-aged woman enter. She carried a large tote bag strapped over her shoulder.

'Hello?' the woman called as she closed the door behind her. Unbidden, she walked towards the rear of the hall, out of Flanagan's view. Flanagan descended the stairs.

'Hello? Mr Garrick, where . . . what's . . .'

Flanagan saw the woman standing in the doorway to the dead man's room, her bag hanging from her hand. She wore a nurse's tunic and trousers, and the kind of plain black shoes favoured by someone who spends the day on their feet.

'Please don't go in there,' Flanagan said.

The woman gasped and spun around. 'Jesus!' She put her free hand to her heart. 'You scared the life out of me. What's going on? Where's Mr Garrick? Who are you?'

Flanagan took her wallet from her jacket pocket and showed the woman her warrant card as she approached. 'I'm Detective Chief Inspector Serena Flanagan. Mr Garrick is dead.'

The woman dropped her bag. 'What? No. How?'

'We believe suicide. I was just locking up when you came in. And you are?'

'Thelma Stinson. I'm a nurse. I come out every other day to change Mr Garrick's dressings and help bath him. I'm used to just letting myself in if the door's not locked. I wondered why all the blinds were drawn. I can't believe it. He was doing so well. Why would he go and do that? God love him.'

She reached down for her bag, looked back into the room.

'I suppose there's no point in me hanging around, then.'

'I suppose not,' Flanagan said.

The nurse nodded a farewell as she passed on her way to the door.

'Actually,' Flanagan called after her, 'maybe we could have a quick chat, if you've time for a few questions.'

'Love, I've got the next two hours free. But do you mind if I step outside for a smoke? Just to settle my nerves.'

Flanagan followed Thelma out to the front step where the nurse's Skoda Fabia sat parked next to her own Volkswagen. Thelma took a ten-pack of Lambert & Butler from her bag, folded back the lid, and removed a cigarette and a disposable lighter. She offered the pack, but Flanagan declined.

Once she'd sparked up, Thelma said, 'Ask away.'

'How long have you been coming here?'

Thelma exhaled a long blue plume that was swiped away by the breeze. 'Ever since he came home from the hospital. That was, what, four months ago, give or take a week?'

'How was Mr Garrick's mood in that time?' Flanagan asked.

'Better than you'd think,' Thelma said. 'I mean, he had his ups and downs, of course. He did better than I ever could if that happened to me. But then, I've no religion.'

'You think his faith helped him?'

43

Another plume of smoke. 'Oh, yes. He always said to me, if that's what God intended for him, then there had to be a reason for it. What was it he said? There's not a leaf falls from a tree without God's say-so. I don't know, if God did that to me, I'd tell him to go fuck himself.'

The nurse turned to Flanagan, open-mouthed, her hand extended in apology. 'Oh, I didn't think, you're not religious, are you?'

Flanagan smiled and shook her head. 'No, not really.'

'Thank God for that, I wouldn't want to offend you. My sister's all into that, but I could never be bothered with it.' She winked at Flanagan. 'I'm always too hung-over on a Sunday morning for church, anyway.'

'How was Mrs Garrick coping?' Flanagan asked.

The smile left Thelma's mouth. 'God love her, I think she took it worse than he did. I mean, she's what, thirty-four, thirty-five, something like that? And now she's got to care for him like he's a baby for the rest of his days. He didn't have much of a life after the accident, but Jesus, it was no laugh for her either. No matter how much you love someone, it's hard to face cleaning up after them day in and day out. And when I say cleaning up, I mean *cleaning up*. Like, down there.'

Thelma waved her fingers at her own crotch while her face creased, and Flanagan knew exactly what she meant. She imagined the rituals the Garricks had to go through morning and night, the shame and resentment that would surely take root and grow between them. True love can only stretch so far.

'And nothing changed recently?' Flanagan asked. 'No mood swings? Any arguments between Mr and Mrs Garrick?'

'Not that I noticed.'

'All right. Thank you, you've been a help.'

Thelma stubbed the cigarette out on the sole of her shoe, slipped the remains into the packet, and stowed it in her bag. 'No worries, love. If you need anything else, you can get me through the local trust.'

She went to her car and paused as she opened the door.

'It's an awful shame,' she said. 'He was a nice man. He'd every right to be bitter about things, but he wasn't. God love him. God love the both of them.'

Flanagan closed the front door as the Skoda's engine hummed away. She went to the hall table and found the two sets of keys there, resting on the open pages of the huge bible. The paper silken and cool against her fingers. In the dimness of the hall, she saw the first page of the New Testament.

The Book of Matthew.

Chapter One. Verse One. The genealogy of Christ, who begat who, the names cascading down the page.

She pulled her gaze away from the words, grabbed the keys, and left.

8

McKay froze when he heard the knock on the door. He'd been standing over his kitchen sink, staring out of the window. He almost lost his grip on the handle of the mug, tea long cooled spilling over the rim, over his fingers and into the steel bowl.

Another knock, and he placed the mug on the draining board before going out to the hall. He saw the form through the rippled glass in the door. Was it Flanagan?

McKay advanced along the hall until he reached the door to the living room. He looked in and saw Roberta staring back at him.

'It's that policewoman,' she said in a voice too angry to be a whisper. 'I don't want to talk to her.'

McKay nodded and went to the door. He paused for a breath before he opened it.

'Yes?' he said, shocking himself with the force of his own voice.

A flicker of concern on Flanagan's face before she said, 'Reverend McKay.'

'Reverend Peter,' he said. 'Or Reverend Mr McKay.'

'Oh, yes,' she said. 'You corrected me earlier on that. I'll try to remember.'

He paused, swallowed, and said, 'Sorry, I don't mean to be rude. It's been a long day.'

'I can imagine,' Flanagan said. 'How's Mrs Garrick holding up?'

'She's resting. She doesn't want to see anyone.'

'I understand.' She held out a set of keys. 'I just came by to drop these off. Mrs Garrick is free to go home any time she wishes. I'd only ask that she stays out of the room Mr Garrick died in and doesn't allow anyone else to enter. Just in case we need to reopen the scene. If she doesn't object, I'll hold on to the other set, to save bothering her if we need access over the next day or two.'

He took the keys from Flanagan's hand. 'That's fine. I think she might stay here at least a couple of days.'

'Okay. I'll need to come by tomorrow and ask some more questions. Routine stuff, so no need to worry. I'll call in advance.'

'All right,' McKay said. 'Thank you.'

He waited for her to leave his doorstep, but she lingered.

'I'd invite you in, but Mrs Garrick . . .'

'No, that's fine,' she said. 'I have to get on, anyway.'

She turned towards the church on the far side of the grounds.

'It's a beautiful building,' she said. 'How old?'

'Mid nineteenth century,' he said.

'How often do you have services?'

'The times are on the board at the gate.'

'Oh,' she said, offering him a polite smile. 'Thank you.'

Without another word, McKay watched her get into her car, start the engine, and pull out of the gate. She did not pause to look at the board. He closed the door and rested his forehead against the cool glass for a moment. Then he went back to the living room where Roberta waited.

'Well?' she said. 'What did she want?'

'To give you these.' He held the keys out to her. When she did not reach for them, he placed them on the coffee table. 'She said you could go back home, but I said you'd maybe stay here for a couple of days.'

'I'll go to a hotel,' she said.

McKay took a step closer to her, knocked his shin on the edge of the coffee table, making the keys rattle. 'No, please, stay here,' he said.

'I can't,' she said. 'How would it look?'

'You don't have to sleep with me,' he said.

'It's not a question of whose bed I'm in.'

'Please,' he said. 'Stay here. With me.'

Roberta closed her eyes for a moment, then said, 'All right. But I need to get some things from home. You'll drive me.'

It was an instruction, not a request. And he didn't mind one bit.

Fifteen minutes later, Roberta unlocked the front door of the house her husband had built for her and stepped inside. McKay followed, sensing that keeping a distance would be best. He closed the door behind him as she walked to the open room in which Mr Garrick had died.

'You're not to go in there,' he called. 'That policewoman said no one's allowed in.'

Roberta changed course as if he had said nothing, as if it was purely her own decision. She walked beneath the staircase and towards the kitchen door on the other side. She opened it and peered into the gloom.

'They closed the blinds,' she said. 'All of them. All over the house.'

'Did they?' he said. 'Out of respect, I suppose.'

48

She turned and he saw the hardness in her features. 'If they'd any respect they'd have left everything alone. I need to get my things.'

He couldn't hold her gaze. Instead, he retreated to the front door and waited there with his back against the wood as she walked upstairs to the double doors of her bedroom. She opened them wide and switched on the light. He watched as she went to one side of the room, out of his view, and returned with a leather bag. Then she froze at the foot of the bed, staring at a place he could not see.

After a while, she said, 'Someone's been in here.'

Her voice resonated in the high-ceilinged hallway, its metallic edge cutting at his senses.

He swallowed and said, 'I suppose they had to search the house.'

If she heard, it did not show. She dropped the bag on the bed and walked towards whatever had caught her attention, disappearing from view once more. A minute later, she reappeared.

'That woman was in my drawer,' she said, anger sharpening her words. 'Where I keep my . . . private things.'

McKay moved closer to the foot of the stairs, daring himself to speak. 'They have to look. I've seen suicides before, and they always look around the house. They always do.'

She stepped out of the room, to the top of the stairs. 'Not my fucking house.'

He moved back to the door, felt the wood against his shoulders, as the last reverberations of her voice faded.

'No,' she said, raising a finger as if admonishing a wilful child. 'She doesn't go through my private things. I won't have it.'

49

Some foolish part of him wanted to argue with her, to tell her nothing was private until it was all settled. But his rational mind closed his mouth.

'Go and wait in the car,' she said. 'I'll get my things, then I want away from this house.'

Reverend Peter McKay did as he was told.

9

Flanagan missed dinner with her children, which was not a rare event, particularly in recent months. When she let herself into the house by the back door she found Alistair at the kitchen table, stacks of exercise books in front of him, marking homework.

'Everyone all right?' she asked as she looked in the fridge for a plate covered with foil.

'Fine,' he said. Barely a grunt.

She set the plate on the worktop, removed the foil. Cottage pie.

Mr Garrick's last meal. Flanagan's appetite deserted her.

'Actually, do you mind if I don't?'

Alistair looked up from a teenager's spidery handwriting. 'Do what you like. Chuck it in the bin, whatever you want. I'm not bothered.'

'I'm sorry, it's just . . .'

He scribbled a note on the exercise book in front of him, not hearing anything she said. She scraped the cold food into the bin and put the plate in the dishwasher.

'How are the kids?' she asked.

'You could ask them yourself if you were ever around.'

'That's not fair,' Flanagan said, surprised more at her own anger than his words.

Alistair rubbed his eyes as he inhaled and exhaled. 'Look, I've got a lot of work to do here. We can argue another time.'

'All right,' Flanagan said, and walked to the kitchen door and the hallway beyond. He called after her, but she pretended not to hear. She went to the stairs and climbed, feeling the smooth varnish on the old wooden banisters. Alistair had sanded and finished them himself, and he had been so proud.

It should have been a happy memory, but instead it made Flanagan mourn for the life they once had. In the quiet hours, when she couldn't sleep, she promised herself they would get back what they'd lost, maybe something even better. If only they could hold it together a little longer, find their way through this.

And what, exactly, was this? She didn't know. How could she fix anything if she didn't know what had been broken?

Reaching the landing, Flanagan found Eli's bedroom door slightly ajar, just as he liked it. But Ruth's was tight shut. When had she started closing her door at night? She was ten years old; Flanagan had been into adolescence before the need for privacy had outweighed her fear of the dark. Even then, she needed a light on in the room. She'd still have one now if Alistair would tolerate it.

She knocked on Ruth's door and listened. After a few seconds, she opened it a crack and peered inside. Ruth stared back from her bed, an open book in her hand.

Flanagan opened the door fully and said, 'Late to be up reading, love.'

'I was just finishing,' Ruth said, folding down the corner of the page.

'Can I come in?' Flanagan asked, realising this was the first time she'd ever sought permission.

'Uh-huh,' Ruth said, the expression on her face seeming to ask if she was in trouble.

Flanagan closed the door behind her and approached the bed. Ruth tucked her legs up to make room, and Flanagan sat down on the edge. She reached for her daughter's hand.

'When did you get so grown up?' she asked. 'How did I miss it?'

'Because you're never here,' Ruth said.

'Nonsense. I saw you this morning. And last night before bed.'

'That's not much. It's not like you hang out with us or anything. It's always Dad takes us if we're going anywhere. You never do anything with us. You're never here, not even just to watch TV.'

Flanagan tightened her hold on Ruth's hand. 'I've been very busy with work, love, you know that. But I'll try to do better, I promise.'

Ruth nodded her acceptance and looked down at her free hand.

After a few moments, Flanagan reached out and touched her cheek. 'What, love? Tell me.'

Ruth took a breath, her eyes brimming. 'Are you and Dad going to split up?'

'No,' Flanagan said, her voice harder than she'd intended, making Ruth flinch. 'No, not at all. Why would you think that?'

'You and Dad haven't been talking to each other for ages, not properly. Not even to argue.'

'Course we have,' Flanagan said, the lie bitter in her mouth. 'We were talking just now, downstairs, before I came up.'

Ruth gave her a hard look that said she knew the truth.

'We were, honest.'

'What about?' Ruth asked.

'You and Eli,' Flanagan said without hesitation.

Ruth shrugged and looked down to her hands once more. 'If you do split up, we'll be all right. I know lots of kids whose mums and dads aren't together, and they're all fine.'

Flanagan was about to dismiss the idea when a question occurred to her. 'Did your father say something?'

Ruth kept her gaze down. She was a terrible liar, always had been, so now she wasn't even going to try.

'What did he say?' Flanagan asked.

Ruth looked to the far corner, biting her lip.

'Tell me.' The sharpness of the words startled them both.

'Just that, sometimes, if a mum and dad aren't happy together, it's better for everybody if they split up.'

Flanagan felt that anger surface again, the same as she'd felt a few minutes ago in the kitchen. She pushed it away, saved it for later.

'Well,' she said, 'sometimes that's true. But me and your dad are happy together. We're just having a bit of a rough patch, like all mums and dads do. We'll get over it and things will be better.'

'When?' Ruth asked in the earnest way only children can.

Flanagan smiled and said, 'Soon. I promise. Now, it's time to go to sleep.'

Ruth lay down, and Flanagan set the book aside. She leaned over and gave her daughter a kiss.

'Light off?'

Ruth nodded against her pillow, and Flanagan did as she was told. She stood and went to the door.

As she stepped through the door, Ruth called, 'Leave it open. Just a little.'

Flanagan did so. Then she went to her own bedroom, lay on the bedclothes, and cried in the dark.

She dreamed of Mr Garrick, dead in his back room, except it was a room in Flanagan's home and she wondered why and how he had come to be here. And dead Mr Garrick pointed to the photographs in their frames, all lined up on the table, facing away from him, facing Flanagan.

Turn them around, dead Mr Garrick said, turn them around, I want to see.

Flanagan reached for the picture of his wife, but he said, no, my baby, I want to see my baby.

She woke the moment her fingertips touched the frame, confused, at first weightless, then heavy on the bed, her body sinking into the mattress. She wanted to go downstairs to the back room, let poor dead Mr Garrick see his baby's photograph, but reality untangled itself from her dream and she knew Mr Garrick lay in a mortuary miles away.

Flanagan moved her arms, felt the clinging of fabric, and realised she had fallen asleep fully dressed. She turned her head on the pillow, saw Alistair staring up at the ceiling.

'You awake?' she asked, even though she knew the answer.

'No, I'm spark out,' he said.

She rolled onto her side, facing him, and inched closer. 'Do you want to talk?'

'I want to sleep.'

She reached for the hand that lay by his side. He did not pull away. 'Seeing as neither of us is doing that, do you want to try the first option?'

'Go on, then,' he said.

She told him what Ruth had said, that their daughter seemed to believe their marriage was over, as if the terrible thing had already been done.

'Is that how you see it?' Flanagan asked. 'Are we done?'

She listened to him breathing for a time before he said, 'I don't know.'

'We can't give up just like that. All these years thrown away. We can't.'

'No?' he said. 'You seem to be giving it a bloody good try.'

'Me? What . . .' She stopped, told herself to not get defensive, it wouldn't help. 'I know I've not been around as much as you'd like, but you know how work is these days.'

'It doesn't make much difference if you're here or there, though, does it? Even when you're here, it's obvious you wish you weren't.'

'That's not true, and it's not fair,' Flanagan said, defensive now whether she liked it or not.

'Really? It's like you're a lodger here, for Christ's sake.'

'Because you've frozen me out. Ever since you were hurt, you've kept me at arm's length.'

'Oh, so it's my fault.'

'I didn't say that. But I know you blame me for what happened, and maybe you're right to, but I can't change it no matter how much I wish I could.'

'Yes,' he said, spitting the word into the darkness. 'You're right. I blame you. It was your fault I got stabbed. It's your fault those boys came into our home. It's your fault I still have nightmares about it. And the one thing I asked of you to try and make it better, you won't do it.'

'What?'

'You know.'

And she did know, much as the idea horrified her. 'Quit my job,' she said.

He remained silent until she had no choice but to speak.

'I won't do that. If that makes me selfish, then so be it, I'm selfish. But I do good work, I help people, or at least I try. Sometimes I wonder what I do it for, sometimes all I get is grief for my trouble, but I try. And I'm going to keep trying.'

Alistair's hand slipped away from hers. 'Then there's nothing more to talk about, is there?'

He pushed back the duvet and got out of bed.

'Alistair, wait,' she said as he pulled on his dressing gown and slippers. 'Wait, darling, please.'

He closed the door softly as he left, and Flanagan placed her hand on the warm place where he had been. She did not know how long passed before she slept again, but she dreamed once more of dead Mr Garrick and the photographs, turn them, please turn them, I want to see . . .

IO

As dawn crept in through the cracks in the shutters, Reverend Peter McKay lay quite still beside Roberta and watched her sleep. He had offered her his bed while he took the small spare room, and she had not hesitated in accepting. At some point in the night he had woken with a start, disorientated in the single bed in the room across the landing. Once his senses had aligned, an idea occurred to him, simple and clear: get up and go to her.

Why not?

They had slept together before on several occasions. Not through the night, of course, but many times, as the sweat cooled on their tangled limbs, they had each drifted into soft warm nothing. Why should they not sleep together now?

Decided, he got out of bed, and left the spare room. Wearing his T-shirt and boxers, he crossed the landing to the door of his own bedroom. He thought about knocking, but dismissed the idea almost as soon as it had appeared. Instead, he reached for the handle and opened the door.

Quiet like a church mouse.

The image almost made him giggle, and he brought a hand to his lips as he closed the door behind him. He crossed the room, mindful of creaking floorboards, and stood over her for a while. So peaceful there, her hair pooled on the pillow, her cheek resting on the palm of one hand. He eased back the covers and lowered himself into the bed.

As he drew up the bedclothes, she lifted her head from the pillow, her eyes barely open, her mind clearly far away.

'But you can't walk,' she said.

He realised she was still tangled in a dream about her dead husband, no wall between the real and the unreal.

'It's all right,' he whispered. 'Go back to sleep.'

She lowered her head to the pillow and closed her eyes. He leaned over and placed a kiss, so soft it wouldn't have woken a baby, on her forehead. At that moment, as he looked up from her, he noticed the framed photograph of Maggie, turned to face the wall. Even though he could not see her face, he couldn't bear to look.

He had slept little in the hours since, stirring every few minutes, roused by the heat of Roberta's body just inches from his own. Now she lay on her back, one arm curled around her head so that he could see the stubble there where he had kissed her so many times. He watched her eyes move behind the lids, listened to her breathing, took in her heated scent.

She had promised.

With his hands clasped in hers, she had sworn on her dead child's soul that they would be together. One day, they would be together. He did not believe in the soul, but he accepted her oath nonetheless, because he wanted her more than anything in the world. He needed her more than he needed his own conscience.

And now, surely, Roberta was his. Wasn't she?

And if she wasn't?

McKay's mouth dried, his stomach turned. Cold on his forehead as sweat seeped from his skin.

No, it was unthinkable. To even consider the possibility would strip away the last of him, unman him as brutally as the Aston's engine had unmanned her husband. So he would not consider the idea. He forced himself, instead, to resume his study of her.

He had lost Maggie a decade ago. Eight years they had together before that. Happy years. From here, it seemed like some soppy television romance, all hazy sunlight and meadow picnics. There had been some sadness – their inability to conceive a child being the darkest stain on the memory – but even so, those eight years retained a golden glow in his mind.

Then one morning, at breakfast, Maggie complained of a headache. As she sat at the kitchen table, head in her hands, a mug of tea going cold in front of her, McKay searched the cupboards for ibuprofen or paracetamol. Eventually, he decided to give up and walk the few hundred yards to the filling station at the other end of the village's main street.

'Don't be too long,' she said. 'It really hurts.'

Five minutes there, five minutes to buy what she needed, five minutes back.

Fifteen minutes, that was all.

He found her on the kitchen floor, the chair toppled over, her face slack, her hands clawed in front of her chest. He wept as he called the ambulance, wept as he kneeled over her, prayed with all his heart.

She died on the way to the hospital. The paramedics restarted her heart twice before they could get her hooked up to the machines. In the early hours of the following morning, the doctor told McKay she was long gone. They could keep her heart beating, keep her lungs inflating and deflating. But Maggie McKay, who blushed when he touched her, who cried at Audrey Hepburn movies, who was kind and sweet to the very root of her being, everything that she was had ceased to exist. Now she was a vessel of organs and blood and bones and skin and nothing more. When they switched the machines off, he crawled onto the bed beside Maggie and held her as the life wheezed and rattled out of her.

Anything you need, Mr Garrick had said, anything at all, just ask.

Mr Garrick's first wife had left him just the year before, had run off with one of the salesmen at the car dealership. But Mr Garrick had his faith to keep him strong, and the fellowship of his church. And so did McKay. The congregation gathered around him in his time of need, and he was grateful. And most of all, McKay had prayer, and the knowledge that his wife's passing had been God's doing. There had to be a reason.

Not a leaf falls against His will. Hadn't he always said that?

Nonsense. All a lie. His wife's passing had been caused by a random malfunction of her brain; God had nothing to do with it.

There is no God, McKay knew. No God, only us and our sordid desires to drive us through our days until we're too old or too sick to desire anything. And then we are meat in a box, or ash in an urn, nothing more.

McKay could recall the exact moment he had ceased to believe. It had not been a process, a gradual degradation of his faith. It had been a sudden and total realisation that it was all a lie. The moment had been when she first brought her mouth to his, four months ago. For days and weeks she had been coming to him so that they could pray together, to help her through the terrible time after her husband's accident.

And they had grown close, talking together long after their praying was done, and as they talked, he noticed her in ways he hadn't before. The curve of her upper lip, the long and slender fingers, the toned form of her thigh as she crossed one leg over the other.

Then one morning, before he knew what was happening, his hands were lost in her red hair, and he felt her warm breath on his neck.

And his mind screamed, *sinner, sinner, sinner!*

But there is no sin. Is there? There is no sin because there is no God.

And then her mouth found his, her tongue quick and nimble and eager, and he knew beyond all certainty. Later that day, when it was done, he turned Maggie's picture to the wall.

The path from there to here had been the only one. There had been no other way but this. No other destination than his bed, the morning sunlight burning in her hair. He reached out, touched the glowing red strands, traced them back to the heat of her scalp.

She gasped, eyes opened wide, her gaze flitting around the room until she found him, inches away, staring back at her.

No recognition there, only confusion. Then realisation, and her expression turned from fear to anger.

'Get out,' she said.

He reached for her again, his fingertips seeking the soft skin of her cheek.

She slapped his hand away. 'Get out.'

'But—'

'Get out!'

A shout now, her voice cracking.

'But we've—'

She struck him, her palm against his cheek, glancing off his nose.

'Get out!'

He brought his hands up as she swiped at him again. Then she pushed, first with her hands against his chest until he teetered at the edge of the bed, then she curled her legs up, and planted her feet against his stomach and pushed again.

McKay landed on the floor, shoulders first, the back of his head cracking on the floorboards. His legs followed, bringing the tangled duvet with them.

Up on her knees now, naked, pointing to the door. 'Get the fuck out!'

He scrambled to his feet, fell, got up again.

'Get out!'

McKay didn't look back as he crossed the room, opened the door, exited, closed it behind him. He stood on the landing, shaking, shame creeping in on him, a sickly wave of it.

He went to the spare room and slipped inside, silent, and climbed back into the small bed. Pulled the duvet up over his head, blacking out everything.

It took an hour for the shaking to pass.

II

At eight a.m., the pathologist's assistant opened the door to the Royal Victoria Hospital's mortuary and allowed DCI Flanagan and DS Murray to enter. Flanagan had spent several minutes assuring Murray that he could leave at any point if he really needed to. Sooner or later, he would have to attend a post-mortem in her stead, and he might as well break his duck with this one. With no trauma involved, no bullet fragments to seek, no stab wounds to count, this would be about as clean as an autopsy gets.

The assistant led them to the post-mortem table. The body bag lay on a trolley beside it, Mr Garrick's remains within. Dr Miriam McCreesh, the forensic pathologist, waited for them. A tall woman, the kind whose girlhood awkwardness turned to grace as an adult, she had an efficiency about her movements and her words. She wore surgical gloves, and a cap that strangely matched the green of her eyes.

'Morning,' she said.

Flanagan and Murray returned the greeting.

McCreesh consulted the clipboard on the wheeled table at her left hand.

'Dr Barr's initial assessment is death by suicide,' she said. 'Do you concur?'

Flanagan hesitated, then said, 'I'm undecided.'

McCreesh looked up from the notes. 'I see.' She returned her attention to the clipboard. 'Going by the liver temperature taken at the scene, the rigor, and the lividity, I'm estimating time of death between eleven p.m. and midnight on Sunday the 4th of October. Dr Barr observed no sign of recent trauma, as well as the presence of ten empty morphine granule sachets. There was an empty yogurt pot, and the spoon with which the yogurt was eaten. I understand the deceased was in the habit of using the yogurt as a means of administering his nightly dose of morphine, correct?'

'That's my understanding,' Flanagan said.

'All right,' McCreesh said. 'Shall we begin?'

Murray endured the early stages of the ritual. Flanagan watched him from the corner of her eye. He showed no signs of defeat as the body was taken from the bag, transferred to the post-mortem table using a ceiling-mounted hoist, and then photographed. Nor when the pyjama top was removed, or even the dressings on the stumps of Mr Garrick's legs. Only when the adult nappy was removed, and the damage to the dead man's lower abdomen was revealed, did Murray flinch.

In truth, so did Flanagan.

They watched as McCreesh took samples – hair, skin, matter from beneath the fingernails. Murray cleared his throat as she swabbed what remained of Mr Garrick's genitalia. Then she began the slow crawling external examination of the body, starting at the head, working down the left side, then up the right. Occasionally, McCreesh paused to lift her magnifying glass and look closer at some hair or fibre, before nodding and putting it back.

Eventually, she said, 'All right. I concur with Dr Barr, no external sign of trauma.'

She looked to her assistant, who immediately acted on the unspoken command, wheeling a trolley laden with tools to the table.

Flanagan leaned in close to Murray. 'How are you holding up?'

'I'm okay, ma'am,' he said. 'So far.'

McCreesh checked Dr Barr's notes once more. 'The FMO mentions that the morphine granules were to be swallowed whole, not chewed, so the dose would be released gradually in the stomach.'

'That's right,' Flanagan said.

McCreesh took a small penlight from her pocket and leaned over Mr Garrick's still open mouth. She shone the light inside, peering into the back of the throat.

'Hm,' she said and reached for a clear plastic tube containing a swab stick. She removed the stick, and inserted the swab into Mr Garrick's mouth, moving it around his back teeth. When she was done, she examined the swab with her magnifying glass.

'I've got a mixture of a pink substance, the yogurt presumably, and crushed granules. I'd say that's the morphine he chewed to get it to release more quickly. Tests will confirm.'

She returned the swab stick to its tube, sealed it, and handed it to her assistant, who wrote on the tube's side with a permanent marker. Then McCreesh turned to her trolley and selected a scalpel.

Murray nodded towards her. 'Is she going to . . .?'

'Yes, she is,' Flanagan said.

Murray exhaled and said, 'I'm okay. I'm okay.'

His breathing deepened as the Y-shaped incision was made from the body's shoulders to its groin. He did not speak again until McCreesh began to saw away the ribs and clavicle to remove the breastplate, the grinding noise resonating between the tiled walls.

Murray leaned in and said, 'Ma'am, may I be excused?'

'Can't you stick it out a little longer?' Flanagan asked. 'The organ examination's where the real work gets done.'

'Oh, Christ,' Murray said, and rushed past her to the doors, where he slapped at the green button with his palm until they swung open.

McCreesh looked up from her work. 'He didn't do too bad.'

'No,' Flanagan said. 'Not too bad at all.'

Two hours later, Flanagan sat at McCreesh's desk, opposite the pathologist. She had sent DS Murray back to Lisburn to chase up the searches made of the Garricks' MacBook and iPad, as well as the notes from the door-to-door inquiries carried out in Morganstown by the two detective constables under his command.

'I'm reporting death by suicide to the coroner,' McCreesh said. Her blonde hair now flowed free of the cap she'd worn during the autopsy.

'All right,' Flanagan said, nodding.

'You don't seem convinced,' McCreesh said.

'I'm not disputing your assessment.'

67

'But?'

'But there's something . . . details, really, just details.'

McCreesh rested her elbows on the desk. 'Go on,' she said.

'I spoke with the nurse who came in to help Mrs Garrick with her husband, change his dressings and so on. She thought he'd been doing well, or as well as could be hoped for. She said his mood was generally good, that he had his faith, that he was strong-willed.'

'Is that so unusual?' McCreesh asked. 'Haven't you ever seen a suicide that came out of the blue, that baffled everybody around the deceased?'

'Of course, but this seems . . . different.'

'Different,' McCreesh said. 'You'll have to do better than "different" to sway the coroner.'

Flanagan swallowed, considered letting it go, then she said, 'It's the photographs.'

McCreesh sat back. 'Photographs?'

'That's the one detail that doesn't sit right. He had photographs of loved ones arranged around him.'

'Suicides often do.'

'But they were facing away from him. If he wanted to see them as he died, they would have been facing him. Why put them there at all if he couldn't see them?'

McCreesh sighed. 'I don't know. We probably never will. What I do know is I found what appear to be crushed morphine granules on his teeth and the rear of his tongue, which is consistent with him chewing them before swallowing. The stomach contained exactly what we expected to find there, the mass spectrometer tests on the liver and blood samples will confirm the lethal morphine levels. All of it adds up. This was a suicide. I can't see it any other way, and I'm going to advise the coroner accordingly. I expect him to sign the interim death certificate, Mrs Garrick will put her husband to rest, and until the inquest, that will be that.'

'Fair enough,' Flanagan said. 'But I can disregard your findings, and the coroner's report, if I so wish.'

McCreesh bristled. 'That's your prerogative. But you're just making grief for yourself.'

A sudden smile burst on Flanagan's lips, in spite of everything, surprising her. 'Oh, I'm good at that.'

McCreesh returned the smile. 'I know,' she said. 'Anyway, enough business. How've you been?'

'Okay,' Flanagan said. 'Still on the tamoxifen for the foreseeable future, still having the check-ups, still terrified I'm going to find another lump. You?'

McCreesh's eyes glistened. She blinked. A tear threatened to spill from the lower lid. 'I found something. I have an appointment at the Cancer Centre first thing on Friday.'

Flanagan reached across the desk, took McCreesh's hand in hers.

'It'll be a cyst,' Flanagan said. 'Just like the last time.'

'That's what I keep telling myself,' McCreesh said. 'Over and over. But I can't drown that other voice out. You know what it's like.'

'I know,' Flanagan said, squeezing McCreesh's fingers tight.

'All I can think of is, how will I tell Eddie, what will I say to the kids? What if it's worse this time? What if it's not been caught soon enough? What if it's spread to the lymphatic system? What if, what if, what if?'

69

Now McCreesh squeezed back, sniffed hard, blinked again.

'But I won't be beaten now,' she said. 'Six years clear. I'm not fucking letting it get the better of me after six years clear.'

'Good,' Flanagan said.

They embraced, and Flanagan walked from the mortuary wing out to the car park. She paid at the kiosk and found her car. Before she inserted the key into the ignition, she closed her eyes and said a small prayer for Miriam McCreesh.

12

Reverend Peter McKay left Roberta Garrick alone in his draughty house and crossed the grounds to the church. The morning prayer service, a daily tradition few parishes maintained. But McKay opened the chapel two mornings a week for the handful of parishioners who still wanted to commune with God on a Tuesday or Thursday morning.

Mr McHugh waited at the vestry door, a folder full of sheet music under his arm. A retired schoolmaster, he'd taught music and religious education at a grammar school in Armagh for forty years. Now he turned up at each service to play organ for the faithful.

'That was a bad doing, yesterday,' Mr McHugh said. 'How's Mrs Garrick?'

'She's coping,' McKay said.

'Well, tell her Cora and I are thinking of her.'

'I will, thank you.'

Mr McHugh touched McKay's sleeve. 'We had the police at the door last night. Asking about it. A fella and a girl, I think they said they were constables. They were asking all sorts. Made me and Cora uncomfortable, if I'm honest.'

'I suppose they have to do these things,' McKay said.

'Well, I didn't like it,' Mr McHugh said. 'It's not respectful. To us or the Garricks.'

McKay gave no response. He opened the door and allowed Mr McHugh into the vestry and through to the church beyond, before entering the code to disable the burglar alarm. Over the next half hour, while McKay donned his black cassock and white surplice, while he scribbled notes on loose sheets of paper he took from the old printer in the vestry, a scattering of people, more women than men, mostly elderly, sat in the pews. More of them than usual. Death brings out the God-fearing.

And there, near the front, Jim Allison, MLA. Forty-something, tanned and well-dressed, owner of a print business on the outskirts of Moira. He'd been an elected Member of the Legislative Assembly at Stormont since the re-establishment of the devolved Northern Ireland government in 2007. A man of influence who'd fought battles for many in the parish, from denied benefits claims to planning refusals, Allison had tackled bureaucrats in every government department on behalf of his constituents.

Although the MLA and his wife were regular attendees on Sundays, McKay struggled to remember a time when Allison had bothered with a weekday service, save for funerals or weddings. But he knew why Allison was here this morning. The parish had suffered a terrible tragedy and the local politician had come to show his solidarity with his people.

Such a cynical thought, but McKay had been given to cynical thinking over the past few months. Since his own faith had left him, he had questioned the belief of every other person who stepped inside his church. We're all just playing along, aren't we? Just going through the motions, doing what's expected of us.

And so McKay worked his way through the service, point-by-point as prescribed by the Book of Common Prayer: the gathering of God's people, the sentence of scripture, the opening hymn, the exhortation, the confession, the Lord's Prayer. Like an actor who'd performed the same lines every night for twenty years, he recited each segment with detached authority.

But today was different, wasn't it?

Today, they listened harder. This morning, every word he spoke carried the weight of Mr Garrick's death. He had chosen the hymns and readings carefully to reflect the sombre mood the congregation expected from him. And this morning, he would go further. A sermon, a rarity in a weekday service. After the canticles and the psalms were done, he turned over two pages of scribbles that would carry him through the next ten minutes.

He heard the door open, felt a cool breeze, and looked up from his own barely legible scrawls. The policewoman, Flanagan. McKay's throat dried. She slipped into the second to last pew, exactly where Roberta Garrick had sat all those months ago. Her eyes met his, held his stare.

Start talking, he told himself.

Start talking now.

'My friends,' he said, or at least he tried. The words came out as a crackling whisper. He cleared his throat, looked down at his notes, and tried again.

'My friends, this morning we come into the Lord's house carrying the great weight of tragedy. You all know the Garrick family, and you all know they have endured more heartbreak than any family should. First, with the loss of little Erin Garrick,

73

not even two years old, in a terrible accident four years ago. Back then, Mr and Mrs Garrick sought the solace of their faith, their Lord God and His son, Jesus Christ. And they sought the support of the congregation of this church, they turned to their friends here, and with your help, and the Saviour's, they survived the loss of their only child.'

McKay glanced up once more. Flanagan still watched him.

And why shouldn't she? Everyone else watched him too. That's what they're here for. Stay calm, he told himself. She can't see inside you. She can't read your thoughts. She doesn't know the terrible things you've done.

And still she watched him.

He coughed once more, and recommenced his sermon.

'Then six months ago, another accident almost took Mr Garrick's life. He survived, but with the loss of his legs, and the cost of a lifetime of pain. And still, Mr and Mrs Garrick turned to the only ones who could help them through such a torturous time: their God and their church.

'Now, if Mr Garrick had reacted to this life-changing accident with anger, all of us would have understood. Wouldn't any one of us have been angry? We'd have had a right, wouldn't we? But Mr Garrick was not angry. He and I talked and prayed together many times over the last few months, and not once did he speak a word of bitterness. What he did say was that if it was God's will that he should survive, there had to be a reason.'

McKay looked once more to the back of the church. Now, at last, Flanagan did not stare at him. Instead, she looked up to the vaults of the ceiling, around at the commemorative plaques, the stained-glass windows, the military standards hanging at intervals along the side walls, the harvest displays of pumpkins, root vegetables, sheaves of wheat, all arranged around the church by Miss Trimble and the other elder ladies of the congregation. He guessed Flanagan seldom visited a church unless someone needed burying. He returned his attention to his notes.

'And this morning, we gather here knowing yet another tragedy has struck the Garrick family. All indications are that, on Sunday evening, Mr Garrick took his own life. I want you all to know that he died peacefully, without pain. We'll never know what brought Mr Garrick to this final decision, but we understand that six months of tremendous suffering have taken their toll. But I want to believe that when Mr Garrick closed his eyes for the last time, he did so with his faith as strong as it had been four years ago when he lost his daughter, and six months ago when he came so close to death. Because without faith, what do we have left?'

McKay knew the answer to that question.

Nothing. Without faith, we have nothing.

13

Then I have nothing, Flanagan thought.

She felt a piercing spike of self-pity, an emotion she detested above all others. Get out of me, she thought, I'll have no more of you.

Reverend McKay wrapped up his sermon and said, 'Let us pray.'

Flanagan kept her head upright while the rest of the congregation lowered theirs. And McKay too, his eyes open as he turned to the prayer desk, side on to the congregation.

'Dear Lord, we pray this morning for the soul of our departed friend, Henry Garrick. We pray that he is now at peace, that the depth of his faith in You brought him into Your eternal embrace, that his suffering is at an end, and that he is made whole again through Your grace and compassion.

'And Our Father, we also pray for Roberta Garrick, that she can find strength in us, her friends, and in You, that You can guide her through this difficult time. Lord, guide us in our efforts to provide comfort for the bereaved.'

McKay looked up from the desk, turned his head. His eyes met Flanagan's.

She felt a hot flush of shame, like a child caught stealing. She dropped her gaze to her hands, bowed her head like the others.

As McKay recommenced the prayer, Flanagan wondered at the power of this place to make a middle-aged woman bow her head even if she didn't believe. The memories a church roused in her, the little girl she had once been, the ritual of putting on her best Sunday clothes, fidgeting beside her mother as a minister droned on, then the Bible classes led by plain women, and how the stories frightened her.

When had Flanagan last attended a service? A year ago, she thought, when her friend Penny Walker had been buried along with her husband. And Flanagan had prayed then, just as she prayed an hour ago for Miriam McCreesh.

Prayed to whom?

If Flanagan did not believe, then why did she pray so often? She rationalised it as a form of self-talk, an internal therapy session. Wasn't that it? Or were those Sunday mornings spent in places like this so rooted in the bones of her that deep down she believed this nonsense, even if her higher mind disagreed?

McKay's voice dragged her back to herself, the words, 'Our Father, who art in heaven.'

With no conscious decision or effort, Flanagan recited the Lord's Prayer along with the rest, every word floating up from her memories of school assembly halls and windswept grave-sides. As the syllables slipped from her tongue she weighed the meaning of each.

And she thought of her daughter, and the question she'd asked last night: was their marriage over? She had denied it, but truthfully, she didn't know. And she thought of the cold distance between her and her husband, his anger stoking hers. If it really happened, if they really split, she knew Alistair would fight for the children. And he might win. With a job like hers, with the hours she kept, she couldn't be sure the court would favour her. There was a real risk she would lose her children because of her job. A job that had once given her days meaning, now a daily mire of futility.

McKay had asked: without faith, what do we have left?

Without the job, Flanagan thought, what do I have left?

Her family should have been the answer. But even that seemed to be slipping beyond her reach.

The service over, the small congregation left their seats and drifted towards the exit. Flanagan felt the cool draught on the back of her neck as the door opened. McKay did not look at her as he joined his people in the late morning light. She heard snatches of hushed conversation between him and the parishioners.

Yes, a tragedy. She's bearing up. Keep her in our prayers.

The church empty now, Flanagan alone, her thoughts seeming to echo in the hollow space around her. She closed her eyes, leaned forward, her hands on the back of the empty pew in front of her, her forehead resting on them.

Oh God, what do I have left?

I am my job. I am my children. What am I without them?

Flanagan turned her mind away from the question, because she knew the answer was there, waiting to snare her and drag her further down. She opened her eyes, lifted her head, and saw Reverend Peter McKay standing over her, his hands in his pockets, his cassock and white gown draped over the back of another pew. Reflexively, her palm went to her cheek, wiped away a tear that wasn't there.

'Sorry,' he said, 'I didn't mean to interrupt your prayer. Please go on.'

'I wasn't praying,' Flanagan said, and immediately wondered why she would lie about such a thing in this of all places. 'Not really. Just thinking.'

'It's a good place to think,' he said, his expression warmed by a soft smile. 'And to pray. Sometimes they're the same thing. Anyway, I quite often come here to do both. At night especially, when it's quiet, when there's no traffic outside, just silence. We all need a peaceful place to hide in now and then.'

Flanagan returned his smile, was about to speak, but he took a breath.

'Listen, I'd like to apologise if I was curt yesterday evening when you dropped the keys off. It'd been a stressful day.'

'No need to apologise,' Flanagan said. 'I understand.'

'So what can I do for you?'

Flanagan stared up at him for a moment before she recalled why she had come here. 'Oh, sorry,' she said, reaching for her bag beside her on the pew, and the pen and notebook within. 'Just a few follow-up questions. All right to do it here?'

'Of course,' McKay said, lowering himself into the pew in front. 'Has the post-mortem been done?'

'This morning,' Flanagan said. 'I've just come from the Royal. Dr McCreesh, the pathologist, is going to report suicide to the coroner, who'll probably issue an interim death certificate in the next day or two. Then the remains will be released to Mrs Garrick.'

'And the inquest?' McKay asked.

He clearly knew the procedures, Flanagan thought; this wasn't the first suicide in his parish, and it wouldn't be the last.

'At least the spring,' Flanagan said. 'Maybe the summer.'

'It takes a long time to decide what everyone already knows,' McKay said. When Flanagan didn't respond, he said, 'You had questions for me.'

She readied her pen. 'About the Garricks. How long have you known them?'

'I've known Mr Garrick as long as I've been here. That's, what, twenty years? His first wife was still around then.'

'And when did they split?'

'About eleven or twelve years ago, I think.'

'What were the circumstances?'

'It's no secret,' McKay said. 'She was having an affair with one of the salesmen at the dealership. It'd been going on for months, apparently. She lifted £50,000 from one savings account, £70,000 from another, and just disappeared one morning. She and the salesman flew to Greece and bought a villa. The money ran out, of course, and the former Mrs Garrick had to take a job in some tourist bar. Last I heard, the salesman left her for some girl who was passing through on holiday.'

'How did Mr Garrick take it at the time?' Flanagan asked.

'He was devastated. But his friends in the church gathered to him, so did I, and we helped him through. That's what people outside don't tend to appreciate. That a church is not a building.' He waved his hands at the empty air around him. 'This is not a church. The stained glass, the altar, the pews, none of this makes a church. A church is a community, a group of human beings brought together by their faith, so close they become a family. And when one of our family is hurt, we help them.'

He dropped his gaze, smiling, ran his fingertips through his salt-and-pepper hair. 'Sorry, I didn't mean that to sound like a recruitment drive. Anyway, you get the picture.'

Flanagan smiled and nodded. 'When did Mr Garrick meet his second wife?'

'About seven, eight years ago,' McKay said. 'They met online. I suppose people do that nowadays.'

'So I hear,' Flanagan said.

'They'd been seeing each other a few months before he brought Mrs Garrick – Roberta Bailey, she was then – before he brought her along one Sunday morning. Everyone was taken with her straight away. She had this glow about her. Like the sun in winter.'

For a moment, McKay was lost in his memory of her. Flanagan measured the distance in his eyes, the years they peered through. Then his mind returned to the present and he focused on Flanagan.

'I married them a couple of months after that. I'd never seen Mr Garrick so happy.'

McKay's smile broadened to emphasise the point, but somehow it stopped at his lips, the rest of his features untouched.

'What about Mrs Garrick's life before that?' Flanagan asked. 'Who was Roberta Bailey?'

The smile left McKay's mouth, his face slackened. 'I don't really know. I suppose I never thought to find out. She just seemed to fit right in here, became a part of the community straight away, joined the choir, everything. There never seemed to be anything outside of the church for her, other than her husband.'

'What about the wedding?' Flanagan asked. 'She would have had friends and family there.'

McKay shook his head. 'She and her parents . . . Listen, does this have to go any further?'

'You're not under caution,' Flanagan said. 'Nothing you say is admissible to the inquest or any other investigation.'

He sat back, his brow creased. 'Any other investigation?'

'If a further investigation of Mr Garrick's death should be required.'

'You said the pathologist was satisfied it was suicide, that he'd made his report.'

'*She* has reported suicide to the coroner. But I am not bound by that report. If I'm not satisfied with the finding, I'm free to look at other possibilities.'

'Surely there are no other possibilities,' McKay said.

'There are always possibilities,' Flanagan said. 'I'm not disputing the pathologist's findings, I'm simply not closing any other doors for the time being. Anyway, as I was saying, nothing you say today is admissible in any court.'

'All right,' McKay said. 'It's just I'm getting reports about your officers doorstepping people from this congregation, asking questions.'

Flanagan opened her mouth to speak, but McKay held up a hand.

'I know, I know, it's routine, you have to do it. But this is a very close-knit community. Everyone talks. If anything I said to you wound up in a question to somebody else, it'd get back to Mrs Garrick. She's been through enough. I don't want to see things get worse for her.'

Flanagan looked him hard in the eye. 'I promise you, this investigation will be handled with discretion. You have my word.'

McKay gave a single nod. 'All right. What I was going to say is, Mrs Garrick had something of a troubled past. She and Mr Garrick told me about it before they married. There were some issues with addiction, alcohol, drugs – nothing too heavy, you understand, but enough to have caused her some problems. Enough to estrange her from her parents. When she found God she left that life behind, including whatever friends and family she had then. So when she and Mr Garrick were married, the bride's side of the church was filled by people from this congregation.'

'They had a child,' Flanagan said.

McKay's face darkened. 'Yes. You know what happened to her?'

'That she drowned. I don't know the detail.'

'Do you need to?'

Flanagan wished she could say no, she didn't need to hear about a child's death. Instead, she said, 'Everything helps.'

McKay's shoulders fell as he exhaled. 'They were on a short holiday in Barcelona. Wee Erin wasn't quite two. They went to the beach, somewhere out of the city centre, I don't know it, I've never been. Anyway, I believe Mr Garrick stayed on the sand while Mrs Garrick took Erin out into the water, paddling at first and then carrying her in her arms. Apparently Mrs Garrick was up to her waist, the water was calm, Erin was giggling, saying the water was cold. Mrs Garrick didn't see the shelf under the water. It dropped a few feet, I was told. She lost her balance, and both she and the baby went under. In the confusion, the child slipped out of Mrs Garrick's arms.

'Mr Garrick didn't know anything was wrong until people started running past him to the water. Mrs Garrick almost drowned trying to save Erin. They were able to revive her. But not the child.'

'You seem to know a lot of detail,' Flanagan said, 'considering you weren't there.'

'Mr and Mrs Garrick told me what happened many times,' McKay said. 'Many, many times. So, three years after I married them here, almost to the day, I conducted their little girl's funeral service. About the worst day of my career, to tell you the truth.'

As he stared at some faraway place, Flanagan had an urge to touch him, offer comfort. She ignored it.

'How did it affect their relationship? Many marriages don't survive a loss like that.'

McKay shrugged. 'They had a difficult year or two, there's no denying it. But once again, they had their faith and their church to cling to.' He turned to Flanagan. 'There's nothing God can't help you survive, if you'll only open your heart to Him.'

Had he aimed those words at her? Maybe, she thought.

'What about more recently, before Mr Garrick's accident? Had there been any problems?'

'None at all,' McKay said. 'At least none that I know of. Erin's death was hard to get past, of course, but they both threw themselves into church life. And community work. Mr Garrick put a lot into the local community. He'd done well in life and he felt he owed something back.'

'And then the accident,' Flanagan said.

'And then the accident,' McKay echoed. 'As if they hadn't been through enough.'

'Some might ask why a benevolent God would do such a thing to a good Christian family. Why would He heap tragedy upon tragedy like that?'

'Believe me, Mr Garrick and I had that conversation many times over.'

'And did you come up with an answer?'

Reverend McKay touched his fingertip to his lips while he thought for a moment, then his gaze met hers. 'May I take a wild guess at something, Inspector Flanagan?'

Flanagan nodded. 'Go on.'

'Doing what you do for a living, I assume you have much faith invested in the science of your work. In the crime scene, all that CSI sort of thing you see on the television. I'm sure it's not terribly accurate, that TV stuff, but I know there's a science to it. Forensics. Fingerprints, DNA, blood spatter, tests, measurements, readings, numbers, results. Correct?'

'Correct,' Flanagan said.

'And even presented with all that science, that evidence, all those hard facts, all these tangible things that you can see and touch, do you always get the answers you need?'

'No,' Flanagan said. 'Far from it.'

'Well then,' McKay said, 'if your faith in science can't answer all of your questions, why expect my faith in God to answer all of mine?'

Flanagan exited the church, tucking her notebook and pen away. She had found the small car park full when she arrived, and had left her Volkswagen out on the road, its inside wheels mounted on a grass verge.

She was halfway to the gate when a voice called, 'Inspector Flanagan, isn't it?'

Flanagan stopped and turned. Jim Allison, MLA, leaning against his Range Rover. She walked back towards him.

'Yes,' she said. 'We've met before, Mr Allison.'

'At the Policing Board meetings,' Allison said.

He extended his hand, and Flanagan shook it. She had sat across a table from him on more than one occasion as he questioned her and other senior officers about their work. The Policing Board was largely a bureaucratic exercise, a sop to those in the community who distrusted the police, but Allison always seemed to take his civic duty more seriously than the other public representatives who had been appointed to the board.

'I would say it's good to see you again, but not under these circumstances. I take it you're investigating Mr Garrick's case.'

'That's right,' Flanagan said. She resisted the urge to wipe her fingers on her trousers.

'Glad to see it's in capable hands,' Allison said. 'I hope you're making progress.'

Flanagan told him she was, and once more explained the pathologist's report to the coroner, and the inquest ahead.

'Good,' he said. 'Listen, here's the thing. I know a suicide requires almost as much digging as a murder case, and I know you have a job to do, and I trust you'll do it thoroughly and diligently. But I'll also ask that you conduct it sensitively. Mrs Garrick is a close personal friend of mine, just as her husband was, and I don't want her to suffer any more distress than she has already.'

86

'Of course,' Flanagan said, offering only enough deference to satisfy his ego. 'I always try to tread as gently as I can when I go about my work. This case will be no different. Have a good day.'

She went to leave, but his fingers closed on her upper arm. She turned back to him, stared down at his hand until he got the message and lifted it away.

'Try won't be good enough this time, Inspector Flanagan. I'll be keeping a close eye on things, and if I suspect Mrs Garrick has been caused any more distress than is absolutely necessary I won't hesitate to go to the Assistant Chief Constable.'

Flanagan took a step closer. 'Like I said, I will conduct this investigation with the utmost sensitivity, as I always do, but let me stress, it is my investigation. One other point, Mr Allison.'

He put his hands in his pockets and leaned back on his car.

She stepped closer still, inches between them, her eyes hard on his. He blinked, but did not look away.

'Do I have your full attention, Mr Allison? Then listen well.' Closer now, so close he couldn't hold her gaze any longer.

'Don't ever touch me again,' she said.

14

McKay slipped out through the vestry, closed the door behind him, locked it. He crossed the grounds to his house, opened the door. Inside, alone, he called out, 'Roberta?'

Not in the living room, he could see from here. Perhaps the bedroom. He hesitated to go up there after what had happened this morning, but he had no choice, he had to talk to her. He took the stairs two at a time, found the bedroom empty.

Where had she gone?

Then he knew.

McKay descended the stairs and let himself out. He crossed back to the church, skirted around to the rear, and the small graveyard on the other side. Only the wealthiest families could afford a burial here. The Garricks were one such family, three generations buried in their plot.

Roberta sat on the low marble wall that surrounded the plot, one hand resting in the gravel, smooth white stones between her long fingers. Two headstones at the top of the grave, one for Mr Garrick's grandparents and parents, the inscription updated over a span of thirty years.

The other headstone bore the name Erin Susan Garrick, the dates only twenty-two months apart: our cherished daughter, taken into the Lord's arms where we will see her again.

McKay slowed his step as he approached, his shoes crunching the loose stones on the concrete path. She heard him, clearly, but did not lift her head to acknowledge his presence. He stopped beside her, considered lowering himself down to sit next to her, decided against it.

'Are you all right?' he asked.

She sighed and said, 'What do you think?'

'I was worried when I didn't find you in the house.'

She kept her eyes on the grave. 'Do I need permission to go out?'

'That policewoman was here.'

Now she looked up. 'Flanagan? What did she want?'

'Follow-up questions.'

Roberta got to her feet. 'What did she ask?'

'About you and Mr Garrick,' McKay said. 'About how long I've known you, about the accident, about Erin.'

Roberta flinched at her daughter's name.

McKay swallowed and said, 'She suspects.'

'No she doesn't,' Roberta said too quickly, shaking her head. 'Why would she? What did she say?'

'Nothing specific. But the questions, they seemed to be leading somewhere.'

She reached for him, grabbed a fistful of sweater. 'Leading where? Tell me exactly what she said.'

He searched his memory, seeking words and intents. His mind scrambled through the fragments, trying to piece them together.

'I . . . I don't remember, not exactly.'

'Think!' She pushed and pulled him. 'What did she say?'

McKay staggered to one side, shuffled his feet for balance. Fear threatened to blot out his higher mind entirely.

'I don't know, I don't remember, I can't think, I can't . . .'

Roberta let go of his sweater and said, 'All right, calm down.'

'What'll we do?' he asked, his throat tightening, his voice rising. 'What'll we do? It's not just her, it's the other police, they're going around the village, asking questions.'

She placed her palm, still cool from the gravel, on his cheek. 'Shut up and calm down.'

'What if she—'

'Shut. Up.' Her fingers moved from his cheek to the side of his neck, warmer now, the heat cutting through the clamour in his mind. 'Calm down. Are you calm?'

She spoke as if he were a child, and in truth, wasn't he? Held here in her palm, he was an infant, blind and helpless, mewling for her succour. And she gave it to him. She reached her arms up and around his neck, drew her body close to his, her nose and mouth seeking the hollow between his jaw and his shoulder. He had no choice but to wrap his arms around her waist, lose himself in her embrace.

'Be strong,' she said, her voice low, her breath rippling across his skin. 'Remember everything we talked about. Everything we're going to have together.'

'Together,' he said. 'You promised. Together.'

'I know,' she said, releasing herself from his arms, bringing her hands to his face. 'And I keep my promises.'

15

Flanagan knocked on the door of DSI Purdy's office and opened it without waiting for permission. She leaned in and saw him at his desk, the telephone handset pressed to his ear. He raised his hand and beckoned her to enter.

'I understand that,' he said into the mouthpiece.

Flanagan took the seat opposite him.

'I do,' he said. 'I do understand.'

She watched as he closed his eyes in exasperation.

'I don't know, but what I can tell you is that DCI Flanagan is one of the best police officers I have ever had the good fortune to work with.'

Flanagan's skin prickled. She pointed to the door, eyebrows raised, silently asking if Purdy wanted her to leave. Purdy shook his head and pointed to the chair she already sat in.

'That's as may be, but this is DCI Flanagan's case, and she will conduct it as she sees fit with no interference from me. If that's not good enough for you, then feel free to complain to the ACC next time you have a round of golf with him. Have a good day.'

He slammed the handset into its cradle and said, 'Fucking prick.'

'Allison?' Flanagan asked, even though she knew the answer.

'Yep,' Purdy said, leaning back in his chair. He took off his glasses, tossed them onto the desk, and rubbed his eyes. 'Was I a little abrupt with him?'

'A little,' Flanagan said.

'Good. If he thinks being on the Policing Board means he can start telling me my job, he's got another think coming. He tries that shit again, I'll bury my boot up his hole.'

Flanagan smiled, partly at the image, partly at the knowledge that Purdy had stood his ground for her. He was a good man. She had spent much of her career working under his command, and although those years weren't without friction – they had both made mistakes they regretted – he had been as good a mentor as she could have wished for. She would miss him when he retired.

Not long now. Boxes were stacked against one wall of the office, his personal items packed in one pile, paperwork filling the rest. A man's career wrapped up and ready to be taken away.

'So, what's the deal with this suicide?' Purdy asked. 'Are you near ready to close it up?'

Flanagan took a breath and said, 'No, I'm not.'

'Explain,' he said as he reached for his glasses.

'It's probably a suicide,' Flanagan said. 'Everything's pointing that way. More than likely, once we've got the coroner's report, I'll close the investigation and leave it to the inquest.'

Purdy tapped the leg of his spectacles against his teeth. 'But?'

'But I'm not sure. Not a hundred per cent.'

'Care to elaborate?'

'Something doesn't feel right.' Purdy went to speak, but Flanagan raised her hand. 'No, let me finish. I know I need more than a feeling to go on, you don't need to tell me that, but there are details that don't add up.'

'Such as?'

'The photographs.'

Flanagan explained the arrangement of the photo frames around the corpse, how they faced away, how Mr Garrick couldn't see his loved ones as he slipped into the dark. She told him of the conversation she'd had with the nurse, how she'd said Mr Garrick had been in good spirits right up to the end.

'That's pretty flimsy,' Purdy said. He rested his chin in his hand and blew air out through his lips. 'Do you need a calculator?'

'Sir?'

'Well, you're adding two and two and coming up with Christ knows what.'

'We won't have the coroner's report for a day or two yet, Murray's still working on the laptop and iPad, the DCs are still doorstepping in the village, and the body won't be released until the end of the week. I've got a few days to dig a little deeper.'

'All right,' Purdy said. 'But go easy. Remember, there's a bereaved woman at the centre of this. Don't cause her any more hardship than you absolutely have to. Understood?'

'Understood,' Flanagan said.

An email from DS Murray awaited Flanagan when she returned to her office. A preliminary examination of the laptop found in Mr Garrick's room showed searches over several weeks for lethal doses of morphine. The cookies stored on the machine showed that whoever made the searches had been logged into Mr Garrick's Google account. There was more information to be gleaned from the computer, but these searches had been what they were primarily looking for. Everything that built towards a suicide, anything that showed intent or planning.

'It's a suicide,' Flanagan said aloud to herself. 'Admit it's a suicide and let it go.'

Problems, Reverend Peter McKay had said. Addiction.

Even so, she logged into her computer and opened the interface for the ViSOR database. She entered the names B-A-I-L-E-Y and R-O-B-E-R-T-A, narrowed the region to Northern Ireland. One result. Flanagan clicked on the name, and the record appeared.

A different woman entirely, this one forty-seven years old, a haggard face, a history of minor assaults and public order offences. Now living in a hostel in Newry.

Flanagan closed the ViSOR interface and opened the DVA database. This time, she entered Roberta Garrick, along with the address of the grand house.

Roberta Bailey had applied for a provisional driving licence twelve years ago, aged twenty-three, and her full licence six months later. Seven years ago, the surname was changed to Garrick, and the address updated. A few months after that, a speeding offence, and three points. Then another, and another.

Those cars, Flanagan thought.

No more points after that. Mrs Garrick's heavy foot could have earned her a driving ban, but she had apparently learned to slow down. The points had expired by the time the licence was renewed two years ago.

'Who are you?' Flanagan asked the screen.

Next, a straight Google search, combinations of the name and social media sites.

"Roberta+Garrick+Twitter"

No Twitter account under that name. She didn't seem the type, anyway.

"Roberta+Garrick+Facebook"

Half a dozen matches, three of them in America, one in New Zealand, one in England, and here, at last, Mrs Garrick smiling from the screen. An informal portrait for her profile picture, a glowing white-toothed smile. A little over a hundred friends. A handful of likes, including her church and her husband's car dealership.

Flanagan scrolled down through the sparse timeline. Nothing but occasional Bible quotes, and photographs she'd been tagged in, the choir here, the floral society there, and precious little else. Had she no life outside her marriage and the church?

She clicked the link to look closer at the Likes list. Almost nothing. No music, no films, no books, only a few local businesses and religious groups.

'Just for show,' Flanagan said aloud. Roberta Garrick had a Facebook account because that's what people do, not because she wanted one for herself. As artificial as keeping the good towels for guests.

'You're a work of fiction,' Flanagan said.

A nonsensical idea. She scolded herself for allowing the very thought to form in her head. Not everyone wants to use social media, or even knows how. Flanagan had never bothered with any of those websites. Why did she expect Mrs Garrick to have any real presence on them?

Roberta Garrick has done nothing wrong, Flanagan thought.

Then why does she bother me so?

Flanagan decided then that she needed to speak with Roberta Garrick today.

16

McKay woke alone, the sheets cool beside him. Roberta had left some time ago.

He had dreamed of Maggie, as he often did. A year ago, he would have woken with the lingering memory of her, despairing that the dream had not been real, that she was not back here with him, returned from whatever strange journey she had taken. Now, he felt relief that she had not come back from the dead to condemn him for what he'd done, that she would never see who he had become.

He reached for the framed photograph on the bedside locker, turned it back from the wall. Maggie smiling, pretty as she'd ever been. So pretty he couldn't stand to look at her for another second. He turned her to face the wall once more.

McKay checked his watch. Two hours he'd been asleep. He swung his legs out of the bed and reached for his clothes. A few minutes later he descended the stairs, slowly, quietly, feeling like a thief come to rob his own house.

He found her at the kitchen table, typing on his old Dell laptop. It took a few moments for her to notice him watching from the doorway. Her eyes flashed in fear or anger for an instant, he couldn't be sure which, before she gave him the faintest of smiles. A few more clicks and keystrokes, then she closed the computer, placed her hands on top of it.

'What are you doing?' McKay asked.

'Nothing,' Roberta said. 'Just reading emails.'

'Be careful. They can check that sort of thing these days. See what you've been saying, what you've been looking at.'

'I know,' she said. 'It's nothing for you to worry about.'

He was about to ask her if she wanted something to eat when the doorbell rang, startling them both. McKay looked back over his shoulder towards the front door. He exhaled when he saw the now familiar shape.

'Is it Flanagan?' Roberta asked.

'Yes,' he said.

'Tell her to go,' she said. 'I'm too distraught to talk.'

'What if she insists?'

'She can't force me to talk to her unless she arrests me. Tell her she can't see me.'

McKay looked from the door to Roberta and back again. The doorbell rang once more. 'It might look bad. Maybe you should—'

'Just fucking tell her,' Roberta said, her words cutting the air between them.

McKay nodded. He was halfway along the hall when he realised he was barefoot, only half dressed. Too late to turn back. She could see him through the frosted glass.

He reached for the chain lock and slid it into place before he opened the door as far as the chain would allow.

'Inspector Flanagan,' he said.

'Reverend,' she said. She looked at the chain. 'No need for that, is there?'

He stared back at her through the gap, his mouth opening and closing, searching for a reason to disagree. When he could find none, he smiled and said, 'Sorry, force of habit. I've been robbed twice by bogus callers.' He slid the lock free, let the chain hang loose. Easing the door open a few inches more, he asked, 'What can I do for you?'

'I'd like to speak with Mrs Garrick,' she said, looking past him into the hall.

He couldn't help but follow her gaze to the closed kitchen door. He imagined Roberta on the other side, her ear pressed against the wood.

'No,' he said, turning back to Flanagan. 'Not today. She's really not fit for it.'

'It won't take long,' she said. 'Fifteen, twenty minutes at most.'

'No, she can't.'

'I will need to speak to Mrs Garrick at some time in the next day or so. If I could get it out of the way now, before the coroner issues the interim death certificate, it'd leave Mrs Garrick to make the arrangements for the funeral.'

'No, I'm sorry,' he said, his voice firm enough to make his point. 'So if there's nothing else I can do for you, I was just going to take a shower.'

Flanagan's shoulders fell as she exhaled. 'All right. But please tell Mrs Garrick I'll need to speak with her by tomorrow at the latest. You have my number. I'd appreciate it if you called me as soon as Mrs Garrick is ready to talk.'

'I will,' he said. He watched her walk back to her car, then closed the door.

Roberta waited in the kitchen, standing by the table. 'Thank you,' she said.

'You'll have to talk to her some time,' McKay said. 'You can't put her off much longer.'

'I need a shower,' she said, and walked past him out of the room.

McKay watched her climb the stairs, heard her enter the bathroom, then running water. Then he went to the table and opened the laptop. The web browser still showed the BBC news article he'd read last night. He clicked on the History tab. Only the last few pages he'd browsed. She'd used the private browser window, the computer recording no traces, no history, no cookies.

She'd been covering her tracks, hiding from him.

Hiding what?

That sick feeling again, deep in his stomach. Like the ground shifting beneath his feet.

I will suffer for this, he thought. I will suffer and I don't care.

17

Flanagan entered the darkened utility room, closed the back door behind her. She passed through the dim kitchen, then out into the hallway. The sound of her footsteps on the wooden floor reverberated in the grand space, rippling through the still air. She froze and listened for a few moments, trapped by the quiet of the house, as if it held its breath, waiting for her to speak.

Intruder, it would say. Get out. Leave us in peace.

But I need to know her better, Flanagan would reply, I need to know her secrets.

She had toured this house the day before, room to room, and saw nothing to shed light on Roberta Garrick. Only the same tasteful shows of wealth Flanagan had already seen and desired for herself.

The bedroom. If the truth lay anywhere in this house, it would be there. Flanagan climbed the stairs to the double doors, opened them, stepped through. Light in here. Someone had opened the blinds. Either Mrs Garrick or the rector. A few items of clothing lay on the bed, considered for wearing and then discarded.

Flanagan's gaze went to the wall above the dresser, the space where the missing picture had been. She walked to the dresser and opened the top drawer. The same portrait of the child, hidden here among the papers and letters. Flanagan lifted a bundle of envelopes and leafed through them. Bank and credit card statements. A car insurance renewal notification. Passports in Mr and Mrs Garrick's names, both with several years left on them. Medical cards. Reissued birth certificates for both of them, a marriage certificate. And here, kept together, the birth and death certificates for the child, the latter issued in Spain.

'Can I help you?'

A cry escaped Flanagan's throat before she could stop it. She turned towards the voice.

Roberta Garrick stared at her from the threshold, her face blank.

'Mrs Garrick,' Flanagan said. She swallowed, searched for something to say. 'How are you feeling?'

'What are you looking for?' Mrs Garrick asked, stepping into the room.

'Nothing specific,' Flanagan said.

'It's hard to find something if you don't know what it is,' Mrs Garrick said. 'I'll give you anything you need, but I'd consider it a courtesy if you'd ask before you go rummaging through my personal items.'

Flanagan held Mrs Garrick's stare. 'I would have asked if I'd been able to speak with you. But Reverend McKay wouldn't allow it.'

Mrs Garrick put her hand to the drawer, began to push it closed.

'Why do you keep your daughter's photograph in there?' Flanagan asked.

Mrs Garrick's hand paused, the drawer still half open. 'Because sometimes it's too hard to look at her. Sometimes I can't bear it, other times I want to see her, then I take the picture out and hang it up.' She pushed the drawer the rest of the way, sealing the framed photograph inside. 'You wanted to talk with me. Let's get it out of the way.'

They sat opposite each other in the living room, the blinds open, sunlight reflecting off the polished surfaces. Flanagan, pen in hand, set her notepad open on her lap.

'Reverend McKay tells me you met your husband online,' Flanagan said.

Mrs Garrick nodded. 'That's right. Lots of people meet like that these days.'

'True,' Flanagan said. 'And how long after that did you marry?'

'A bit less than a year.'

'That was quick,' Flanagan said.

'We knew we were right for each other,' Mrs Garrick said. 'Why wait?'

'And you had your little girl within a year. Was she planned?'

'Not really. Harry was a bit older than me. He wasn't sure about having a baby at his age. But when I realised I was expecting, then we accepted the Lord's blessing.'

'How did he take your child's death?'

Mrs Garrick's features hardened, her lips thinned. 'That's a ridiculous question,' she said. 'How do you think he took it?'

'Well, I'm told he coped well with the consequences of his car accident, under the circumstances. Was he able to deal with your child's death in the same way?'

'No. No, he wasn't. It almost destroyed him. It almost destroyed us both. We put a brave face on it, but we barely held our marriage together. It took a year to come back to anything resembling a normal life. Even then, it was still difficult. But the Lord got us through it eventually.'

'And Reverend McKay helped.'

'He's been very good to us. I don't think we could have coped without him.'

'You and he are particularly close,' Flanagan said.

Mrs Garrick nodded. 'He's a good friend.'

An idea flitted across Flanagan's mind, a question. Too much? Too hard? She asked anyway. 'More than that?'

Mrs Garrick stared, her eyes burning. 'How dare you?'

Yes, it had been too much, but Flanagan kept her face impassive, would not take it back. 'It's just a question.'

Mrs Garrick stood. 'We'll have to do this another time.'

Flanagan remained seated. 'Can't we just keep—'

'Another time,' Mrs Garrick repeated, a tremor in her voice now. 'Please.'

'Mrs Garrick, if we can—'

'Isn't it enough?' she asked, her voice rising, breaking. Her hands shaking. 'When is it enough? I have nothing left to give.'

Now Flanagan stared. 'I don't understand,' she said.

Mrs Garrick blinked, seemed to return from somewhere. 'First my little girl,' she said, her voice thinner, softer. 'Now my husband. Just when I think God might let me breathe, let me live, He burns it all down again. I don't know if I can take any more.'

Mrs Garrick collapsed back onto the couch, her body limp. Tears spilled.

Flanagan sat frozen, caught between her instinct to comfort this bereaved woman and the need to follow her suspicion.

Mrs Garrick shook her head as she spoke, her face contorting as she turned it up to the ceiling, her voice aimed beyond. 'I can't, I can't take any more. If you want to kill me, then kill me. Don't make me suffer this, please, I've had enough. No more, please, no more.'

Flanagan thought of the white coffin, the devastated car, the body she'd watched being taken apart that morning.

'Christ,' she whispered. She set her pen and notebook aside, then crossed to the couch, beside Mrs Garrick. She slipped her arm around the other woman's quivering shoulders, gathered her in.

Mrs Garrick curled into Flanagan's lap, muttering, 'No more, no more, no more . . .'

Back in her car, Flanagan called DS Murray's mobile.

'Are you at the station?' she asked.

'Yes, ma'am. Just got the last of the info back from the computer searches.'

'Anything to trouble us?'

'No, ma'am, not that I can see.'

'All right,' Flanagan said.

She closed her eyes, placed her free hand on the dashboard, concentrated on the sensation of the soft plastic on her skin, the coolness of it, allowed it to settle her mind.

'Ma'am?'

Flanagan opened her eyes again. 'Gather up all the paperwork, all the reports, get everything in order for me to sign off on.'

'You're going with suicide?'

'Yes,' Flanagan said. 'Yes I am.'

18

McKay waited for her in the kitchen, a mug of tea long cold in front of him. It had occurred to him to prepare a meal, but he didn't know what she'd want to eat. What if he made something she didn't like? The idea of displeasing her caused a small terror in him.

Could that be right? If he loved Roberta, how could he be afraid of her? And yet he was. McKay banished the thought. To seek logic in the madness of recent days was the maddest idea of all.

Roberta had said she wouldn't be long, no more than an hour. It had been more than two going by the clock over the kitchen door, and he had been picking at a thread of worry for thirty minutes now. As the notion that she might not return, that she had fled, began to take form in his mind, the front door opened.

From the kitchen table, McKay watched Roberta, the fading evening light silhouetting her on the threshold as his fear dissolved. She closed the door and approached the kitchen.

'Don't worry about the policewoman,' she said.

'Why?' McKay asked, fear returning, colder and brighter than before. 'What happened?'

'Never mind why,' Roberta said. 'We don't have to worry about her any more, that's all.'

McKay studied her face, but it was unreadable. He wiped his fingers across his dry lips and said, 'There was a call from the coroner's liaison. They've declared it suicide, pending the inquest, and they'll have the interim death certificate ready by tomorrow.'

'What does that mean?' she asked.

'It means you can bury him.'

Her shoulders fell. She placed a hand on the table to steady herself.

'Then it's all done,' McKay said. 'It's over.'

She exhaled, a long, whispery expulsion of air. 'Over,' she said. She pulled out the chair opposite McKay and sat down, rested her palms on the table. Stared at some point miles beyond his shoulder.

'We can talk after the funeral.'

Her gaze returned to him. 'About what?' she asked.

He swallowed. 'About us.'

She blinked once and said, 'I'll go back home first thing tomorrow morning.'

'You don't have to.'

'It'd be best.'

He looked down at his hands. 'All right.'

Without speaking further, she stood and left the kitchen. When she reached the bottom of the stairs, he called after her.

'Can I bring you something to eat?'

She did not reply as she climbed the stairs, and the idea that he had lost her reared up again. And again, he told himself no, no she is mine now, always and for ever.

To think otherwise might kill him. Might kill them both.

19

Alistair looked up from his plate as Flanagan let herself through the back door and into the kitchen. Ruth and Eli both glanced in her direction, but neither spoke. Bolognese sauce smeared Eli's chin. Ruth went back to spinning spaghetti onto her fork.

'Anything for me?' Flanagan asked.

Alistair nodded towards the hob. 'There's a little left in the pot. I wasn't expecting you home.'

Flanagan put her bag on the worktop, slung her jacket over the back of a chair. 'Well, I wanted to make sure and eat with everyone tonight. I haven't done that enough lately.'

Alistair shrugged and picked up his fork. 'If you'd let me know, I would've made more.'

She scooped the few spoonfuls of minced beef and pasta from the pot onto a plate. 'This is plenty,' she said, even though it wasn't. An empty jar of ready-made sauce sat by the cooker. She took a fork from the drawer and brought the plate to the table. She sat down opposite Alistair, with Ruth and Eli at either side.

The children stared at their food. Alistair stared at the wall.

Flanagan reached for the last piece of garlic bread, broke it in two, chewed a mouthful without tasting it. She swallowed and said, 'So, any news?'

No one answered.

'Ruth, what about school? Anything happening?'

Ruth shrugged and said, 'Same as usual.'

Flanagan reached for Eli's hand and asked, 'What about you, wee man?'

Eli looked down at Flanagan's hand, kept his gaze there until she released her hold on him. His hand retreated to his lap.

'All right,' she said, forcing a laugh into her voice. 'I'll just shut up, then, will I?'

Alistair's fork clanked on his plate. 'You can't just waltz in here and expect us to act like everything's fine. You've barely spoken to your children in months, and you think they're going to be all over you just because you decided to show up tonight? You know I had to go and see Eli's teacher today?'

Flanagan shook her head.

'Mrs Cuthbertson,' Alistair said. 'Do you even know that's who his teacher is? No? Well, I had to go and see her today and be told he's been picking on other kids.'

She turned to her son. 'Oh, Eli, why—'

'Save your breath, I've already talked to him about it. The point is, you have no idea what's going on with your own family. You think it's just another late night on the job, what does it matter? And every night I'm having to make excuses for you when they ask where you are. Now, I'm at the end of my bloody rope with this. You need to decide if you're part of this family or not.'

Ruth pushed her plate away and left the table. Only when she'd gone did Flanagan notice the tiny pools where her tears had fallen.

'If you want to stay with us,' Alistair continued, 'then stay with us. But be *here* with us. Or else there's no point. Or else you might as well pack up and get out.'

Now Eli stood and left. His fork rang as it hit the tiled floor.

'Well?' Alistair said. 'Are you going to say anything?'

Flanagan brought her hands together to suppress the tremor of anger. 'Of course I want to stay here. This is my home. Those are my children. But what are you? You've been pushing me away for a year now. Longer than that. Ever since I was first diagnosed, it's like I was tainted.'

'That's not fair.' Alistair sat back, his hands on the table. 'I did everything I could for you while you were having the treatment.'

'Everything except be my husband.'

'What does that mean?'

'You know what it means.'

Alistair's chair scraped on the tiles as he stood. He said nothing as he left.

Flanagan brought her hands to her face, rested her elbows on the table.

'Fuck,' she said. 'Fuck.'

Flanagan woke in the night, stirred by her son's cry.

A few seconds of disorientation scrambled past before she remembered she had gone to sleep in the spare room, on the lower landing, next to the bathroom. Eli's cry had come from in there, echoing against the tiles. She threw back the duvet and went to the door, the creeping tendrils of a dream still snaking through her mind.

She found Eli crouched over a puddle on the floor, his soaked pyjama bottoms bundled beside it. He held a wad of toilet paper in his hand, mopped at the liquid with it. He looked up as she entered, shame and fear on his round face.

'I couldn't hold on,' he said, tears coming. 'I tried really hard, but I couldn't.'

Flanagan kneeled down next to him. 'It's all right, love, don't worry about it. It's just an accident, that's all. We'll get it sorted.'

She pulled more paper from the roll and mopped up the rest then tossed the pyjama bottoms in the laundry hamper. After washing her hands, she reached for the buttons on Eli's pyjama top.

'Let's pop you in the shower for a second.'

Eli pulled away. 'I want Dad to do it.'

Flanagan reached again. 'Dad's sleeping.'

'No, I want Dad.'

'He's sleeping. Come on, I can do it.'

'I want Dad!' His voice rang in her ears.

Flanagan stood and said, 'Okay.' She left Eli there, climbed the short flight of stairs to the top floor and entered the bedroom she should have shared with her husband. She nudged him and said, 'Eli needs you.'

Alistair sat up in the bed, blinking in the light from the landing. 'What?'

'Eli needs you,' she said. 'He's in the bathroom.'

She returned to the spare room, closed the door, and got back into the cold bed. The tears came then, and she covered her mouth and nose so no one would hear.

20

McKay set Roberta's bags on the hall floor.

'I can bring them upstairs for you if you want,' he said.

Roberta followed his gaze up to the double doors of her bedroom. 'No,' she said. 'They're fine here.'

She turned and walked to the end of the hall and the closed door to her husband's death bed. She turned the handle, opened it. McKay saw the bed, the wheeled table, the photographs. The framed verse on the wall.

'Just two days ago,' she said.

'It's done now,' McKay said. 'No going back.'

'No,' she said as she pulled the door closed. 'No going back.'

They stood at opposite ends of the hall for a time, he staring at her, she staring at the door.

'Look,' he said eventually, 'I'll leave you in peace. I can come over this evening, if you like.'

'Why?' she asked.

That cold feeling in his stomach again. He realised it was somehow worse that she hadn't understood why he offered than if she'd simply said no.

He cleared his throat. 'Well, they're bringing him home tomorrow. With the wake and all the fuss, tonight might be the last chance we have to . . . to . . .'

He waved his hand towards her bedroom door, feeling heat creep up his neck and into his cheeks. Don't make me say it out loud, he thought.

She walked the length of the hall to him, the click-clack of her heels resonating through the house. 'It's best we be discreet,' she said before placing a dry kiss on his cheek.

'For now,' he said. 'You're probably right, let's keep things simple for now.'

She nodded, smiled, took his elbow and turned him towards the door.

McKay saw DCI Flanagan's Volkswagen Golf as he pulled into the church grounds. He parked his Fiesta by the house and crossed to where she waited, the driver's door open. She looked up at him as he approached, but couldn't hold his gaze.

With terror in his heart, McKay asked, 'What can I do for you, Inspector?'

She glanced up at him and away again, indicated the building that cast a shadow over them both. 'I thought I might come to the morning service,' she said.

'Oh,' he said, unable to keep the surprise from his voice. 'Sorry, only Tuesdays, Thursdays and Saturdays for matins.'

'Matins?'

'Morning prayers.'

'I see,' she said. A tear rolled down her cheek. 'It's just . . . I . . . I think I need to pray.'

She took a seat at the end of the third row, gripped the rolled top of the pew in front of her. Her fingers flexed and relaxed, gripped again. Real strength there, but they were not masculine hands. McKay's eyes were always drawn to a woman's hands before any other part of her. The touch of cool soft skin, hard bones within. These were the sensations he recalled when he thought of the few women he had been with in his life.

'Am I supposed to kneel?' Flanagan asked.

He looked from her hands, along her arms, her shoulders, up to her face. How frightened she looked. And yet he suspected this was a woman who feared little in the world.

'You can kneel if you want,' he said. 'Or you can sit, or you can stand, or you can run laps around the church.'

He gave her a smile, but the joke seemed lost on her.

'Sorry,' he said. 'What I'm trying to say is, God doesn't much care what you do when you pray. All He wants is for you to open your heart to Him.'

'Okay,' she said, returning his smile now, if only a flicker. She looked towards the altar, her eyes wet, reflecting the greens and reds of the stained-glass windows.

'Shall I leave you alone?' he asked, pointing his thumb back to the vestry.

She opened her mouth, her voice crackling in her throat before she found the words. 'I don't know what to do. I don't know what to say. I don't believe in this.'

'Then why are you here?' McKay asked.

Flanagan shook her head. 'I don't know.'

McKay hesitated a moment before sliding into the pew in front of her. He rested his arm on the back. Her hands lifted from the wood, hung in the cool air, then returned, knuckles showing white beneath the skin as she gripped.

'In my experience,' he said, 'whether you believe in prayer or not, just saying something out loud can make it smaller, take away the power it has over you.'

'I've been having counselling sessions,' she said. 'Dr Brady, once a fortnight, fifty minutes of me talking and him pretending to listen.'

'Has it helped?'

'Not one fucking bit.' She gave him a shamed glance, then dipped her head. 'I'm sorry.'

'Don't be,' he said. 'Swearing does the soul good. Keep it to yourself, but I've been known to let the odd f-word slip myself.'

She smiled, held it on her lips a little longer this time before it slipped away. She took a breath before she spoke. 'There was an incident a few months ago. I suppose it wasn't a full-blown breakdown, but it wasn't far off. A man died. I didn't kill him, it was entirely his own doing, but all the same I felt like I had. He and another man had tried to shoot me five years ago. The shooter was the pillion passenger on a motorcycle. His pistol jammed, and I shot him. One in the head, one in the chest. He died right there.

'The other, the one driving the bike, he took off. A couple of streets away, he ran a red light right into the path of a bus. Took him five years to die. Like I said, it was his own stupid bloody fault, but when I found out he'd died, I fell to pieces. I know it doesn't make any sense. I've spent my career dealing with killers. I've seen the cost of what they do. And I'm one of them. Doesn't matter that I didn't choose to be.'

McKay's mouth dried as she spoke. He put a hand over his lips and nodded.

She can't see inside me, he thought. She can't.

'Have you buried any murder victims?' Flanagan asked.

He managed a nod as he took his hand from his mouth. 'Just one,' he said, his voice a whisper.

'Then you know what it does to the people left behind. It blows families apart. Destroys marriages. Ruins children's lives.'

Tell her.

The thought rang clear and bright in his mind.

Tell her and be done with it.

His hand went to his mouth once more, teeth hard on his palm. He nodded again.

Tell her or save yourself, he thought. One or the other. Do it now.

Flanagan stared at him. His skin burned where her gaze touched. She went to speak.

Do it now.

'But that's not why you're here,' McKay said. No quiver in his voice. 'Is it?'

She dropped her eyes, and he exhaled.

'Is it?' he asked again.

Flanagan's left hand shook as she lifted it from the pew back and wiped fresh tears from her cheeks. McKay waited, left room for her, knowing the confession would come before long.

Finally, she said, 'I'm losing my family.'

A sob from deep in her chest, and she looked away.

Fear leaving him, relief taking its place, McKay put a hand on her wrist and said, 'Tell me.'

21

Flanagan couldn't be sure what had brought her here this morning. She'd left the house before Alistair rose, before the children stirred, and had driven to Lisburn and the fortress-like station. Her office door locked, she sat at her desk, paperwork laid out across its surface. All of it meaningless to her, nothing but shapes and scrawls on pages.

Some time before nine, she messaged DSI Purdy, said she was going to follow up on the last details for the Garrick suicide. She went to her car and drove the small roads across country as far as Lurgan, then circled back east towards Moira, with the intention of going home for an hour. Just an hour to think, that was all.

But to get there, she had to pass through Morganstown, with its one main street, the church at one end, the filling station at the other. She made no conscious decision to hit the indicator, to slow, to pull the steering wheel to the right. And yet she found herself parked by the grey wall of the church, reaching for the key to kill the ignition.

She sat there for a time listening to her own breathing, hearing its strange dry resonance in the car, before it seemed the glass all around was only an inch from her skin. Then she opened the driver's door and felt the cool morning air wash in.

So quiet here. No traffic on the street. Nothing but the whisper of leaves on trees, silvery threads of birdsong between the branches.

She knew no one else was here, hers was the only car on the grounds, even McKay's was gone. Looking across the car park, she saw the old house and wondered if Mrs Garrick was in there, grieving the desperate angry grief of those robbed by suicide. She remembered the widow's tears and felt a sting of guilt.

Why had she been so determined to find some dark stain on this woman? A woman who had borne more loss than most would in a lifetime. What had Flanagan seen in Mrs Garrick that she wanted to believe her husband's death had been anything more than it appeared? Was it bitter envy for all Mrs Garrick had?

Flanagan would never have believed herself capable of such a base emotion, but there it was. She had been ready to torment Roberta Garrick further in her time of grief in pursuit of a truth that existed only in her own mind. Mrs Garrick's husband had been physically devastated by a terrible accident, and months of agonising recovery had left him unable to face more. That was all, and Flanagan had to let it go.

But the photographs . . .

No, too thin. Too much of a reach. Still wanting Mrs Garrick to be guilty of something just because she disliked her.

'Enough,' she said aloud, startling herself.

Only when she looked around to see if anyone had heard did she notice Reverend Peter McKay walking towards her. Now he was sitting in the pew in front of her, his warm hand on her wrist, and she wanted to tell him every rotten thing that festered in her soul.

She told him about the Devine brothers, Ciaran and Thomas, how they came to her home a year ago with the intent to do her harm, and how instead Ciaran stabbed her husband in their bedroom while their children cowered downstairs. She told him how the case came to an end on a beach near Newcastle, how everything that she'd done had helped no one, least of all the young man the brothers had murdered in a Belfast alleyway. Over the following twelve months, as she drifted from her husband and children's reach, she had wondered over and over what she had achieved in her career. Had it been worth the loss of her family?

'Then quit,' McKay said.

She stared at him for a moment, disoriented at being pulled from her spoken thoughts. 'What?'

'If your job's making you miserable, then quit,' he said. 'Simple, isn't it?'

Flanagan shook her head, fumbling for an answer. 'No, it's . . . it's not . . .'

He smiled that kind smile of his, the one that warmed his eyes. 'No, it's not that simple, is it? We have this in common, you know. Neither of us has a nine-to-five job we can leave behind at the end of the day. We don't work in some office, watching the clock, waiting for home time. You don't stop being a police officer when you go home any more than I stop being a priest. Not even when we go to sleep at night. Do you dream much?'

'Every night,' Flanagan said. 'About the ones I couldn't help. They stare at me. They point at me. They tell me I should have tried harder, asked one more question, turned over one more stone.'

'Then you are your job, your job is you. Same for me.'

'And I am my family. I need them, even if they don't need me.'

His fingers tightened on her wrist, a small pressure. 'Then the answer lies somewhere between the two. It's like two sides of an arch. One can't stand without the other.'

'Then what do I do?' she asked, another sob catching in her throat.

'What you came here for,' McKay said. 'You pray.'

As new, hot tears spilled from her eyes, McKay got to his feet.

'Now I'll leave you to it,' he said. 'Let yourself out when you're ready.'

As he stepped away, Flanagan reached for his hand. He turned and looked down at her, and she suddenly realised how tired he appeared, darkness beneath his eyes, lines deepened by the light and shade of the church. She regretted the insinuation she'd made the day before when interviewing Mrs Garrick, that there might be more to the minister's and the new widow's relationship. It had been unfair and uncalled for. She decided she would apologise to Mrs Garrick, if she got the chance.

'Thank you,' Flanagan said. 'You're a good man.'

Something flashed across his face, something quick and furtive, gone before she could fully see it.

'A good man,' she said again.

He nodded, smiled, squeezed her hand, then left her alone with the God she did not believe in.

22

McKay closed the vestry door behind him, leaned his forehead against the wood.

Shakes erupted out from his core, to his hands, to his legs. His knees buckled and he collapsed into the door, then staggered across to the desk beneath the window.

A good man.

The words clawed at him.

'I am not,' he whispered. 'I am not.'

A good man.

Maybe once. But not now.

I killed a man so I could have his wife.

Go back out. Go back out and tell her.

Tell her there is no God, that she is praying to air and stone and glass and nothing else.

Tell her this good man is a killer who deserves hellfire for his sins.

But McKay went nowhere. Instead, he remained at the desk, wishing he had a God to pray to.

23

Flanagan spent the next two days in prayer. An hour in the silence of the church before the stillness of the air seemed to press against her, squeezing her chest tight. Then in the car. Then in her office with the door locked. Then in the bed in the spare room, duvet pulled up to her mouth.

On the second night, she left the spare room, climbed the small flight of stairs to the master bedroom. She knocked lightly on the door. After a few moments, Alistair opened it.

'Can I sleep with you tonight?' she asked.

'It's your bed,' he said. 'You don't need to ask. And you don't need to knock.'

She followed him to the bed, climbed in beside him, into his open arms. Warm and familiar and shocking. She rested her head on his chest.

'I'm sorry,' she said.

A few seconds passed before he asked, 'What for?'

'For not being here for you and the kids. And for the distance I've put between us.'

She felt his chest fall as he exhaled.

'I'm as responsible for that as you are,' he said. 'I've been thinking about it all day. I've been pushing you away since before what happened last year. I think I need to talk to somebody about it. Get some counselling.'

She almost told him about the prayer that had brought her back to their bed, but felt suddenly shy. They did not believe in such things, she and her husband. And anyway, her prayers were between her and whatever listened.

'Maybe we should both talk to someone,' she said. 'As a couple, I mean.'

'Maybe,' he said.

'But listen.' She moved her head so she could see the profile of his features in the darkness. 'You have to understand, I need to do my job. It's what I'm good at. It's what I've worked for my whole adult life. You can't ask me to choose between my job and my family, because it's not really a choice. I need both. I'm not me without them. Both of them.'

Quiet, the only sound their breathing in the dark.

Then Alistair spoke. 'All right. But you have to leave your work outside. When you come into our home, all that other stuff, it stays outside.'

'Says the man who spends his evenings marking homework,' she said, smiling.

'I'm serious.'

'I know. And I promise I'll try. And you have to promise not to push me away.'

'I promise,' he said.

They kissed and slept hard into the morning.

Flanagan arrived early at the church, but still she had to park a hundred yards down the road, wheels up on the kerb. She had known it would be a big funeral – Henry Garrick had been a well-liked man in the community – but even so, she was surprised. Before she got out of the car, she sent a text message to Miriam McCreesh, wishing her luck with the appointment at the Cancer Centre.

Before she pressed send, she checked her watch, realised the test might have already happened. She knew the routine: the probing, the scanning, the sting of the biopsy. The hours between being sent away and coming back for the results. A long and lonely day, even if you had someone to hold your hand.

Flanagan walked towards the church, buttoning her black jacket. Groups of men and women, some younger, most older, moved in the same direction, and Flanagan found herself part of the tide. She listened as people exchanged greetings, their polite laughs, their remembrances of past encounters. A strange comfort in these voices, and she recalled funerals she'd attended in the past, the coming together of family and friends, aunts or uncles seldom seen, cousins she barely recognised.

The farewell to an elderly relative often had a muted joy about it. If their time was due, and the suffering and indignities of their withering years were at an end, then wasn't that a good thing? Sad, yes, but wasn't life itself?

But this kind of funeral was different. Mr Garrick had not been taken by heart failure after days wired to machines in a hospital side ward. There had been no long and slow decline to be endured. True, Mr Garrick had spent his last months in terrible pain, but even so, it was not his time. Flanagan had gone to enough suicide funerals to know there was no joy or gratitude to be found here.

Police cones at the gates to the grounds to keep them clear for the hearse and the family cars. As Flanagan walked towards the church, she checked her watch. Quarter past eleven. The service was to start at noon. As she entered, an elderly gentleman handed her an order of service printed on folded A4 paper. He smiled and said good morning as he did so, and Flanagan couldn't help but return the smile.

Inside, she found a place in a pew two rows from the back. Soft organ music played, sending warm waves of sound through the church. It was already two thirds full. With the first two rows reserved for family, the place would be packed tight.

As she let her gaze wander the congregation, Flanagan noticed a middle-aged man, slender, well dressed. Mid fifties, or perhaps younger but prematurely grey. It was difficult to tell from this angle. He sat across the aisle, two rows forward. Flanagan watched as he bowed his head, rested his knees on the prayer stool, and clasped his hands together. She could just make out the movement of his jaw as he spoke to his God.

Right there in front of everyone. As if it was the most natural thing in the world.

And wasn't it?

It is a church, after all, Flanagan thought. If he can't do it here, where can he?

She looked around. No one paid him any attention. No one cared.

Flanagan put her hands on the back of the pew before her, brought them together, twined her fingers. Then she slid forward until her knees rested on the padded bench. She took one more look around, saw no one watching, then bowed and closed her eyes.

'Dear God,' she whispered in a voice so low only the Creator could possibly hear. 'Thank you for my blessings. Thank you for my children, for my husband, for keeping them well, and for keeping us together. Thank you. And please help Miriam with her test this morning. Please let it be good news.'

She raised her head and said aloud, 'Amen.'

When she got back up onto the seat, she looked back towards the middle-aged man whose prayer had inspired her own. He sat turned in his pew, watching her. Flanagan froze as if caught in some misdeed. She saw now that the man was older, perhaps near sixty, and his eyes were tearful and hollow. He nodded to her, and she returned the gesture, realising his features were familiar. The man turned away, and Flanagan studied the back of him, digging for a memory, anything to reveal his identity.

She spent the next forty-five minutes wondering about him as the church filled. By the time the coffin arrived, shoulders pressed against hers at either side. The hum of chatter faded as the widowed Mrs Garrick arrived, walked up the aisle to the reserved seats, arm-in-arm with another woman.

Then Flanagan heard Reverend McKay's voice behind her, coming from the vestibule. She turned her head, but she could not see him.

'We receive the body of our brother Henry Garrick with confidence in God, the giver of life, who raised the Lord Jesus from the dead.'

When he finished the verse, the congregation said, 'Amen.' Flanagan said it too.

She watched as McKay led the group of six men along the aisle, the coffin resting on their shoulders. Two undertakers guided the coffin onto the waiting trolley at the front.

McKay went to the lectern and said, 'We meet in the name of Christ who died and was raised by the glory of God the Father. Grace and mercy be with you all.'

The congregation said, 'And also with you.'

Flanagan said it too, beats behind everyone else. As she said the words, McKay's eyes met hers, and from the back of the church, even over this distance, she saw despair in them.

24

McKay recited the words with no awareness of their meaning. They were only shapes in his mouth, movements his tongue had made hundreds of times over the years.

He looked out to the people, his gaze finding Flanagan.

Save me, he thought.

She stared back, and she saw it on him, he was sure. He looked away, looked anywhere but at her. Then he found Roberta in the front row, and she did not look at him.

She had barely looked at him the day before, during the wake. All the same people, the congregation of this church, milling around the house. Cups of tea, small sandwiches, biscuits, cakes, sausage rolls. The kitchen a production line of kindly women, the hall lined with folding chairs, borrowed by the vanload from the old school hall across the road from the church that served as a community centre, now bearing the weight of middle-aged men holding cups and saucers.

The chatter of voices and the clink of china, this was the sound of a wake to Reverend Peter McKay. The smell of tea and sweat.

Roberta had the coffin put in the back room where Mr Garrick had spent his last weeks. McKay didn't want to see it, didn't want to look at the face of the man he'd killed. But such was his duty. When he arrived at the house in the early afternoon he lingered in the hall as long as he could, shaking hands, patting shoulders, refusing cups of tea.

Soon there was no more avoiding it. He walked to the room at the rear of the hall, paused in the doorway. A small cluster of men greeted him, and he stepped inside. They moved out of his way, allowed him space. As fear pushed up from his belly and into his throat, threatening to choke him, McKay approached the coffin. Varnished oak, gold-plated handles, glistening in the light from the window. McKay swallowed and looked inside.

Silk covered the body to the waist, disguising the missing legs, the gnarled hands powdered to hide the scarring. And the face, waxen and hollow, like a doll.

I'm sorry, he wanted to say. I wish I could take it back. I shouldn't have done this terrible thing, and I'd give anything to take the poison from your mouth.

And every unspoken word was true. As he fought the urge to weep, McKay startled at the sound of a voice at his shoulder.

'Sure, you'd think he was sleeping, wouldn't you?'

He turned to see Mr McHugh staring into the coffin.

'They can do wonderful things, these days, the undertakers. I remember when we buried Cora's mother it looked as if they'd made her up as a clown.'

McKay knew he should have replied, perhaps enquired after Cora's health, was she getting out at all lately? Instead, he walked away, out of the room, and struggled through the kitchen full of trays and steam and gossip until he found the door to the utility room and the small bathroom off that.

Had he still believed in God, McKay would have thanked Him that the bathroom was unoccupied. He closed and locked the door, leaned against it. A small space, no more than six feet by four, the toilet at one end, a washbasin at the other, lit by a narrow frosted window.

For the first time in a decade, he felt the craving for a cigarette. That dry need at the back of his throat, in his lungs, waiting for tarry blue smoke. He had never smoked more than ten a day, even as a young man, but still the desire was great.

Later.

Later, he would go to a shop in some other town and buy a packet of cigarettes and smoke them until he hacked up grey phlegm, until he was dizzy and nauseous. But now he had to pull himself together. Get through the next forty-eight hours. That was all.

Last night she had given him hope.

Roberta still hadn't wanted him to come over – discreet, she'd said – but her voice had been warm and kind. Loving, even. Enough to let him think there might be an after, a beyond. If he survived, there could be a future for him and Roberta, as tainted as it might be.

His thin surface of calm restored, McKay left the bathroom, back out through the kitchen, into the hall, avoiding every hand that reached out for him, every seeking face that wanted to snare him in banal conversation. He kept his focus on the door to the good sitting room, where he knew Roberta would be, the queen on her throne holding dominion over her subjects.

She did not look up as he entered the room. A cup of tea on a saucer held on her lap. Black skirt, white blouse, minimal make-up. A beautiful young widow mourning her husband. McKay crossed the room, swerving between the feet and knees of those seated here, towards the one narrow space on the couch, opposite her.

'Excuse me,' he said to Miss Trimble, the aged spinster who always insisted on giving him a critique of his sermons. She moved sideways, leaving him just enough cushion to squeeze onto.

Now the widow saw him.

'Reverend Peter,' she said.

'Mrs Garrick,' he said. 'How are you holding up?'

A gentle smile. She tilted her head. 'Not too bad.' She shared the smile with the people all around. 'Everyone's been very kind.'

With that, she turned away from him. A clear instruction. Don't talk to her.

And he wanted to slap the cup and saucer from her hand, grab her shoulders, shake her. And tell her what? He loved her? He hated her?

He said nothing. Sat with his hands on his knees, exchanged greetings with the good people as they came and went, while magnificent fury burned inside him.

'We have come here today to remember our dear friend Henry Garrick,' McKay said, his voice carrying over the congregation. The echo of the loudspeakers sent his words back to him, a booming muddle of vowels and dull consonants. 'To give thanks for his life, to leave him in the keeping of God his creator, redeemer and judge, to commit his body to be buried, and to comfort one another in our grief, in the hope that is ours through the death and resurrection of Jesus Christ.'

Words upon words upon words. He worked through each stage of the ceremony, the prayers, the hymns, the psalm, the calls and responses, the standing and sitting. All the time he avoided the policewoman's gaze, and Roberta avoided his.

He read from the First Epistle of John, asking the congregation to reflect on the fleeting nature of life on this earth, because one's gaze should be beyond. He almost choked on his hypocrisy as he came to verse fifteen.

'Love not the world, neither the things that are in the world. If any man love the world, the love of the Father is not in him. For all that is in the world, the lust of the flesh, and the lust of the eyes, and the pride of life, is not of the Father, but is of the world. And the world passeth away, and the lust thereof: but he that doeth the will of God abideth for ever.'

He watched Roberta as he read the words lust and flesh, but she did not react.

Then he moved to the pulpit for the sermon, the usual recounting of the deceased's life and loves, their hobbies, their foibles, their losses, their victories. Roberta smiled and nodded when appropriate. When McKay spoke of the drowned child, she bowed her head, pulled a tissue from her sleeve and dabbed at her cheeks while Miss Trimble put a comforting hand on her shoulder.

Now a final glance up at him, so quick, so sly. Barely enough for him to see the dryness of her eyes as he said her dead daughter's name once more.

He stared down into the open grave, the fine wood of the coffin marred by the handfuls of earth that had broken on its surface. The Lord's Prayer murmured around him, and for an insane moment he wondered who had prompted the gathered people to recite it before he realised he spoke it himself. He faltered over the final lines, but the voices around him carried him to the finish.

'Lord,' he said, 'you will show us the path of life: in your presence is fullness of joy, and from your right hand flow delights for evermore.'

A moment of stillness, only the breeze rustling through the trees, then the crowd began to disperse. McKay shook hands with a few as they passed on their way to Roberta to give their final condolences.

He backed away, worked towards the periphery. The day was far from over; tea and sandwiches were to be served in the community centre, please join us, all welcome. At least two more hours of small talk and handshakes, two more hours of swallowing the scream that had been coiled in his throat since the coffin entered the church.

But a moment, please, a moment of quiet. He made for the church, imagining the silence of the vestry. He could take his time removing his cassock and surplice, hanging them up, putting on his jacket. The half-full packet of Marlboros was hidden in the safe, along with a packet of mints. No one would miss him for fifteen minutes, surely? He nodded and smiled to the stragglers on the path back to the church, ignored any attempt to slow him, to talk to him.

'Reverend McKay.'

A woman's voice, behind him.

'Reverend McKay?'

He knew whose. He kept his head down, quickened his step. She was quicker.

DCI Flanagan touched his arm. 'Reverend McKay.'

He turned, feigned surprise, hoped she wouldn't see the fear on him. 'Ah, sorry, Inspector, I was in a world of my own. And it's Reverend Peter.'

'Reverend Peter,' she echoed. 'Sorry to keep you back. I just wanted to thank you for the other day. For taking the time to talk with me. It helped, it really did.'

McKay felt the fear slip away almost entirely, replaced by something else. What was it? He couldn't be sure; his emotions had become a confused jumble in recent days, and he struggled to tell one from another.

He wetted his lips and asked, 'And did the prayer do any good?'

'Yes,' she said, a smile blooming on her mouth. 'I'm still not sure who or what I was praying to, maybe I was just talking to myself, but it helped me see things more clearly. My husband and I had a good talk last night. Things are looking better.'

'Good, I'm glad,' he said, meaning it.

In that moment, he saw something in Flanagan that alarmed and calmed him all at once: her decency. In all the filth he had allowed himself to wallow in for the last few months he had lost sight of that most human of qualities. And here, confronted by this woman's basic goodness, he felt awed by her. Once more he wanted to tell her everything, throw himself on her mercy.

It must have told on his features, because a crease appeared on her brow.

'Is everything all right?' she asked, putting her hand on his arm again.

'Fine, fine,' he said, backing away. 'It's been one long day after another, is all. Sorry, I need to get these robes off and get over to the hall. Will you be joining us? You're very welcome.'

Even as he asked the question, he regretted it. A small burst of relief when she shook her head.

'I have to get to work,' she said, moving towards the gates. 'Thanks again.'

She walked to the drift of people exiting the grounds. When he'd lost her among them, he went back to the church, into the cool and the quiet. He ignored Mr McHugh who was packing away his sheet music at the organ and headed straight for the vestry. The door closed and locked behind him, he pulled the surplice over his head, let it fall to the floor, unbuckled the belt at his waist, threw the cassock off. He got down on his knees, hit the four-digit combination on the safe, reached inside for the lighter and cigarettes, pinched one between his lips, sparked the thumbwheel, inhaled.

Oh, glorious heat, filling his chest, that crackling through his veins, into his skull.

He exhaled a long plume of smoke, felt a dizzy wave wash across his forehead, took another drag. Once the wave passed, he got to his feet and went to the small window protected by a wire grille. He opened the top pane, blew smoke through.

I've gotten away with it, he thought.

Such a certain and reasonable idea, he couldn't question it. Flanagan had moved on, more concerned with her own life now than his or Roberta's. The coroner had ruled it suicide. If he held his nerve just a little longer, if he could keep a wall around the crushing guilt that threatened to break him, if he could do that, he had gotten away with it.

A high whoop of a laugh escaped him, followed by a stream of tears.

He had gotten away with it.

They had gotten away with it.

25

Flanagan edged through the cluster of mourners at the gate, fighting against the flow towards the community centre. She wanted to turn right, head towards her car, but she was swept onto the road. She persevered through the dark suits and sharp-cornered handbags, excuse me, excuse me, thank you, excuse me, until she emerged into clear air. There, she joined the thin trickle of people who didn't want to partake of tea and sandwiches.

Her Volkswagen in sight, she kept her head down, walking along the roadway, avoiding the bottlenecks of people on the footpath.

From behind, 'Excuse me!'

Another person trying to escape the crowd. She kept going.

'Excuse me! Hello?'

Footsteps jogging behind her. Flanagan turned, feeling suddenly defensive for no reason she could comprehend.

That man, from the church. The middle-aged man who knelt in prayer, the familiarity of whose features had nagged at her throughout the ceremony. He slowed his pace, fighting for breath.

'Can I help you?' she asked, trying to ignore her growing wariness.

'Are you the police officer who's handling Harry's case?' he asked between gulps of air.

'That's right,' she said. 'DCI Flanagan. What can I do for you?'

'My name's George Garrick,' he said. 'Harry's brother.'

It made sense, then, the familiarity. The scarring had blurred the dead man's features, but enough remained for the likeness to his brother to be clear. For a moment, Flanagan felt she knew what Henry Garrick had looked like in life, tall and gently handsome. She wondered if he had spoken with the same country softness to the consonants as George Garrick. With the wondering came a sadness that he had gone and no one would hear his voice again.

She pushed the thought aside and said, 'I see. I'm sorry for your loss.'

He fussed at his well-worn suit jacket. 'Thank you. I recognised you from the news. I wanted to have a word, if you've time.'

She looked towards her car, thought of the paperwork at the station that needed doing, then turned back to him. 'Of course.'

'It's about Harry,' he said. He looked to the crowd filtering into the old school hall before speaking again. 'And Roberta. I need to tell you something about her.'

'Go ahead,' Flanagan said.

She noticed the redness of his eyes, realised he had been weeping for his brother. The grief lingered beneath the surface, its vague form visible to her through his skin.

'That woman,' George Garrick said. 'She's evil.'

* * *

'I stayed near the back,' he said. 'Out of the way. I daren't have let her see me there.'

George Garrick sat in the passenger seat of her car, his knees pressed against the glovebox, his head nearly touching the roof lining. Some of the other cars had started to move away. He looked over his shoulder, put his elbow on the door, his forearm shielding his face from outside.

'Why not?' Flanagan asked.

'She would've made sure I got driven out. She wouldn't stand to have me about the place. I haven't been welcome around here for four years now.'

'Why?' Flanagan asked.

'Roberta made sure of it. The lies she told about me. The things she accused me of.'

The last words caught in his throat, and he brought his hand to his mouth, his eyes brimming. Flanagan did not prompt him, allowed him to find his own way.

'I never touched her,' he said eventually, wiping at his veined cheeks. 'I swear to my Lord God above, I never touched her. I swore to Harry, I swore to the rest of them, and I swear to you, I never laid one hand on that woman.'

He wept now, tears running free to drip onto his shirt.

'And I have to tell you this. I've never said it to anyone, not once. But I have to say it now.'

Flanagan reached across, put her hand on his forearm. 'Go on,' she said.

'Oh God,' he said. He hissed through his teeth as if the pressure of his secrets might burst him at the seams. He looked skyward, then closed his eyes. 'Oh God. Dear God forgive me, I think she killed her child.'

Fat raindrops slapped against the car's windscreen. Flanagan's nerves jangled, electricity coursed across her skin.

'From the start,' she said. 'Tell me what happened.'

He sat there for a while, his head gently shaking, a tiny movement, almost nothing at all. His breathing settled, the tears dried. He took a breath and began.

'I was so happy for Harry when he met her,' he said. 'He'd been struggling since his first wife cleared out. He put a brave face on it, he was always a proud man. Not in a sinful way, I mean, but he was the sort of fella wouldn't tell anyone his problems. But I knew he was struggling. He was lonely. He had all this money, and no one to share it with. All he had was his business, that and the church. If he'd been a drinker like me, he probably would've let that eat him up.

'Anyway, when Roberta came along I was delighted for him, the same as everyone else. You could see how happy he was. I knew he was going to marry her before he did. I was best man at his wedding. Second time I did that for him. I started to see less of him after the wedding, but I thought, sure, that's only natural. He's got a lovely wife now, why would he be bothered with his useless auld lump of a brother.

'She threw herself into the church, joined in all the activities, all the clubs. Really made herself a part of the community. Everyone loved her. So did I. She just pulled people to her. Then she got pregnant and everyone was over the moon. You'd think the whole town and country was an uncle or an aunt to that child.'

A smile broke on his face, wide and toothy. Flanagan couldn't help but reflect it. He blushed, dropped his gaze.

'Wee Erin. She was a beautiful wee girl. An awful good baby. They never had any trouble with her. She fed well, she slept well. She was talking away by the time they went to Barcelona. She couldn't make a whole pile of sense, but you could see the personality coming through, who she was going to grow into. Who she might have been.

'It was Reverend Peter phoned me to let me know. I remember it like it was five minutes ago. It was evening time, I was having a wee whiskey, watching the snooker on TV. The wife was washing up. I answered the phone and he told me, and I hung up and I went and put that bottle to my mouth and I never took another breath till it was gone.

'Oh God, the funeral. It was the worst I'd ever seen. The crying. People cry at funerals, course they do, but not like this. And me and Harry carried that wee white coffin and, oh God, I wanted to take Harry and pull all the pain out of him and take it for myself.

'And I remember, I stood by the graveside, that same grave she stood by today, and I looked across and I saw Roberta. And I knew it was an act. Everyone else was too worked up to see it, but I saw it, like she was wearing a mask.

'I started wondering then. I started drinking, too, more than I should have. Maybe if I'd laid off the drink for those few months, maybe I would've made more sense of it. But here's the thing. She was a swimmer. A good swimmer. Not everyone knew that, but I did. She used to go to Lisburn, and I saw her there, doing lengths. She cut through that water like she could win a medal. And somehow she goes out into the sea and loses her child? Nearly drowns herself?

'The more I thought about it, the more I couldn't make sense of it. And the way she'd looked at the funeral. Maybe I should've gone to Harry about it, or the police, or just kept my bloody mouth shut. But one Sunday after church, Harry and Roberta had me and the wife to theirs for lunch. I'd had a few wee nips from a quarter bottle in my pocket, the wife didn't approve, but I felt like I needed it. Anyway, usually Janet and Roberta would've done the dishes, but I insisted Janet sit down and take it easy.

'So there's me and Roberta in the kitchen, loading up the dishwasher, sorting out the pans, and I says to her about wee Erin. I say, tell me again how it happened, and she sort of closed up, said she didn't want to go over it again. But I didn't let it go. I says to her, I don't understand it, as good a swimmer as her, and she couldn't help wee Erin. Even if she lost hold of her, how come she couldn't get her back? How come she nearly drowned herself?'

George went quiet, his eyes distant, the memory holding his mind there in the past. Flanagan wondered how many hours he'd lost to it over the years, locked there.

'How did she react?' Flanagan asked.

'She just stared at me for a minute,' George said. 'I remember the two of us standing there, her with a stack of plates in her hands, me with my hands in my pockets. And then I saw who she really was. Like she'd taken off this disguise she was wearing, and I could see what she really was underneath. And I knew then she killed her daughter. And she knew I knew.

We stood still like that for I don't know how long, not saying anything, just knowing each other. I saw something inside her, something that's sick, that's not human. I see it every night when I try to sleep. I see it every time I think of my brother, and when I remember wee Erin. I think of the monster she showed me that day.

'She dropped the plates. There was this almighty crash, pieces going everywhere. And then she screamed, stop it, stop it, let go of me, and she ran for the door. Harry came in then, and she ran right past him and upstairs. I went and got Janet and said, let's go, and I got out of there.

'Harry called me that night. He said he didn't want to see me ever again, not at home, not in the street, and not at church. Before I know it, it's all around the town and country that I grabbed my brother's wife, tried to feel her up when she's still grieving for her child. And of course, the rumour got worse the further it spread. Janet started hearing all sorts of things on the street. She stuck by me for a month, but it got too much for her, all the talk and all the looks she got. She couldn't take it any longer, even though she knew it was nonsense. She moved back to Bushmills, where she's from.'

He seemed diminished, shrunken into the seat, as if telling all this to Flanagan had bled something out of him. He shook his head and looked at her.

'That woman destroyed me. She might as well have put a gun to my head and pulled the trigger. It's years since I set foot on this street. And now my brother's dead. My brother, who was the strongest man I ever knew in my life, who thought suicide was the worst sin a person could commit. I tried, but I never got to see him after the accident. I know he was in bad shape, but if he had a thread of life to hang on to, he never would have given up. I know that. I know it in my heart. My brother did not kill himself.'

Flanagan remained silent and still, her mind racing.

'Have you nothing to say?' he asked. 'Tell me I'm mad, at least. Tell me something.'

'The coroner has reported it as suicide,' she said.

'I know that, but—'

'I was there when the pathologist did the post-mortem examination. Everything pointed towards suicide. Everything.'

'You sound like you're trying to convince yourself more than me,' he said.

Flanagan shook her head. 'I don't know what else to say.'

'Well, at least I told someone.' He reached for the door handle. 'I don't have to go to my grave carrying this thing around with me. I suppose what you do with it is up to you. But I had to tell you. You understand that, don't you?'

'I do,' Flanagan said. She put her hand on his arm. 'And again, I'm sorry for your loss, I really am.'

He nodded and opened the passenger door, climbed out, ducked down to look in at her.

'Whatever happens,' he said, 'just remember what she really is.'

He closed the door before Flanagan could reply, and she watched in her rear-view mirror as George Garrick slipped between the parked cars and out of her vision.

26

'You're looking terrible, Reverend Peter,' Miss Trimble said.

McKay had tried to avoid her, had veered around a row of chairs, but she had ducked through a gap and headed him off.

'Have you not been sleeping?' she asked.

He looked past her, beyond the rows of people with their combination plates and saucers, cups of tea or coffee balanced on one side, mounds of sandwiches and sausage rolls on the other. At the long table at the top of the hall, by the curtained stage, Roberta sat, people leaning in from all sides to offer their kinship, like Christ at the Last Supper. One empty chair at the table where McKay should have sat. He had spent as much time as he could touring the room, shaking hands, smiling, saying thank you for the compliments on his sermon. Miss Trimble had not been the first to comment on his gaunt appearance.

Now, as people began to say farewell, the room emptying, he had no choice but to take his seat. First, he went to the long table laden with trays and cups and plates, two large urns at one end. He took a plate, lifted a few scraps of food, paying no mind to what he had chosen.

'Tea or coffee, Reverend?' Mr Wellesley asked.

'Yes, please,' McKay said, watching her across the hall.

'Which?'

'Oh,' McKay said, turning back to Mr Wellesley. 'Tea, please.'

Mr Wellesley poured him a cup and set it on the outstretched plate. McKay thanked him and walked towards the stage, and the table before it. She glanced up as he approached, looked away again, leaning across to listen to whatever drivel Jim Allison spouted.

McKay sat down between them, forcing Allison to speak around him.

'I was just saying, it was a good service.'

'Thank you,' McKay said.

'I saw that policewoman talking to you outside the church,' Allison said. 'Has she been bothering you? I can deal with her if she has.'

McKay shook his head. 'No. She's been nothing but courteous and professional. I think we'll not be hearing from her again until the inquest next year.'

'Okay, good,' Allison said. 'I need to be off, but I'll see you on Sunday.'

He stood and patted McKay's shoulder before crouching down and putting an arm around Roberta. 'Take care, now, and let me know if you need anything. Anything at all.'

McKay watched Allison's back as he left, saw him shake hands and smile his way through the thinning crowd.

'You don't like him, do you?'

He turned to Roberta, startled at the teasing in her voice. 'It's not up to me to like or dislike my congregation. My job is to care for them, whoever they are.'

'He's not that different from you,' she said.

'He's nothing like me.'

'You sure about that?'

He tried to read her face, even though he should have known by now that she was unreadable. Was she mocking him? Was it playfulness or spite? Or were they the same thing to her?

'You were right,' he said.

'About what?'

'About DCI Flanagan,' he said. 'We don't have to worry about her. She's not—'

Roberta squeezed his arm, stopping the words in his mouth. She looked around the room, at those close by, those still at the table.

'I need the bathroom,' she said. Then she lowered her voice. 'Follow me in two minutes.'

She left the table without waiting for a reply. McKay watched her walk to the entrance hall, avoiding encounters with sympathetic friends, moving through the people like a snake through grass. He checked his watch, counted the seconds. Someone at the table spoke his name. He pretended he didn't hear.

When two minutes had passed, exactly, to the second, he rose from his chair and made his way to the entrance hall. No one tried to talk to him, no one reached for his elbow. He rounded the corner to the two unisex toilets out of view of the hall. One stood open and empty, the other an inch ajar. He went to it, put his fingertips to the wood, pushed.

Roberta stood at the washbasin, examining her face in the mirror above. She turned to him as he closed the door, locking them both inside.

McKay opened his mouth to speak, but before a word could find his tongue, her hand lashed out, her palm hard across his

147

cheek. He staggered back, tried to speak again, but she lunged at him, caught his throat between her fingers, pushed him against the door. The back of his head connected with the wood. Her fingers tightened, closing his windpipe. Black dots speckled his vision.

'Don't ever talk like that again in public,' she said through bared teeth. 'If someone heard, we'd both be finished. Watch your fucking mouth. Do you understand me?'

He tried to speak, but no air could pass through his throat.

She eased her grip and repeated, 'Do you understand me?'

'Yes,' he said, a thin croak between gulps of air. He put a hand on the wall to steady himself as his head seemed to drift away from his shoulders.

'Good,' she said, stepping back. She wiped the back of her hand across her mouth, her eyes burning. Then she lunged forward again.

McKay said, 'No,' and brought his hands up, tried to keep her away. But she grabbed his wrists, pulled his arms aside.

Please don't, he would have said, but her lips closed on his, her tongue soft and warm, her body in tight to him. Her hands went to his waist, his belt, the button, the fly. She took his lower lip between her teeth, and he felt a hot sting and tasted metal.

As chattering voices drifted in through the small bathroom window, Roberta dropped to her knees. She pulled fabric aside, baring him to her.

She grinned up at him, a red smear of his blood on her teeth.

27

Flanagan found DS Murray at his desk, engrossed in paperwork. She knocked on the wood to get his attention. He looked up, startled.

'Sorry, ma'am,' he said, blinking as if he'd come out of a slumber.

'Get on the phone to Barcelona, get hold of whoever in the Mossos d'Esquadra dealt with the death of Erin Garrick four years ago.'

'Who?'

'The Garricks' little girl,' Flanagan said, her voice rising with her impatience. 'She drowned at a beach there. I want to speak with whoever dealt with the case. Today, if possible. Organise a translator if one's needed.'

She walked away, and he called after her.

'Ma'am, what's going on?'

'Just get it sorted,' she said without looking back.

Flanagan went to her office, fired up her computer. A minute later she had the telephone number for the British Consulate in Barcelona. One minute more and she was on hold for the Third Secretary. She had to wait five more before an answer came.

'This is Julia Heston-Charles, how can I help?'

The accent was stiffly English, public school through and through.

'This is Detective Chief Inspector Serena Flanagan, Police Service of Northern Ireland, based in Lisburn. I need to discuss the case of a child, a British national, who drowned at the beach in Barcelona four years ago. Her name was Erin Garrick, her parents were Henry and Roberta Garrick.'

A moment of hiss in the earpiece before Heston-Charles said, 'Yes, I remember.'

'You dealt with this?'

'Yes. It was just before I went on maternity leave. I was seven or eight months pregnant at the time. Not a pleasant case to deal with when you're about to have a child of your own.'

'No, I suppose not,' Flanagan said.

'What do you need to know?'

'Anything,' Flanagan said, her pen ready. 'Whatever you can remember about it.'

'All right,' Heston-Charles said. The line went quiet as she gathered her memories. 'If I recall correctly, the initial contact came from the police officer who dealt with the case. Can't think of his name, but he was an inspector. He called a few hours after the accident. In these situations, the Consulate needs to liaise with the police, the coroner, the local government, the undertakers, the airline for getting the body home, all on the family's behalf. It's quite an operation to oversee.'

'Did you have much contact with the Garricks themselves?' Flanagan asked.

'Some. They were still at the hospital when I first met them. The mother was in the emergency ward herself, she almost drowned trying to save the little girl. The father was just wandering the corridors, he didn't know what to do with himself. I sat him down and talked him through the procedures. He was in a terrible state, understandably. Confused, angry, despairing. It was a difficult conversation.'

'I can imagine,' Flanagan said, remembering the many death notices she'd delivered, facing the denial and fury of the bereaved. 'And what about the mother? How was Mrs Garrick?'

'She was different,' Heston-Charles said. 'Whoever pumped the water out of her lungs cracked one of her ribs in the process, so she was in physical pain as well as emotional. The doctors had given her morphine, as much to sedate her as to kill the pain, I think. It all seemed to be washing over her, as if she was watching this happen to someone else. She was almost serene, I remember. Almost smiling, at times. I didn't deal with her much; it was mostly Mr Garrick after that. He pulled himself together over those few days, got everything dealt with. I believe his brother flew over to help, too.'

Flanagan took a breath before asking, 'Were there ever any questions about what happened?'

A pause, then, 'What do you mean?'

'The police, the coroner, did anyone dispute the Garricks' version of events?'

'Goodness, no. Can I ask, what's this about? That little girl drowned four years ago. Why are you digging into it now?'

'Sorry, I can't discuss that,' Flanagan said. 'It's nothing for you to be concerned about.'

Heston-Charles's voice hardened. 'But it concerns me enough that you need to interrupt my working day to question me about it.'

'I do appreciate your time,' Flanagan said. 'I'm sure you understand why I can't discuss what I'm dealing with here.'

'I understand. Doesn't mean I have to like it. Now, is there anything else you need to know?'

Flanagan scanned her notes. 'Not at the moment. You've been very helpful, thank you. Can I get back in touch if need be?'

'I suppose so. Good afternoon.'

The line died, and Flanagan looked at the handset. 'Fuck you too,' she whispered before hanging up.

Her fingers hadn't left the telephone before it rang. She picked it up.

'DCI Flanagan,' she said.

'What's going on?' DSI Purdy asked, not even bothering with a greeting.

Flanagan closed her eyes as she searched for something convincing. 'Just following up on some details, sir,' she said, knowing he wouldn't accept such a weak explanation.

'Some details,' he echoed. 'I was chasing young Murray for some paperwork and he tells me you have him tracking down someone in Spain for you. To do with the Garrick case, I'm told. Exactly what details can a cop in Barcelona clarify for you?'

Flanagan winced as she spoke. 'I just had a few questions about the little girl's death.'

'I fail to see the relevance,' Purdy said.

She would have to tell him, there was no getting around it. 'This morning, at the funeral, Henry Garrick's brother found me, said he had to talk to me.'

'And?'

Flanagan told him all of it, every detail. When she'd finished, he said nothing for a while. When he did speak, he said, 'All right, but tread carefully. I don't need that Allison prick annoying me because you stuck your nose where it didn't belong. Understood?'

'Understood, sir,' Flanagan said. 'Thank you.'

Relieved, Flanagan hung up and turned back to her computer and its web browser. A few search phrases later, she had Roberta Garrick's Facebook profile open once more. A string of condolence messages had been posted by her friends, but otherwise nothing had changed. Including the irrational feeling that this woman did not really exist in the world. No schools listed, no former places of work. As if she'd sprung into life fully formed seven years ago.

Flanagan returned to Google and combined Roberta Garrick's name with that of every social network site she could think of, even those that had fallen from fashion years ago, as well as every major shopping site in case she'd ever reviewed anything online.

Still nothing.

After an hour's fruitless searching, Flanagan realised she had forgotten to eat. She went to the canteen and ordered some toast and a coffee. She ate alone, the only other customers being a cluster of uniformed officers discussing a protest they were to attend in Belfast city centre to make sure it didn't get out of hand. Their relaxed manner suggested they didn't expect any trouble.

Just as she swallowed the last mouthful of toast, her mobile pinged to tell her a text message had arrived. Flanagan looked at the display. From Miriam: *You were right – it was a cyst. Thank*

God! A smiley-face emoticon finished the message, and Flanagan felt a smile spread on her own face.

She went to reply, but the phone trilled and vibrated in her hand. DS Murray's desk number on the display.

'Yes?'

'Ma'am, I have an Inspector Guillermo Sala, retired, on the line for you.'

Flanagan smiled at Murray's fumbling at a Spanish accent when he said the name. She got to her feet and walked towards the canteen exit. 'Give me a minute, I'll take it in my office.'

Once at her desk, she turned over to a fresh notebook page, lifted the telephone handset, and hit the blinking call waiting button. Murray had said the retired inspector's English was excellent, so no translator was needed.

When Murray had connected them, Flanagan said, 'Inspector Sala?'

'Yes,' he said. She could hear the grit of age in his voice.

'I'm Detective Chief Inspector Serena Flanagan, Police Service of Northern Ireland. I'd like to ask you about a case you dealt with four years ago.'

'Yes, the sergeant, he told me this,' Sala said. 'About the baby girl.'

'That's right,' Flanagan said.

'It was very sad,' he said. 'I don't like to remember. What do you ask me?'

'If you can, please tell me what happened the day the child died.'

He exhaled a sorrowful sigh, and Flanagan sensed the recollection pained him. 'I come to the beach after. A *Sotsinpector*, he go first, then he call me. When I go, the mother, she is already gone to hospital. The father, he is there on the beach. He is crying, crying, crying, he says do something for her, the baby, but the paramedics say, no, she is gone, we can do nothing. It was difficult. It is more time before I know what happened. The mother carries the baby out into the sea, but there is a drop, the water is deeper, and she lets go of the baby. She cannot get her back, and she goes under water also.'

Flanagan noted it all down, the events matching what McKay had told her a few days before.

'The mother, she is hurt. A broken rib. They stay her in the hospital, and I call the British Consulate. I talk to the mother and the father the next day.'

'What was your impression of them?' she asked.

'Ah, I don't know this meaning.'

'What did you think of them?' Flanagan said. 'Did you like them? Not like them?'

'Ah, *si*. Yes, first I like them. They are good people. The mother is, how do I say it, cold? No feeling. But, you know, a child dies, how do you act? The father is very sad, very angry, he cries all the time. I am sad for him.'

'You said, at first you liked them. Did something change?'

Sala clicked his tongue as he thought. 'I don't know I should tell. The father, Mr Garrick, he tells me say to no one. Is a secret.'

'Inspector Sala,' Flanagan said, 'anything you can tell me will be helpful. I'd really appreciate it.'

'Why do you call me?' he asked. 'Four years ago, this is. Why call now? What happens there?'

'I'm investigating the apparent suicide of Mr Garrick,' Flanagan said.

155

'Ay, ay. This is bad news. Tell me, please, did they have more children?'

'No, they didn't.'

'Is sad. Is very sad. He was a good man. A good father, I think.'

'Inspector Sala, can you tell me what Mr Garrick said to you?'

Silence as he considered it, before he said, 'Okay. Mr Garrick is dead, so I can tell. He was very sad in this time, you understand, very weak. So weak he tells me this thing.'

'What did he tell you, Inspector Sala?'

'He tells me, she beat him. Not all the time, but some time, she beat him. And she calls him stupid, weak, a bad man. He cries when he tells me this in my office. He tells me he is afraid of her. Then he tell me not to say.'

'And you agreed?'

'What can I do? They take the baby home, back to Ireland, they go together. I cannot arrest her for what he tells me. I tell him go home, go to police, ask they help you.'

'Seems like he didn't,' Flanagan said.

'You know, I think Mr Garrick is big in his heart, how to say it . . . proud, yes?'

'Proud,' Flanagan echoed, thinking of what George Garrick had told her about his brother.

'A proud man, is difficult to say a woman beat him. It makes him feel like he is not a man. Do you understand?'

'I do,' Flanagan said. And pride was not an exclusively male trait. She had known women who refused to report abuse by their husbands simply because they couldn't bear the shame of it. It was easier to take the beatings than it was to admit they had been taken.

'One last question,' she said. 'Was there ever any doubt about what happened on the beach that day?'

Sala's voice thinned, as if the speaking of his answer diminished him. 'I wondered,' he said. 'I wondered about the mother. I think, maybe, can she do this? Then I think, no, a mother cannot do this. And the coroner says an accident, I don't argue. But sometimes at night, when I don't sleep. I lie in bed and I think, maybe? Maybe?'

A pause before he spoke again.

'Please, Inspector Flanagan, will you make a promise to me?'

'All right,' she said.

'If you find out maybe is yes? If you find out she kill the baby? Please. Don't tell me. I don't want to know.'

28

McKay stared at the ceiling, Roberta beside him on his bed.

They had emerged from the bathroom five minutes apart. No one had seen them, no one had noticed their absence in the time they were gone. When McKay had returned to the main hall, only a few stragglers remained; the ladies had already begun clearing the tables.

Ten minutes later, within earshot of Miss Trimble, Roberta had said she felt tired, unwell, could she please go over to Reverend McKay's house for a lie-down? Of course, he had said, and he escorted her through the hall, pausing for a few polite farewells, and across the road to the church grounds.

She had taken everything he could give her, taken it so voraciously it had frightened him. Now they both lay spent and exhausted, the blinds drawn, the room dim around them. They had lain for an hour, neither of them speaking. He had drifted in and out of a thin and whispery sleep, jerking awake as the images that played in his mind grew more scarred and bloody.

The drowsiness passed, and the urge to move took its place. Perhaps she sensed the change in him because she rolled onto her side to face him. He turned to look at her. Her eyes just inches from him, glittering in the points of light that pierced the blinds. She brought her hand up, rested her palm on his cheek.

'I've been thinking,' she said.

'Yes?'

'Maybe we shouldn't see each other for a while.'

She waited as if to let him argue, object, but his mouth was empty.

'Just for a few months,' she continued. 'Maybe six. Until the dust settles. Then we won't have to sneak around any more. We can be together, like we talked about.'

He searched for something to say to her, a reason they shouldn't be apart, even if it was only for a few months. But he couldn't defend against her cold logic.

Her hand moved to his chest, her fingers spread wide.

'I'm going to go away for a couple of weeks,' she said. 'Maybe more. I need to get out of this village for a while. Miss Trimble and all that lot will be torturing me, bringing me cakes and cottage pies and lasagnes when all I really need is to be left alone.'

At last he found a word to speak. 'Where?'

'Somewhere warm,' she said. 'South of France, Montpellier's lovely, or the Canaries. Just so long as it's away from here.'

'Away from me?'

The words escaped him before his right mind could intervene. He felt her body first stiffen against him, then go loose once more.

'Don't be silly,' she said. 'We've come this far together. It won't fall apart now. I just need some space. We need to think about the long term.'

'It's just . . .'

He lacked the courage to finish the sentence.

She propped herself up on her elbow. 'Just what?'

'I feel like you've been pushing me away since . . . you know . . . like I'm being closed out. Like you're putting distance between us.'

'Nonsense,' she said.

'And you've been . . . angry at me.'

'It's been a stressful few days. You know that.'

She seemed so calm, so reasonable, his fears seemed trivial when spoken aloud. But inside him they remained barbed and tangled. Try to explain, he thought. Make her see.

'If all this was for nothing,' he said. 'If I did what I did just for you to turn away from me, then I don't think I could survive that.'

She kissed him and said, 'I'm not turning away. Just being pragmatic. Now, I need a shower.'

The bed rocked as she got up. He watched her naked back as she left the room and he told himself to believe her, not to let the doubt eat at him. Truly, he didn't know what he would do to himself if she left him now. He didn't know what he would do to her.

He imagined her throat squeezed between his hands.

No, he could not do that.

But hadn't he thought, all those weeks ago, that he'd never be able to kill a man?

In this very bed, another sunny afternoon sealed out of the room, when she said, 'Kill him for me.' Hadn't he said, 'No, no I can't?' And she hadn't argued. Simply gone quiet, clinging to him as if he was all she needed in the world.

She had asked again two days later.

Like before, she had been talking about her husband's suffering. How the pain never left him except at night, when the morphine shut him down. The indignities of his existence. The urine and the excrement she had to clean away in their daily rituals. The ruin of him. How he would never be a husband to her again.

'But he'll get better,' McKay had said. 'It'll be hard, but things will improve. The pain, the healing, all that has to be got through to get to the other side. He'll be mobile again one day, even if it's just a wheelchair.'

'Years,' she said. 'The doctors say it'll take years before he can even try to move. And they said there's a good chance he won't be able to use artificial limbs when there's so little left of his legs. And the suffering he'll have to go through to get there.'

'But he's strong,' McKay said. 'He's been so positive when I've prayed with him.'

She buried her face in the pillow. Her shoulders fell and rose again. 'That's what everyone says.' The pillow muted her voice, but the bitterness still cut through. 'They come and visit for half an hour, they can't stand any more than that, and they come out of his room saying, oh, isn't he doing well? Isn't he cheerful, considering.' She lifted her face, and he saw the tears as her voice cracked. 'But when they're gone, when you're gone, I see what it's really like for him. He can barely stand breathing, it's so hard for him. He tells me when I wake him in the mornings, he's sorry he didn't slip away in the night. That's what he told me: he wants to just go to sleep one night and not wake up.'

She covered her eyes and wept, tears dripping onto McKay's arm.

'Just imagine what it's like for him,' she said between sobs. 'Imagine living in constant pain. Imagine being unable to move, to care for yourself. Imagine staring at the same four walls all day, every day, for years and years. Imagine being a grown man and your wife having to clean up your shit and your piss like you're a baby.'

He couldn't look at her. He couldn't get past the truth of it. 'It'll get better,' he said, knowing what he said meant nothing.

'When?' she asked. She spat the words at him. 'When will it get better? Tell me. When will I be able to face a day that doesn't feel like hell to me and him both. For Christ's sake, we're kinder to dogs.'

So the following day, Reverend Peter McKay went to Mr and Mrs Garrick's beautiful house outside the village. He sat down with Roberta on the luxurious couch in the living room and took her hands in his.

He asked, 'How do I do it?'

The answer was simpler than he could have believed. Every night, Mr Garrick ate a pot of yogurt – he preferred straw-berry flavour – laced with the prescribed morphine granules the pharmacist delivered once every two weeks. One sachet per night, fourteen sachets per delivery. The granules were to be swallowed whole to allow them to disperse slowly in the stomach. The doctor had given dire warnings that they shouldn't be chewed lest too much of the drug be released at once: mixed with yogurt was the best way to consume the granules. And so had begun the nightly ritual of Mr Garrick finishing his small evening meal – he didn't need a great deal of calories, but the nutritionist had insisted on an abundance of protein to promote healing – followed by a pot of yogurt spoon-fed to him by his wife, or occasionally by a concerned friend. Like McKay.

They talked about it over the weeks that followed. It seemed an abstract idea, not something they would actually do. Like the way a couple might talk about leaving their jobs to buy a vineyard in France, or take a round-the-world trip. A fantasy to pass time in each other's arms, not a real act to be undertaken in earnest. But the plan grew flesh, details emerged, problems were revealed and resolved.

The granules would have to be crushed, but that was easy, just use a pestle and mortar, ditch them after. But surely they'd know he hadn't chewed them? Simply rub some of the yogurt and crushed granule mix onto his teeth with a cotton bud. But wouldn't the cotton bud leave traces of its fabric on the teeth? Then use a finger in a rubber glove.

But even though a course of action emerged clear and firm from their wonderings, McKay never truly believed it to be real. Even on Sunday night past, when he arrived at the Garricks' house, he didn't truly think he'd go through with it. Even when he saw the ceramic pestle and mortar on the kitchen worktop, the open box of morphine sachets beside it, along with a box of the surgical gloves she used when cleaning her husband.

'There,' she said, pointing at them, as if he hadn't seen them as he entered the room. She took a step back, showed him she would take no further part in it. It was up to him, and him alone.

He looked at her, and she saw the question on his face.

'Yes, tonight,' she said. 'Just like we talked about. It has to be tonight.'

He stayed where he was. 'Are you sure?' he asked.

'Yes,' she said. 'Go on.'

McKay moved to the worktop. Slow steps, as if a noose waited for him there. He reached for a sachet.

'Gloves first,' she said.

A latex glove protruded from the dispenser box. He plucked it, then the second that sprouted in its place. Tight. He struggled to put one on, then the other.

'Two pairs,' she said. 'To be safe.'

He took another pair, pulled them on over the first. Talcum powder dusted the worktop.

'You'll need to wipe this down,' he said.

She did not answer. He took the first sachet, tore along its top edge, and poured the milky white granules into the pestle.

'Ten, you reckon?'

'I think so,' she said.

One after another, he tore them open, emptied their contents into the bowl until ten empty packets lay on the worktop and granules mounded in the pestle. He gripped the pestle in his right hand, the edge of the mortar in his left, and set to work. It didn't take long. The cracking and crunching of the larger pieces breaking down gave way to a sandy grinding that made him think of the beach in Cushendun where he had spent childhood summer Saturdays.

When the morphine had been reduced to a gritty powder, McKay lifted the bowl and showed it to Roberta.

'Good enough?' he asked.

'Good enough,' she said.

She went to the fridge and fetched a large pot of strawberry yogurt, the expensive kind, the kind they advertised with beautiful actresses licking the spoons, purring words like creamy and decadent. Not the type he usually had, the type the supermarkets sold in packs of six, bound together at the rim to be snapped apart.

Roberta took a teaspoon from a drawer and joined McKay at the worktop. She set the pot down and peeled back the lid, put it aside. McKay held the pestle for her while she scooped spoonfuls of powdered morphine into the yogurt. She worked with a steady care and precision, not letting a single grain fall from the spoon, stirring occasionally as she went.

When the last of the morphine had been scraped from the pestle, McKay set it down next to the yogurt pot. Roberta pulled a crumpled-up carrier bag from the cupboard beneath the sink, opened it wide while McKay put the pestle and mortar inside, along with the gloves. She tied the handles in a loose knot.

'Are you ready?' Roberta asked.

'I'm ready,' he said.

She lifted the yogurt pot, the spoon standing inside it, and handed them to him. He followed her out of the kitchen, across the hall, to the closed door of Mr Garrick's room. Roberta knocked once and opened it.

Mr Garrick lay on the bed, its back raised, pillows propping him up. He seemed to be adrift somewhere inside himself, his eyes open but unfocused. A sharp breath and he came back, looked towards the door.

'Oh, what's this?' he said, the scarred mouth stretching into a smile.

'Reverend Peter dropped in to see you,' Roberta said.

'Oh, that's nice,' he said. 'Good to see you, Peter. It's been a while.'

Mr Garrick had always called McKay by his first name, ever since he first took over the parish.

'Been busy,' McKay said, following Roberta into the room. It was a lie. In truth, he had avoided seeing Mr Garrick as much as possible since he'd taken the poor bastard's wife into his bed. 'I brought you your pudding.'

'Good man,' Mr Garrick said.

Cheery. Always cheery. When he had all the reasons in the world not to be.

Roberta gathered up the plate and cutlery from dinner, clearing space on the wheeled table that overhung the bed.

'Thanks, love,' Mr Garrick said.

As McKay went to the chair by the bed, Roberta carried the plate to the door, out into the hall, and started to close it behind her.

'Are you going?' McKay asked, a hard edge to his voice he hadn't intended. He cleared his throat. 'I thought you might stay and chat with us.'

She shook her head. 'Sure, you boys chat away and I'll get the dishes done.'

If not for the panic in his breast, he might have noted for the hundredth time how her accent took on her husband's soft country lilt when she was around him.

The door closed, and McKay stared at the wood until Mr Garrick said, 'Sit down, Peter, sit down.'

McKay did so, holding out the yogurt pot.

'Oh, she's got me the fancy stuff this time. Set it on the table, there, I'll have it in a wee bit.'

McKay put the pot on the table, then put his hands on his knees. His mind scrambled for something to say, anything, anything at all.

'For a man who came to chat, you're awful quiet tonight,' Mr Garrick said. 'No crack with you?'

McKay swallowed and said, 'No, nothing at all, just work at the minute. How've you been?'

'Oh, much the same, good days and bad days. More bad than good, if I'm honest. If it wasn't for Ro, I wouldn't be able to stick it.'

Ro. His pet name for her. McKay could never call her that.

Mr Garrick winked, the gesture creasing the pink scar tissue on his cheek. 'Still no movement in your love life, then? No wee Dilsey-Janes chasing after you?'

McKay felt heat in his cheeks. 'No,' he said. 'I've no time for that.'

'Then make time.' Mr Garrick raised a clawed hand to him. '*Cherchez la femme*, as the man says. You should try online. There's no shame in it these days. Sure, I did all right out of it, didn't I?'

'Yes, you did,' McKay said. 'You have that to be thankful for, at least.'

'At least,' Mr Garrick echoed. 'Speaking of thanks, maybe we should say a few words to Him upstairs, what do you think?'

'Would you like to?'

Mr Garrick's eyes glistened. 'Yes, I'd like to.'

Even though there was nothing he wanted less at that moment, McKay said, 'All right.'

He leaned forward, bowed his head, put his hands on the edge of the bed, brought them together. He inhaled, ready to speak, but Mr Garrick started first.

'Dear Lord,' he said, 'I just want to thank you for all my blessings. I've had some hard times, but You've blessed me with good friends. And I thank You for bringing Ro to me, and I pray that You give her the strength to care for me the way she has done so far.'

McKay felt knuckles nudge his shoulder.

'And Dear God, I pray You put some sense into this man's head, and help him get up off his backside and find a decent woman, because he deserves one as much as he needs one. Amen.'

In spite of himself, McKay smiled and said, 'Amen.'

He looked up at the table, the yogurt pot, the spoon.

'Maybe you don't want that,' he said, standing as he reached for it. 'I'll put it into the bin for you.'

Mr Garrick hooked his clawed hand around the pot. 'No, you're not taking that off me. That's the good stuff, and I'm not wasting it.'

With his right hand he was able to grip the spoon between his thumb and index finger. He scooped yogurt into his mouth, worked it around his tongue, and swallowed. He opened and closed his mouth a few times.

McKay sat down again, watching.

'Texture's a bit funny,' Mr Garrick said. 'Tastes good, though.'

He took another spoonful, then another. With the next one, the spoon slipped in his grasp before it reached his lips, spilling yogurt down his chin. He tutted and shook his head.

'Here, let me,' McKay said. He reached for a napkin from the table.

'These spoons are too small,' Mr Garrick said. 'I can't keep hold of them like the big spoons.'

'I'll help,' McKay said.

He used the napkin to grip the spoon handle, scooped some yogurt out of the pot and into Mr Garrick's mouth.

When he'd swallowed, Mr Garrick gave a dry laugh. 'Look at me, like a baby. Don't be making choo-choo noises, now.'

He giggled, and his head rocked forward then back onto the pillow. 'She's kicking in quick tonight, boy.'

'Good,' McKay said, scooping as much as he could into the spoon. 'The sleep will do you good.'

Into his mouth, there, don't spill.

'I remember feeding our wee Erin,' Mr Garrick said, his eyes focusing and defocusing, the pupils growing. 'She was a great eater. You remember our wee Erin?'

Another spoonful.

'Of course I do,' McKay said.

Mr Garrick's head nodded forward but didn't fall back again. 'She's getting big,' he said. 'She's near up to my . . . what?'

McKay put a finger beneath Mr Garrick's chin, lifted it until the weight of the head carried it back. His eyes glassy now.

Don't go yet, McKay thought. If he passed out too soon he might not get enough morphine. He might wake and know what they'd tried to do. McKay clicked his fingers in front of Mr Garrick's face until he blinked and said, 'What?'

Another spoonful in, and Mr Garrick swallowed by reflex. And another.

The eyelids fluttering.

'I . . . I . . . don . . . wan . . .'

Another, and another, then McKay scraped the bottom of the pot for the last drops. He tipped them into the open mouth. Mr Garrick smacked his lips together then went very still. McKay stood there over the bed, the napkin-wrapped spoon suspended in one hand. He held his breath, felt the silence press in on him.

Then Mr Garrick inhaled with a long, low, guttural snore and McKay let the air out of his lungs. He reached across and placed the spoon handle between the fingers of Mr Garrick's right hand, feeling the dying man's breath upon his cheek. He shivered and stood up straight.

Simple as that.

And wasn't Roberta right? Wasn't it a mercy?

No, it wasn't. McKay was a murderer. The truth of it threatened to flood his mind, drive all reason from him. Be calm, he thought. You're not done yet.

Roberta had googled suicide, the methods and investigation. Often people place photographs around themselves, watch them as they die. McKay took another napkin from the bundle on the table. He moved each of the framed pictures from the bedside locker and arranged them in front of Mr Garrick. There, good.

He went to the door, opened it, out into the hall, across to the kitchen.

Where was Roberta? No time to think of that now.

He squeezed his hands into another two pairs of surgical gloves then gathered up the empty morphine sachets, bundled them in one hand, lifted the box with the other. Back in Mr Garrick's room, he spread the sachets on the table, put the box on the bedclothes, just within Mr Garrick's reach.

That done, he surveyed his work. Yes, everything was as they'd discussed and planned. All he had to do now was leave the room and close the door.

Then he noticed the utter silence. No snoring. Not even a whisper of a breath.

Some time between McKay's leaving this room and returning, Mr Garrick had died.

A wave of panic swelled in him, and he began to shake as adrenalin surged through his body, telling him to run, run, get away, get out of here.

'Stop it,' he said. 'Stop it now.'

Breathe. For Christ's sake, breathe.

He willed his lungs to obey, air in, air out, until the tremors subsided enough for him to be able to step back through the door and close it behind him.

Done.

God help him, he had done it.

Suddenly, all air left the hallway. McKay inhaled as deep as his lungs would allow, but there was no air. Breathed out, and in again. No air. He reached for his collar, pulled aside the white tabard, found the button at his throat, undid it. Inhaled again, but no good, there was no air. His vision narrowed, closed in.

McKay's legs gave way, and he tried to put his hands out to break his fall. The wooden floor slammed into his knees. His heart boomed behind his breastbone, and he felt that the next thunderous beat would burst it inside him.

An idea pierced through the chaos behind his eyes: Heart attack. I'm having a heart attack and I'm dying. One hand on the floor to stop him toppling over, the other clutched at his heaving chest, his lungs pulling at the air that wasn't in the hallway.

He didn't see Roberta approach, didn't hear her shoes on the floor, only realised she was by his side when her hands gathered him up to her.

'Panic attack,' she said. 'It's just a panic attack. Try to breathe. Come on. Breathe.'

And he did. Somehow, slowly, sweet air returned to the world. Thin at first, but thickening so that he could take a gulp, then another, and another until the booming of his heart eased.

He didn't know how long passed as he kneeled on the floor, his head on her breast. Eventually she said, 'It's over. It's done.'

'Yes,' he whispered as he pushed himself up to sit alongside her.

'I'll find him in the morning,' she said. 'Just like we talked about.'

'Then you'll call me,' he said between breaths.

'That's right. You should go now. I'll take care of everything else.'

She helped him to his feet as he asked, 'What about the pestle and mortar, the bag?'

'I'll take care of them.' She pushed him towards the front door. 'Now go.'

A minute later, he steered his Ford Fiesta through the gates at the end of the driveway. Branches and hedgerows blurred as they passed through the glare of his headlights. Without thinking, he headed west, skirted Moira, and found his way onto the motorway, south, left it again.

Lurgan, the signs said. A service station. Houses, sixties boxes and newbuilds.

After a few turns, he came to a roundabout. He circled it once, twice, three times, unable to choose which exit to take. Finally, he jerked the wheel at the next junction he saw, not caring where it might lead. He found himself on a straight stretch of road, railings on either side. Then he saw the wide stretch of water he crossed, reflecting the weak moonlight: the River Bann. He slowed the car, stopped at the centre of the bridge, the river rolling away either side of him. Darkness everywhere.

He climbed out of the car, put his hands on the metal railing, felt the cold of it seep through the flesh and into the bones. Trees hissed at him. He wondered for a moment what it would feel like, the fall, only a second or two, then the sudden cold of the water. Would his body fight to live? Or could he allow himself to sink, to drown down there in the black?

He saw the beam of the headlights illuminating the pale skin of his hands before he heard the engine. It'll pass, he thought. The driver will see me and think I'm odd standing here at night, but that's all.

The car did not pass. Its engine note dropped in pitch, stepping down as the driver moved through the gears. McKay heard the tyres rumble on the road, a faint high whine as the brakes gripped the wheels, then the engine died. He didn't have to turn his head to know the car had pulled in behind his own. But when he heard one door open, then another, he did turn his head and his heart froze.

Two police officers closed the doors of their patrol car. One, the driver, lit a torch and shone it at McKay. He squinted, brought his hand up to shield his eyes.

Did they know what he'd done? Had they tracked him here? Would they arrest him?

No, no, they can't know. Be calm.

'Everything all right, sir?' the policeman asked.

If he answered, would they hear the terror in his voice? He had no choice. He swallowed and said, 'Fine.'

The policeman paused as the torchlight found the white collar at McKay's throat. 'Any reason why you're out here this time of night?'

McKay put his hands in his pockets to hide his trembling. 'Oh . . . I, uh . . . well, I was just out for a drive, and I saw how pretty the moonlight on the river was, so I wanted to just stop and have a look. Take it all in, you know?'

'Just out for a drive,' the policeman echoed. 'Do that often, do you?'

'Occasionally,' McKay said. 'I have trouble sleeping some-times, so I find a nice drive settles me a little bit.'

The policeman turned his torch towards McKay's car, shone it through the windows, examined the empty seats. 'I see,' he said. 'Will you do me a favour, though?'

'Yes?'

'Get on the move again. We've had a few hijackings in the area over the last couple of weeks, young lads taking cars and rallying them around the place then burning them out. I wouldn't want them getting a hold of you. These wee bastards wouldn't go easy on you just because you're a minister.'

McKay nodded as the torch beam glared at him once more. 'All right,' he said. 'I'll do that. Thanks for the warning.'

He went to his car, opened the driver's door.

'Take care, now,' the policeman called as he and his colleague returned to their vehicle.

'You too,' McKay said as he lowered himself in. He watched the rear-view mirror as he closed the door and put on his seat-belt. Waved as the patrol car pulled out and passed him. When the other car was out of sight, he leaned his head against the steering wheel, kept it there until the shaking stopped.

29

Flanagan took the seat opposite DSI Purdy.

'Well?' he said.

'I want to question Roberta Garrick,' Flanagan said.

'I thought you already did.'

'Here,' Flanagan said. 'I want to bring her in, do it in an interview room, put the fear of God into her.'

Purdy chewed the end of his spectacle arm for a few seconds before saying, 'No, absolutely not. You can't hit her that hard with so little to go on.'

She considered arguing, but knew this was not a fight worth having. 'Do you have any objection to me questioning her at home?'

'What sort of tone?' he asked.

'Firm,' Flanagan said. 'I'll not let her know what I'm after specifically, but I want her to know I'm suspicious. If she's innocent, it'll probably go over her head. If she's guilty, it'll rattle her. Put her on the back foot. I'll learn a lot just from her reaction.'

'Prearranged or drop-in?'

'Drop-in. Not tonight, of course, but tomorrow.'

Purdy nodded and put his glasses back on. He leaned back and said, 'You know, I've got mixed feelings about this. On the one hand, I've no desire for this to turn into a murder investigation, so I hope you're wrong. On the other, if you are wrong, if you've been pursuing a recently bereaved woman for no good reason, then you'll have gone down in my estimation.'

'I understand that, sir,' she said, feeling the weight of his gaze on her.

'This will be the last investigation of yours that I oversee before my retirement. What I said to Allison on the phone the other day, that was true, you're probably the best I've ever worked with. I don't want my last memory of you to be a monumental fuck-up.'

She looked at her lap. 'No, sir.'

He leaned forward, his elbows on the table. 'Look at me,' he said.

She did so. 'Sir?'

'I'll give you one chance, right now, to drop this. You let it go, and I'll forget everything you told me about the brother and the baby, all of that. You can put this case behind you and move on, no harm done.'

'I can't do that,' she said, keeping her eyes hard on his.

'All right. But know this: if you go chasing after a murder and the whole thing blows up in your face, there'll be sweet fuck all I can do for you.'

'I know, sir.'

'Okay. Have at it, then.'

Flanagan made it home before dinner, in time to eat with her family. It seemed like the first time in forever. She called Alistair on the way, asked if he'd started cooking anything yet. He hadn't, and she offered to grab a Chinese takeaway. She picked

177

up a bottle of wine and some beer while she was at it, and now all four of them sat around the table, sharing sweet and spicy food. Flanagan took a mouthful of cold Czech lager, savoured the sharp taste, the burn of the carbonation on her tongue, and felt a gladness in her heart.

Ruth and Eli talked about school, their friends, the film they were looking forward to at the cinema. Some new superhero nonsense with a character Flanagan had never heard of.

'We'll go tomorrow,' Alistair said. 'Let me see.'

He thumbed his smartphone, clicked his tongue behind his teeth as he searched. 'There,' he said. 'There's a morning showing in Lisburn – 2D, I'm not squinting at the screen for two hours in those stupid 3D glasses – and we can go and get burgers after. How does that sound?'

Ruth and Eli threw their hands up and cheered.

'Actually,' Flanagan said.

Alistair's smile fell away. He stared across the table at her. 'Actually, what?'

'I need to do something for work in the morning,' she said.

'On a Saturday morning?'

'Yes.' She felt the temperature drop around the table, the smiles gone. 'But I'll probably be done by lunchtime. I can meet you guys in Lisburn, we can get something to eat, then go to an afternoon showing. Have a look, see what times there are.'

He sighed and swiped his thumb up and down the phone's screen. 'Well, yes, but the times aren't so good. We'd be hanging around for an hour and a half.'

'Then we can go bowling for an hour,' she said. 'We haven't done that in ages. Or Sunday. What about Sunday?'

Alistair put his phone down. 'Sure, we'll figure something out.'

'Don't be like that,' Flanagan said. 'Let's just pick a time and go.'

'Never mind,' Alistair said. 'I'll just take the kids to the film in the morning, and if you're done in time, you can meet us for lunch. Or you can leave it. Or whatever.'

She felt anger build, but held it back. The children ate, quiet now, their disappointment tainting the air between them. Flanagan would not have another argument in front of them. She forced a smile and said, 'All right, we'll play it by ear, then.'

They didn't speak for the rest of the meal.

That night in bed, Alistair reached for her hand. 'Sorry about earlier,' he said.

'Me too.'

He squeezed her hand and let go. Sleep soon took her, but she was woken in the dark hours by Alistair's gasping. She lay quiet and still as he woke from his nightmare, got up and went downstairs. Flanagan returned to her rest by the soft murmur of the television downstairs. Her last thought before her mind darkened was that she'd forgotten to reply to Miriam McCreesh's text message. Never mind, she would do it in the morning.

But she didn't.

Flanagan drove the short distance to Morganstown in less than ten minutes, passing along its main street as the clock on the Volkswagen's dashboard showed eleven. Another few minutes took her out the other side and to the driveway of the Garrick house. She applied the handbrake and shut off the engine. The house seemed quieter now, more grey, less grand on this overcast morning.

As Flanagan got out of the car, she looked at the sitting room window. Roberta Garrick stood there, looking back, wearing a dressing gown, a mug held in both hands. By the time Flanagan got to the front door, Mrs Garrick had already opened it.

'Good morning,' she said, a polite smile on her mouth. 'What can I do for you?'

Flanagan put one foot on the doorstep. 'Just a few follow-up questions,' she said. 'Can I come inside?'

Mrs Garrick's smile remained in place, but her eyes narrowed. 'I thought everything was settled.'

'Almost,' Flanagan said. 'I'll try not to take up too much of your time.'

'I was hoping to have today to myself. It's been a difficult week, and I'd like some peace.'

Flanagan moved her other foot onto the doorstep, closer to Mrs Garrick. 'Like I said, it won't take too long.'

Mrs Garrick gave her a hard stare, then said, 'All right.'

She stepped back, allowed room for Flanagan to enter.

'Coffee smells good,' Flanagan said, looking at the mug in Mrs Garrick's hand.

With a rigid smile, Mrs Garrick asked, 'Would you like some?'

'Yes, please,' Flanagan said. 'Black.' Without invitation, she walked towards the kitchen.

'Why don't you take a seat in the living room?' Mrs Garrick asked.

'No, kitchen's fine,' Flanagan said, not looking back. She proceeded to the tiled and shining room, placed her bag on the granite-topped island at the centre.

Mrs Garrick followed her into the room and went to the coffee machine. She placed a mug beneath the spout, put a pod in the top, pressed a button. The machine gurgled.

'I've been meaning to get one of those machines,' Flanagan said.

Mrs Garrick turned to her. 'Shall we get started?'

Flanagan ran her fingertips over the shining black granite. 'You have a beautiful home.'

'Thank you,' Mrs Garrick said. 'Can we start?'

'Your husband had it built, is that right?'

'Yes, when we married. Please, can we start?'

Flanagan sat on a stool by the island and took her notebook and pen from her bag. She opened the book to a fresh page and asked, 'How long ago? We have started, by the way.'

Another hard stare. 'It'd be seven years now.'

'How did you two meet?'

'Online.'

'So, he saw your profile and messaged you, or was it the other way around?'

'Actually, I messaged him.'

'What did you say?'

'I don't think that's any of your business.'

Flanagan gave her an apologetic smile. 'I'm just trying to get the broader picture.'

'I don't remember what I said in the message. Something short, I think, that I liked his profile, the usual sort of thing.'

'What about your relationship history before then?' Flanagan asked.

Mrs Garrick raised her eyebrows. 'I don't see the relevance of that.'

'Like I said, the broader picture.'

'I had a few boyfriends over the years.'

'Serious? Casual? Long term? Flings?'

Mrs Garrick bristled, folded her arms across her chest. 'Both.'

'Which was the longest?'

'Three years, on and off.'

'Tell me about him.'

'Why?'

'The broader picture.'

'His name was Malachi. He was a drug user. So was I at the time. Cannabis, speed, MDMA, that sort of thing. Cocaine, sometimes. When he moved on to heroin, that's when I knew I had to leave him.' Her features softened, as did her voice, her gaze distant. Then she came back to herself and said, 'That's when I cleaned myself up. That's when I found Jesus and turned my life around. Is that enough for you?'

'Malachi. What was his surname?'

'I don't remember.'

Flanagan met her gaze. 'Yes you do.'

'I do, but I'm not going to tell you because it's none of your business.'

'Were you ever violent towards Malachi?'

Mrs Garrick paled. 'Excuse me?'

'Were you ever violent towards him?'

Mrs Garrick shook her head. 'That's a ridiculous question.'

'Is it? I thought it worth asking seeing as I was told you were violent towards your husband.'

Mrs Garrick took a step forward. 'That's a lie. Who told you that?'

'The police officer in Barcelona who investigated your daughter's death,' Flanagan said. 'Your husband told him in what I suppose was a moment of weakness.'

'I think you should leave now,' Mrs Garrick said. 'If you want to ask further questions, it'll be with a lawyer present.'

'I haven't had my coffee yet,' Flanagan said, indicating the machine, which had ceased gurgling and hissing.

'I'm sorry, you'll have to do without.' Mrs Garrick took the cup from beneath the spout and poured the steaming contents down the sink. 'Please leave now.'

Flanagan did not move from the stool. 'Mrs Garrick, how did your daughter really die?'

Silence. Mrs Garrick stared at Flanagan, wide-eyed. Then she threw the empty mug into the sink. Fragments exploded from the bowl.

'Get out of my house,' she said. 'Get out and don't come back.'

'What did you do, Mrs Garrick?'

'Go,' Mrs Garrick said. 'Right now. Leave.'

Flanagan stood, packed her notepad and pen away, slung her bag over her shoulder. 'Thank you for your time,' she said, heading for the kitchen door. 'I'll be in touch soon.'

As Flanagan walked to her car, Mrs Garrick slammed the front door behind her. Once behind the wheel, she looked back to the house and saw Mrs Garrick through the living room window. She had a phone pressed to her ear.

Reverend McKay or Jim Allison, one of the two.

Mrs Garrick stared back at Flanagan, her anger burning through the glass.

Flanagan gave her a nod, started the car's engine, and pulled away.

30

McKay hung up his cassock and lifted his mobile phone from the desk. He had kept the morning prayer service short, and some of the congregation had seemed confused to be leaving so early. Instead of bidding farewell to the stragglers, he had come straight to the vestry. After a sleepless night, he intended to cross to his house and try for a doze, though he was not optimistic.

What little sleep he'd managed had been riven with dreams of Henry Garrick dragging him to the hell to which he was surely damned. Except McKay didn't believe in hell. But even so, no matter how he protested, Mr Garrick dragged him there anyway, down into the fire and the tangled screaming souls.

At one point in the night, McKay had gone to the bathroom to relieve his bladder. Washing his hands, he saw a strange and hollow man in the mirror. He remembered that he had neglected to eat again, so he went downstairs and toasted some stale bread, chewed it without tasting, swallowed it without satisfaction. Then he fetched the cigarette packet and lighter from the cutlery drawer and smoked one to the butt before lighting another from its embers.

He had realised then that it was only a matter of time. Roberta would cast him aside now that he had served his purpose, leaving him with the dreams of burning and nothing else. He had wept.

Like a child, desperate hacking sobs like he cried when Maggie died.

Let it end, he thought. Just let it end.

Now, as morning light hazed through the small vestry window, he felt little better. But another cigarette would help. Another drive into Moira, to the filling station or the super-market. Remove the white collar, undo the top button, and he'd be nothing but a man in a black suit.

He switched on the phone, put it in his pocket while it booted up. It was quiet outside now, so he slipped out of the side door, locked it behind him. The phone pinged and vibrated against his thigh. He was about to reach for it when he saw DCI Flanagan leaning against her car. Frozen, he could only watch as she approached.

'Reverend McKay,' she said, 'can you spare a few minutes?'

As hard as he tried, he could think of no reason why he couldn't. 'All right,' he said. He considered correcting how she addressed him, but he had grown weary of that. Instead, he unlocked the side door again and led her into the vestry, pulled a chair out from the table. Flanagan sat, and he took the seat opposite.

'I'd thought everything was all wrapped up,' he said, watching her take a notebook and pen from her bag.

'More or less,' she said. 'Just a few loose ends. Have you heard from Mrs Garrick this morning?'

'No, my phone's been turned off,' he said. 'I've been busy with the morning service.'

Was that surprise on her face? Gone before he could really see it, her expression turned to concern.

'Are you feeling all right? You don't look well.'

'Tired,' he said. 'It's been a difficult week.'

'Of course. I'll try to make this quick. Did something happen?'

She brought a finger to her lower lip, mirroring the redness on his.

'Oh, this.' His fingertip found the tender spot on his own lip. 'Stupid. I was leaning in to get something out of the car, and I misjudged it. So what do you need to know?'

'I wanted to ask about Mr Garrick's brother, George Garrick.'

'George,' McKay said, picturing the tall man who looked so much like his brother. 'I spotted him at the funeral yesterday, right at the back. That was the first time I'd seen him in a few years. It was a shame what happened.'

'And what did happen, to your knowledge?'

'I suppose it's no secret. Not long after Erin died, George . . . touched Mrs Garrick inappropriately. In their home, while Mr Garrick was in the other room. I think George had been drinking at the time.'

'Did George Garrick ever give you his version of events?'

McKay nodded. 'Yes, he came to see me a few days after. He denied it.'

'Did you believe him?'

'It wasn't up to me to believe or disbelieve him. It was my job just to listen. Anyway, it was too late by then. Word had gotten around the congregation. He couldn't show his face around here any more.'

'You couldn't have supported him?'

'I could, but that would mean turning my back on Mr and Mrs Garrick. You understand, a congregation is like a family, a very tight-knit family. And sometimes families split. The tighter they are, the harder the split. Churches sometimes break in two. Even in a small town, you'll get two churches of the same denomination because somewhere along the way there was a split. If I'd stood by George Garrick, this church would have been blown apart. It was a difficult choice, but it was the right one for my congregation.'

'Even if George Garrick might have been innocent?'

McKay thought about the cigarettes in his kitchen drawer. 'I don't get everything right. Do you?'

She did not drop her gaze. 'No. I don't.'

'Sorry,' he said, looking away. 'I didn't mean to be confrontational.'

She dismissed his apology with a shake of her head. 'You were close to Mr and Mrs Garrick.'

'That's right.'

'More so than others in the congregation.'

'I suppose so,' McKay said. 'Mr Garrick was very generous in his support of the church. And he was very good to me when my wife died.'

'Did he ever speak to you in confidence?'

'Sometimes.'

'Did he ever talk to you about his relationship with his wife?'

'Not really. They were very happy together.'

'Did he ever indicate that Mrs Garrick might have been abusive towards him? Violent?'

McKay pictured his own blood on her teeth. Felt her hand at his throat. He had to fight to keep his fingers from going to the red swelling on his lip again.

'No,' he said. 'Never. Why?'

'Just an avenue I'm exploring. Did he ever show up with any marks or injuries that he couldn't explain?'

'No, not that I can remember.'

She turned to a fresh page in her notepad. 'Okay. Let's talk about Jim Allison.'

McKay felt a strange sensation, like cold sparks running up his spine to his brain. 'What about him?'

'What's the nature of his relationship with Mrs Garrick?'

'What do you mean?'

Flanagan shrugged. 'He seems very protective of her. Defensive, even. I wondered exactly how close they are.'

The cold sparks turned to hot flashes of anger. 'What are you suggesting?' he asked.

'Nothing specific. I don't know them like you do. Have you ever wondered if their relationship went further than friendship?'

No, McKay had never wondered that. Not until now. He clenched his fists under the table and shook his head, no.

'You're certain of that?' Flanagan asked.

'I'm certain,' he said, keeping his voice low and calm as he pictured Allison's hands on Roberta's body. 'Why, have you seen something? Heard something?'

'No,' she said. 'But I find it useful to explore all possibilities.'

Perhaps he should have felt relief in that, but he didn't.

She closed her notebook. 'Okay, I think that's all for now. While I'm here, I wanted to thank you again for the other day. It did help a lot.'

He forced a smile. 'That's what I'm here for.'

'I might come to the service tomorrow morning. See if I can convince the kids to come too. I don't think they've ever seen the inside of a church.'

'You'll be very welcome,' he said, wishing she would hurry up and leave.

At last, she stood. 'Hopefully see you tomorrow, then,' she said.

He nodded, stood, and showed her to the door. From the vestry window, he watched her get into her car. She sat there for an agonising time.

'Go,' he said to the window. 'Just go.'

There, her hands moved on the steering wheel and the car moved off, turning towards the gate. He reached into his pocket, retrieved his phone and his keys. He exited through the side door, locked it, and thumbed the phone as he crossed the grounds to his house. The display showed a missed call from Roberta. As he unlocked his front door, he pressed the callback option and put the phone to his ear. It connected as he reached the kitchen, and he listened to the dial tone as he took the cigarettes and lighter from the drawer. By the time the answerphone message played, he had breathed a lungful of tarry smoke.

A cloud of blue billowed around him as he said, 'It's me. Flanagan was here. Call me back.'

He sat down at the table and finished the cigarette, holding it between quivering fingers. Twenty minutes later, the packet was empty and the phone still silent. McKay returned it to his pocket and lifted his car keys.

31

Flanagan had checked her watch as she returned to the car. Maybe time to meet Alistair and the kids. In the driver's seat, she opened the favourites list on her phone and called her husband. As she listened to the dial tone, she saw McKay through the vestry window, watching her.

A realisation hit her, sure and clear in her mind: Reverend McKay loved Roberta Garrick.

He couldn't hide his shock and anger when she mentioned Jim Allison's name. Jealousy had been clear and plain on his face. Had he ever acted on it? Surely not. Not a man like him. McKay had a decency about him, and not just something she inferred from his vocation and his collar.

Before she could consider it further, Alistair's impatient voice sounded in the phone's earpiece. 'Hello? Are you there?'

How long had he been on the line? 'Sorry,' she said. 'Yes, I'm here, I got distracted. Where are you?'

'In Lisburn, we're just out of the cinema. Will you make the restaurant?'

'I'll be fifteen, twenty minutes. Go ahead and order for me.'

'All right,' he said.

Flanagan hung up and looked back towards the vestry. McKay still stood there, watching her.

Another idea formed in her mind, clearer, brighter, colder than the first.

Was it you?

No. She looked away and shook her head. She had already reached far enough on this case. Her mind had been slipping into irrationality too often recently. Enough. She turned the key in the ignition and set off, chiding herself for letting her thoughts run away like that. Keep control. Reach within your grasp.

Flanagan turned right out of the gate, towards the far end of Morganstown's main street. As she neared the filling station, without thinking, she slowed her Volkswagen to a halt. She gripped the steering wheel tight.

No, not him. Couldn't be.

A car horn blasted behind her. She flicked the indicator stalk and pulled onto the filling station's forecourt, manoeuvred into a parking space by the exit, shut off the engine.

Think about it.

She played out scenarios in her mind. Desires. Impulses. Actions. She sought logic in them, even if – especially if – it was in intent rather than deed. Was there a sequence of events that could fit such an unlikely answer? She closed her eyes and imagined threads intersecting, each a course of action, each intersection a choice made, and the end of every thread led to a dead man surrounded by photographs of his loved ones that he could not see.

'Evidence,' she said aloud as she opened her eyes. 'There is no evidence.'

Forget it, she thought. You're chasing a phantom.

No reason, no logic. Let it go.

Flanagan thought of her husband and her children, that she could be with them now, enjoying them, not sitting here, torturing herself over something far beyond her control. She turned the key in the ignition once more, felt the resonance of the engine starting.

She reversed out of the space, shifted into first, and approached the forecourt's exit. As the car idled and she looked for oncoming traffic, she saw McKay's Ford Fiesta pull out of the church grounds at the far end of the street.

Flanagan knew where he was going: to the Garrick house.

Follow him?

And what would that achieve?

Once more, Flanagan thought of her family, and she pulled out of the forecourt, drove towards Lisburn and her children.

32

McKay rang the bell once more, rapped the door with his knuckles, hard enough to hurt. And again, leaving a trace of red on the wood.

The door opened, Roberta's face in the few inches between it and the frame.

'What are you doing here?' she asked.

'I need to talk to you.'

'Now's not a good time,' she said.

'I don't care,' he said. 'We need to talk.'

'Not now,' she said, her voice hardening.

He pushed the door inward, making her stagger back into the hall.

'What are you doing?' she asked as he walked past her.

He looked into the living room, saw it empty, headed towards the kitchen. There he was. Casually dressed in polo shirt and beige chinos. A mug of something steaming on the island in front of him. Sitting there like he belonged in this house. Like he belonged with her.

'Peter,' Jim Allison said. 'Is everything all right?'

'Why are you here?' McKay asked.

'Roberta called me,' Allison said.

'Why?'

Roberta entered, came to McKay's side. Put a hand on his arm. He shook it away.

'Reverend Peter,' she said, 'I think you should go home and get some sleep.'

'Why did you call him?' he asked.

Allison answered for her. 'That policewoman Flanagan called here this morning and questioned Roberta. She's crossed the line into harassment. I'm going to see what can be done about it.'

McKay stepped forward and put his hands on the black granite. 'Why are you here?'

Allison gave a nervous smile. 'I just told you. Roberta was—'

'Why are you here?!'

The shout reverberated off the tiles, made all three of them flinch. Allison raised his hands, palms out.

'Peter, I really think you need to calm yourself down, get some rest. Pardon my language, but you look like shit.'

McKay felt his face contort with hatred as he said, 'Go fuck yourself.'

Allison's mouth dropped open.

McKay turned to Roberta. 'I need to talk to you.'

'Later,' she said, reaching for his arm again. 'What you really need is—'

'Now,' he said. 'We're going to talk now, whether you want to or not.'

She went quiet for a moment, her eyes flickering, before she said, 'Okay.' She turned to Allison. 'You go on, Jim. I'll call you later.'

Allison shook his head. 'No, no, I'm not leaving you alone with him when he's like this.'

'It'll be fine,' she said. 'I'm going to make sure he gets some rest.'

'Roberta, no.'

McKay flinched at the tenderness in Allison's voice.

'Jim, go,' she said. 'I can handle this.'

'Roberta—'

'Go!'

Allison shook his head, but he stood and reached for the jacket and keys on the island. 'I'll call you later,' he said as he headed for the door. 'And don't worry, I'll deal with Flanagan.'

Alone now, McKay turned to her.

'It's over,' he said.

'What do you mean?' she asked.

'I'm going to confess,' he said.

Roberta stared at him for long seconds before she said, 'No you're not. Calm down.'

McKay watched her pace the kitchen, arms folded across her chest, and realised that he was indeed calm. For the first time since Mr Garrick had taken his last guttural snoring breath, McKay felt peace in his heart.

'I am calm,' he said, and as much as it shocked him, a smile found its way to his mouth. And a feeling of lightness behind his eyes, and on his shoulders. A terrible weight lifted away so it felt as if his feet hovered an inch above the floor. Heat in his eyes.

He recognised this feeling, a sensation rooted deep in his youth. The euphoria he felt when he first accepted Christ into his heart, when he first felt his sin washed away by the Lord.

I am saved, he thought.

Roberta stopped pacing. 'What are you smiling at?'

'I'm saved,' he said.

A high laugh escaped him, and he put his hand over his mouth. Roberta watched him, concern on her face.

'You need to get some rest,' she said. 'Sleep for a couple of hours. Then you'll feel better. You'll see things differently.'

'No.' He shook his head, the words clarifying his feelings as he spoke. 'I don't need to sleep. I need to tell the truth. I need to get this over with.'

'You're not in your right mind,' she said. 'You don't know what you're saying.'

'My right mind?' He laughed again. 'I haven't been in my right mind since the first time I touched you. And I can't take any more. It's time to stop this.'

She walked slowly around the island to him, and he knew that look on her face, the mask she wore. The seductress, Eve with the serpent's whisper in her ear, the taste of apple on her tongue. She came close, spoke softly.

'Just come upstairs and lie down,' she said. 'I'll lie with you.'

She went to put her arms around his neck, lace herself around him like so many times before, but he took her wrists in his hands and lifted them away, held them tight against his chest.

'I see what you are now,' he said. 'I should have seen it months ago, but I was weak, and you knew it. Just like you knew your husband was weak, when you found him, and you knew you could bleed him dry. Until you were faced with caring for him for the rest of his days, and you couldn't have that, could you? So you came after me. Because I was weak.'

She tried to pull her wrists away from him but he held them firm.

197

'And Jim Allison is weak too, isn't he? What is it you want from him? You've got all the money you could ever want. What can you take from him? Protection? Is that it? You think he can protect you from Flanagan, don't you? Does he know what we did?'

Now she pulled with a strength he didn't know she possessed, wrenched her wrists from his grasp. He saw the rage in her, burning and crackling, barely held in check.

'You've lost your mind,' she said.

'Maybe,' he said. 'Or maybe I've just found it again. Either way, tonight or tomorrow morning, whenever I've got the courage, I'm going to call the police. I'm going to call Flanagan and tell her everything. I just wanted to warn you so you can prepare yourself.'

He walked to the kitchen door, but she called after him.

'I'll deny it,' she said, closing the distance between them, anger and hate in her eyes. 'You go ahead and tell them what you did. But remember, *you* did it. Not me. You have no proof that I knew anything about what you planned to do. After all, you'd been chasing after me, hadn't you? Trying it on with me for the last six months, you were, all the time my poor husband was lying there suffering. You were trying to take advantage of a poor woman coping with a terrible situation.'

A grin, familiar to him, stretched her mouth as the lie took form. Close now so he could feel the heat of her. 'You tried to exploit me. You tried to exploit my vulnerability. And when you couldn't, when I wouldn't let you because I loved my husband so dearly, you decided to kill him. As far as I'm concerned, that's what happened, and that's exactly how I'll tell it. And there isn't a single piece of evidence to say otherwise.'

McKay laughed once more. Not the near hysterical laughter of before, but the calm and easy laugh of a man who knows he's right.

'You don't get it, do you?' he said. 'I don't care what you say. I don't care what you do. You can tell them anything you want. All I need is to tell the truth. Nothing else matters.'

He walked along the hall to the front door, reached for the handle.

'I'll kill myself,' she shouted from the kitchen doorway, her voice rising with each syllable.

He looked back over his shoulder and said, 'I don't care.'

She screamed as he closed the door behind him.

33

Flanagan's phone rang as she parked outside the restaurant. A number she didn't know. She should have rejected the call, she knew that, but she didn't.

'Flanagan,' she said.

'Good afternoon, Inspector, this is Jim Allison.'

She closed her eyes and mouthed a string of the worst curses she could bring to mind. Then she said, 'Good afternoon, Mr Allison, what can I do for you?'

'What can you do for me?' She heard the sneer in his voice, and anger. 'What you can do for me is stop harassing my friend Mrs Garrick.'

Flanagan took a slow and deep breath, in and out, willed her temper to be still. 'Mr Allison, it's Saturday, and I'm late for lunch with my family. Do you think we could keep this conversation for Monday morning? I can give you a call, say, ten—'

'That's right, it's Saturday, but you were happy enough to call at Mrs Garrick's home this morning. And Peter McKay. You've pushed that poor man to breaking point, and you're trying to do the same with Roberta.'

Her temper roused whether she wanted it to or not. 'What I'm trying to do is my job, and I'd thank you to let me get on with it without interference.'

'You might think it's your job to intimidate a grieving woman in her home, but I think otherwise. As an elected representative of this constituency, and a member of the Policing Board, it is my job to protect people from this kind of—'

'Oh, fuck off.'

Flanagan listened to the silence, already stinging with regret. She winced and put her hand over her eyes.

'Excuse me?'

I should apologise, she thought. I should beg forgiveness and back off. Even as those ideas moved through her mind, she knew she would ignore them.

'Let me rephrase that,' she said. 'I would very much appreciate it if you'd save your grandstanding for the Assembly. You might be on the Policing Board, but your job is to tick whatever boxes and sign whatever declarations the civil servants put in front of you, nothing more, nothing less. Some people might be impressed when you start swinging your dick around, but I'm not one of them. Now kindly shove your indignation up your arse while I go and spend a little time with my family. Goodbye.'

She hung up before he could get a word out in response, held the phone in her fist.

'Stupid, stupid, stupid,' she whispered, shaking her head.

Doesn't matter, she thought. It's done now.

She stowed the phone in her bag, got out of the car, locked it, and made her way to the restaurant. Inside, she craned her neck and stood on tiptoe, scanning the booths full of parents and children, young teens on dates, middle-aged couples looking out of place. There, near the back corner, Alistair and the children. Ruth and Eli staring wide-eyed at the ice cream sundaes the waitress was placing before them; she had a coffee on the tray for Alistair. She went to lift the untouched plate of food, chicken wings and fries, but Flanagan interrupted her.

'That's mine, thanks.'

Alistair looked up at the sound of her voice, surprise on his face at first, followed by anger, then a blank coldness that cut her deepest of all.

The waitress smiled and left them. As Flanagan lowered herself into the booth beside Eli, Alistair said, 'Hardly worth your while sitting down.'

'I can throw this into me while you have your coffee,' she said.

'Suit yourself,' he said.

'Look, I'm sorry for being late. I couldn't avoid it.'

Flanagan felt a faint itch of guilt at the lie as she took a bite of chicken from the bone. There had been a choice: go to see McKay or not. She still couldn't be sure if she'd made the right choice. She supposed she'd find out soon enough.

'So, what did you guys have?' she asked, a cheer in her voice that probably sounded as fake to them as it did to her.

'Burgers,' Ruth said.

'Were they any good?'

Ruth shrugged and resumed pushing ice cream around with her spoon. Eli hadn't even acknowledged her presence.

Flanagan put down the chicken, wiped her fingers on her napkin, reached for each of their hands, grasped them tight. 'I'm sorry,' she said. 'Honestly. I'll make it up to you tomorrow, I promise.'

'You promise,' Ruth echoed, her voice flat. 'You always promise.'

Flanagan let go of their hands, brought hers together on the tabletop. She considered arguing, pleading, but knew it was useless. Let them be angry, she thought. They're right to be angry. She ate her food, all four of them silent apart from the clink of spoons on glass.

By the time Flanagan had eaten all she could stomach, which was barely a third of the plate, the children had cleared their bowls and Alistair's cup was empty.

She set down her knife and fork, pushed the plate away. They all looked at her, knowing she meant to speak. She cleared her throat.

'I know this is difficult to understand,' she said, 'but I have a very important, very difficult job. A lot of people depend on me to do this job. And sometimes that means I can't be around as much as I want to be. I know that's difficult for you, that you think it's not fair, but I can't let those people down.'

'But you let us down,' Ruth said. 'All the time.'

Flanagan felt Alistair's eyes on her, gauging her reaction. Don't get defensive, she warned herself. It won't help.

'I know,' Flanagan said. 'Sometimes I let you down. And sometimes I let down the people I'm trying to help. But I want to do better, for you and them both.'

She reached across the table for Ruth's hand.

'Will you let me try?'

Ruth did not answer, but neither did she pull her hand away. Flanagan was glad of that.

Alistair ran his fingers through Ruth's hair, leaned over and kissed the top of her head. He exchanged a glance with Flanagan, a hint of a smile. Flanagan returned it.

'Doesn't mean I'm not angry,' he said.

'I know,' she said. 'Tomorrow will be better. We'll do something.' She reached for her children once more. 'Come on, what'll we do tomorrow? What about the zoo? We haven't been in ages.'

Ruth shook her head. 'I don't like the zoo. The way the elephants walk up and down like they're crazy people. It makes me sad.'

'All right, what else?'

Eli spoke for the first time, a smile breaking on his face that lit a flame in Flanagan's heart. 'The museum,' he said. 'The one with the dinosaurs.'

'The Ulster Museum,' she said. 'Good idea. We can go to the park after. What does everyone else think?'

Her phone trilled in her bag before anyone could answer. She squeezed her eyes shut, cursed under her breath. Without looking at Alistair, she fished it from her bag, looked at the screen.

DSI Purdy.

'Shit,' she said.

Now she looked to Alistair. With an expression of defeat and a wave of his hand, he indicated, go on, take it. She squeezed her husband's shoulder as she passed on the way to the corridor that led to the toilets. As the door swung closed behind her, she thumbed the green button.

'You know what I'm calling about,' Purdy said. It wasn't a question.

'Allison,' she said.

'What in the name of Christ did you say to him?'

'We had a disagreement about my methods,' she said.

'I'm supposed to be here preparing for my last week in this bloody job, not dealing with your mess.'

'Yes, sir,' she said. 'I'm sorry.'

I'm so tired of apologising, she thought, feeling a heavy weariness like sand in her soul.

'Sorry my arse,' he said. 'Allison tells me you're harassing his good friend Mrs Garrick.'

'His *very* good friend,' she said.

'What's that supposed to mean?'

'Sir, I think you know what it means.'

'Watch your mouth, Flanagan.'

She bowed her head, covered her eyes with her palm. 'Sorry, sir.'

The men's toilet door opened and a tubby teenager in goth gear stepped past her and out through the door to the restaurant.

'All right. Whatever you think the relationship is between Jim Allison and Roberta Garrick, you don't allude to it again without proof.'

'Yes, sir.'

'Allison says you insulted him, effed-and-blinded at him,' Purdy said.

'Maybe,' Flanagan said. 'And I might have said something about his dick.'

'Oh, fuck me pink,' Purdy said with a despairing sigh.

'Is he going to pursue this?'

'He said he'd drop it if you left Mrs Garrick alone,' Purdy said. 'I told him that would be your choice to make.'

'Thank you, sir,' Flanagan said. 'Thank you.'

'It's all right,' Purdy said. 'Listen, there's not a thing in the world Jim Allison can do to stop me drawing my pension in a week. He tries to give me grief in my last few days here, I'll happily tie his bollocks in a knot and whistle as I head out the door. But Flanagan . . . Serena . . . you need to think hard about your future. I don't know if Allison really has the clout to damage your career, but if you push him, I have no doubt he'll try.'

Flanagan leaned her shoulder against the wall. 'I won't let that stop me any more than you would, sir.'

She heard a small laugh in her ear.

'I'd be a liar if I said I wasn't glad to hear that,' Purdy said. 'But tread carefully. Promise me that.'

The tiled wall cooled her forehead. 'I don't keep promises,' she said.

'What?'

'Nothing, sir. I'll try to keep out of trouble.'

'Good,' he said. 'Take care.'

The phone silent in her hand, Flanagan remained against the wall for a minute, fighting the desire to weep for herself. She sniffed, straightened, and left the corridor. Back in the restaurant, the place had quietened, patrons finishing their meals, wait staff clearing the tables after the lunchtime rush.

Flanagan felt sure Alistair and the kids had been at the last booth on the far wall, but wondered if she was mistaken as she approached and found it deserted. Then she saw the empty coffee cup, the glass dishes scraped clean of ice cream, her own plate still two thirds full.

Anger bloomed in her, the urge to cry once again. Then a wash of relief as she saw her husband and children over by the till, coats on, waiting for her. Alistair took his debit card from the machine, placed a ten-pound note on the counter. The waitress thanked him.

As they walked towards the exit together, Flanagan took Ruth's hand in hers. Ruth resisted at first, but Flanagan tightened her fingers. Outside, Ruth said, 'I'm too big to hold hands.'

'But I'm not,' Flanagan said. 'Do you want to come home in my car? Girls' club. Let Eli and Daddy go together. They can be the boys' club.'

Ruth worked her hand free. 'No. I want to go with Daddy.'

Flanagan nodded, said, 'All right. See you at home.'

She held the tears back until she was in her car, the doors locked against the world.

34

McKay spent the rest of the day driving: motorways, country roads, through villages and towns. At some point he realised he had gone as far as the north coast and he pulled into a lay-by to get his bearings. Beyond the rolling countryside, a sliver of grey sea. He checked the map on his phone, saw he was between Ballycastle and Cushendun.

Cushendun, where he and his parents – long gone now – spent summer weekends in a caravan. As a child, he had loved it. The beach there, the thunder of the water. On a clear day, you could see Scotland, sometimes even the white specks of dwellings on the Mull of Kintyre. By the time he was a teenager, he hated it. Weekends of rainy boredom cooped up with his mother and father. By the time he was an adult, of course, he found he loved the place again. Or at least the memory of it. His parents were too elderly and infirm by that time to spend a night in a caravan.

McKay had brought Maggie there not long after they married. They had kissed in the grassy dunes, neither of them brave enough to take it further. Only the once. They never came back, though they talked about it often before she died.

'I miss you,' he said aloud.

What would she make of him now? Damned murderer, a monstrous distortion of the man he had been before she fell dying to their kitchen floor.

Only a few miles to Cushendun. He pulled out of the lay-by, turned the car, and headed east.

Twenty minutes and a wrong turn brought him to the small car park on the bay, the mouth of the river on one side, the long golden stretch of sand on the other. He got out of the car, didn't bother to lock it, and walked along the path to the knots of grass and the beach beyond.

The wind came in hard off the water, grey out there, sea and sky meeting at their darkest points. Spray prickled his skin and he tasted salt on his lips. Last time he'd been here, it had been quiet. Now a scattering of tourists wandered from the caves beyond the river along the length of the bay. All brought here by the location being used in a television fantasy programme he'd never seen.

Sand dragged at his shoes as he trudged out towards the water, moving further away from the car park and the river mouth. Still wearing his black shirt and white collar, he wrapped his jacket tight around himself, but it did little to keep out the wind's bite. Passers-by gave him sideways looks, most of them more appropriately dressed in anoraks and outdoor shoes.

He stopped at the water's edge, the foaming lip of the sea a matter of inches from his feet.

I could just keep walking, he thought. Keep walking until the cold stops the blood in my legs, until the salt water fills my lungs. He thought of the case he'd read about last year, two brothers drowning themselves in the sea further down the eastern coast. How would it feel, to die like that? He closed his eyes and imagined.

Cold swallowed his feet, and he looked down to see a murky wash lap at his shoes. He should have stepped back, moved clear, but instead he watched the water draw back towards the sea again. Still as the sweeping hills around him, he waited for it to return.

As it did, a large brown dog galloped past, splashing water up as it went. McKay felt it chill his thighs, his belly. He followed the dog – a Weimaraner? – with his gaze as it looped around, back across the sand to its owner, a woman in a red and black coat, the kind they sell in outdoor sports shops alongside camping gear and hiking boots. She patted the back of the dog's neck, and it bounded in circles around her.

McKay realised she was staring back at him. He looked out to sea again, feeling a ridiculous blush on his cheeks.

'You're getting your feet wet,' the woman called as she approached.

McKay looked down, feigned surprise, and stepped back.

Close now, she asked, 'Are you all right?'

He reached for something to say, but could only look around as if searching for a lost companion.

'Do you need help?' she asked. Closer still, she put her hand on his arm.

Tell her something. 'I'm just . . . out for a walk.'

She reached for the zip at the neck of her anorak and pulled it down, revealing a grey shirt and a white collar.

'I work for the Big Man too,' she said, a smile wide on her mouth. The first real smile McKay had seen in so long he couldn't remember. 'Come on, I'll get you a cup of tea.'

* * *

They sat opposite each other at a picnic table on the grass above the beach. Young men played Gaelic football on a pitch behind them, shouting to each other, the referee's whistle chirping. The dog lay on the ground beside McKay's shoes and socks. Deborah had insisted he take them off.

Reverend Deborah Sansom, rector of three churches in the locality. The scant Protestant population in the area meant her work was spread over the countryside, she explained, as she poured steaming tea from a thermos into a plastic cup.

'Forgive me for saying, but you didn't look like a man at ease with the world when I saw you there.'

'I suppose not,' McKay said.

'Talk if you feel like talking,' she said. 'Or just drink your tea.'

He reached for the cup and took a mouthful. Sweet and hot enough to leave his tongue tingling. It stung his lower lip.

'Tea it is then,' she said.

Deborah Sansom had brown hair streaked with grey, round cheeks reddened by the wind, sparks in her eyes as she smiled.

'I did a terrible thing,' McKay said.

'Oh?' The smile dimmed. 'Do you want to tell me?'

McKay shook his head.

'Can you put it right?'

'No,' he said. 'Never.'

She raised a finger skyward. 'Did the Big Man have anything to say about it when you asked him?'

He shook his head again. 'I didn't pray.'

'No?'

He took another swig of hot sweet tea and said, 'I don't believe any more.'

'My goodness,' she said. 'No wonder you looked like you wanted to throw yourself in. Have you spoken to anyone else about this? Your bishop, maybe?'

'No one.'

'When did you lose your faith?'

'A few months ago,' he said. He looked up from the cup and into her eyes. 'No, not then. Not really. It was ten years ago. When my wife died. It just took all that time to admit it to myself.'

'How did she die?'

He told her. The headache, the short walk, the return to find her rigid on the floor.

Deborah reached across the table and took his hand. 'I'm sorry. That would make anyone question things, no matter how strong their faith.'

She removed her hand, and they both sat quiet for a time, listening to the waves, watching the walkers on the beach.

Eventually, she said, 'Look at it.'

McKay raised his head, looked out to sea.

'All of it,' she said, her free hand sweeping across the horizon, from the sloping hills in the north to the cliffs in the south. 'Even today, when it's grim like this, it's still beautiful. I know it's possible all this is an accident. Billions of years of dust aggregating in space until it makes this. Until it makes us. But my goodness, what a sad and lonely thought. That this is just chance. That there's nothing deliberate about us. That we are chaos.'

'Chaos,' McKay echoed.

'Chaos or faith,' she said. 'It's one or the other. I know which I prefer.'

'It's not a matter of preference,' McKay said, already regretting the hardness in his voice. 'It's a matter of reality. What's real and what's just a story to cling to.'

'You were thinking about suicide when I came along,' Deborah said. 'Weren't you?'

He couldn't look at her.

'Don't worry, I didn't read your mind. But a person doesn't stand with his feet in the sea if he's not thinking about drowning.'

'I wouldn't go through with it,' he said.

'Why not?'

'Because I'm a coward.'

'I don't think that's true. I think somewhere inside, buried deep, you still believe.'

'No,' he said. 'I don't.'

She pointed at the crashing water. 'Then go on and do it. If all is chaos, then submit to the chaos. What difference will it make? If we're just random clusters of cells clinging to a rock in space, if that's what you really believe, then why live in pain? Just go and bloody do it. The universe will go on as if you'd never been here.'

McKay got to his feet, walked across the grass, feeling each blade beneath his bare soles, between his toes. Do it, he thought. She's right. Nothing matters anyway.

He reached the edge of the grass, the sandy slope down to the beach another footstep away. Just a step. He went no further. After a while, he turned and went back to the table and sat.

'Glad to have you back,' Deborah said. 'You didn't get too far, mind you.'

He looked her in the eye, challenged her to contradict him. 'I told you, I'm a coward.'

'Bollocks,' she said. 'Then we're all cowards.'

'I should go,' he said.

'Home?'

'I suppose. There's nowhere else.'

'Where's home? Where's your church?'

'Morganstown.'

'Ah, I know it. I went to a wedding there, oh, must have been twenty years ago. It's a lovely little church. Do me a favour when you get there, will you?'

'What's that?'

'Pray.'

'I can't.'

She smiled. 'Course you can. It's easy. You just go into your church, get down on your knees, close your eyes, and talk to God for a bit. Or if not God, then talk to yourself. Someone. Anyone. Just say it out loud, whatever it is that's eating you up. Do it for me. I gave you that nice cup of tea. You owe me something in return. Make me feel like I did you some good.'

McKay stood and said, 'I'll think about it.'

He bent and picked up his shoes and socks, carried them towards the car park that lay two hundred yards along the beach. After a few paces, he stopped, turned back to her.

'Thank you,' he said.

She nodded and waved.

The dog followed him along the grass almost to the end of the beach, an escort, a guardian, until it missed its master. It gave him a nudge on the hand, and he gave it a scratch, then it turned and ran back to where she stood watching.

35

Flanagan sat at the kitchen table, a mostly empty bottle of Shiraz in front of her, a mostly full glass beside that. Her tongue felt gritty from the wine, a pleasing sway behind her eyes. She took another mouthful, swallowed.

Alistair was upstairs with the kids, putting them to bed. She could hear their voices, him ordering them to brush their teeth, them screeching as he tickled them instead of getting them into their pyjamas, the soft murmur as he read them stories. Ruth said she was too old for them now, she only played along for Eli's benefit.

Flanagan smiled, but the smile faded from her mouth, unable to gain purchase there.

She had arrived home not long after them, and everyone had behaved as if nothing was wrong, only that they had entered a world of silence. Alistair had barely looked at her. The children had insisted their father do their bedtime, had given her begrudging kisses goodnight at Alistair's instruction.

Is this really it? Is this how it ends?

Not with an explosive row, nor a discovered affair. No final betrayal to sever them. Just a slow decline of bitter reproaches and fake apologies until there was nothing left but a festering resentment between them all.

Flanagan buried her face in her hands, thought about the cool space of the church, the salve of prayer whether she believed in it or not. She kept her eyes closed, brought her hands together. Formed the words in her mind.

Not like this. Please, not like this. Help me save us. Please, God, I don't want to lose my family. Please tell me what to do. Please show me—

She cried out, raised her head, as glass clinked against glass.

Alistair poured the last of the wine into a fresh glass. 'Don't mind, do you?'

Flanagan inhaled, steadied her breathing. 'Course not.'

'What were you doing?' he asked, taking the seat opposite.

She considered lying, but said, 'Praying.'

'You?' He smiled, a gentle smile, no mockery in it.

'Yes, me. I've been doing it more often lately. It helps.'

'My mother prayed a lot,' he said.

'I remember. She swore by it. Said it could cure anything.'

He took a sip of wine. 'And can it?'

'I don't know what it does,' she said. 'Maybe nothing. Maybe something. Who knows?'

He gave her a coy look. 'Were you praying for us?'

'Yes,' she said.

'You think we need praying for?'

'Christ, we need something,' she said with a weak laugh.

He smiled then, and she wanted to kiss him.

Want?

Do it.

Flanagan stood, went around the table to him. As he watched, confusion in his eyes, she got down on her knees beside him, took his face in her hands. Brought her mouth to his. He remained still for a few seconds, then he wrapped his arms around her, brought her in close.

'Listen,' he said, 'what you said earlier, about your work, about trying to do better for everyone. I think it got through to Ruth.'

Flanagan sat back, arms still around his neck. 'Oh?'

'She asked me about it upstairs. If what you did really helped people. I told her yes, and she said, well, then that's what Mummy needs to do. And maybe we shouldn't expect to have you all to ourselves.'

'And what did you say to that?'

Alistair sighed, rested his forehead against her cheek. 'I told her she was a very smart and grown-up girl. That maybe Daddy's been asking too much of Mummy. Maybe Daddy needs to get his head out of his arse and acknowledge the fact that he's not the centre of the universe. Well, I didn't put it like that, exactly, but you get the gist.'

'I do.' She kissed him once more. 'Thank you.'

Then her phone vibrated on the table.

Alistair stiffened. She did not pull away. She kissed him harder, feeling his teeth through his lips. The phone vibrated again.

Now she let go, and so did he. She got to her feet, reached for the phone. A mobile number she did not recognise. Alistair started to get up from the chair, but she put a hand on his shoulder, pushed him back down.

'Wait,' she said. 'Just wait.'

She thumbed the green button and brought the phone to her ear.

'DCI Serena Flanagan,' she said. 'Who is this?'

A pause, then, 'Peter McKay. I'm sorry to disturb you on a Saturday night.'

'Yes,' she said, not allowing him an acceptance of his apology.

'I need to talk to you.'

She hesitated, looked down at Alistair. 'I'm sorry, now's not a good time.'

'It's important. Can you come to the church?'

His voice sounded thin and far away, as if a shadow of a man spoke in his place.

Alistair went to say something, but she put her fingertips on his lips.

'No, I can't, I'm sorry. I've had a glass of wine, so I can't drive.'

'I can't do it over the phone,' McKay said. 'Can I come to you?'

'No,' Flanagan said. 'I'm sorry, really, but not right now, not tonight. The morning. I can come to you first thing in the morning, before your service.'

Silence as he considered. 'All right,' he said. 'The morning. Eight-thirty?'

'The morning,' Flanagan said, looking to Alistair, her eyebrows raised. 'Eight-thirty?'

Alistair nodded his assent.

'Yes, eight-thirty.'

'Okay,' McKay said. 'Thank you.'

She hung up and dropped her phone to the table. Alistair drew her down to him, sat her on his lap as if they were a boy and girl, still in love with the joyful newness of it all.

He kissed her and said, 'Thank you.'

Flanagan returned the kiss and tried not to think of Reverend McKay and the terrible things he knew.

36

McKay placed the phone on the passenger seat beside him. Tomorrow. He could tell her tomorrow. One more night wouldn't change things. He got out of the car into the darkness outside his house, the keys in his hand. The glass of the front door showed the black inside there, that cold and hollow house, where his wife had died and he had years later betrayed her with a monster dressed as a woman.

He looked across the grounds to the church, a spired silhouette against the dark blue. A beautiful building, it really was. He remembered when he had first inherited this parish. He and Maggie had sat inside on that first night, the building dark around them, street and moon light illuminating the stained glass, making strange shadows. They had embraced and thanked God together.

Do it for me, the woman had said.

No, he thought. I'll do it for Maggie.

He dropped his house keys back into his pocket and found the long spindly keys for the church. His fingers wrapped around them as he crossed to the building, feeling for the familiar lines of the vestry key. He found it by the time he reached the door and let himself inside. Dark in here, a weak orange sheen from the street lights outside. The burglar alarm buzzed until he entered the code: 1606, Maggie's birthday. He found the small desktop lamp, flicked it on. As he passed the open closet he brushed his cassock and surplice with his fingertips, coarse black fabric and smooth white silk.

Out into the church where the stained-glass windows rose above and looked like angels come to observe his hypocrisy. Weariness crept into his arms and legs as he crossed in front of the pulpit and into the aisle.

He chose a pew three rows back, slid down and into the hard wooden seat. Rested his forearms on the back of the pew in front. Lowered his knees onto the padded bench. Clasped his hands together. Closed his eyes.

'Maggie,' he said. 'Maggie, I'm sorry. I don't know what I've become. I'm not who I used to be before you left me. I've changed. Everything's changed. You would hate me. No. You never hated anybody. But you could never love me. Not the way I am now. I betrayed you. I turned your picture away so you wouldn't see what I did. I didn't want you to see me with her.

'Oh, Maggie, I've done an awful thing. I've done a thing so awful I'm glad you're not alive to see it. Do you understand? Do you see what I did to myself? I made myself glad you died.'

He wept then. Hard choking sobs trapped his voice in his throat. He swallowed, forced the tears back, the words out.

'I want you back,' he said. 'I prayed for you not to die and you died anyway. And now I want you back. I want everything back like before. I know it's not possible, it'll never be, but that's what I want. I want it so badly it's been killing me all these years. And God, I'm so angry at You. You took her from me for no reason at all, You took her just because You could and I'm so fucking angry and I hate You, God, I fucking hate You for doing that to me, I fucking hate You, I hate You, and I want her back, please give her back.'

A movement in the darkness by the vestry startled him.

'She's gone,' a voice said. 'There is no giving back.'

He got to his feet and said, 'Come out where I can see you.'

She moved into the dim light. Roberta, dressed in a hooded top and jeans.

'What do you want?' he asked.

'To talk,' she said.

A quiver in her voice, as if she held back tears.

'We've nothing to talk about,' he said. 'Go home.'

'Please,' she said. 'I've got no one else.'

He stepped out of the pew and into the aisle, but went no closer to her. 'You never really needed anyone else, did you? Not unless you had some use for them. Now go.'

'I'm going to kill myself,' she said.

'No, you're not.'

'I am. And I want to do it here. Before God.'

'You don't believe in God,' he said.

'Do you?' she asked.

He went to speak, but realised he did not know the answer to that question. This morning he had certainty, absolute faith in his disbelief. Now the certainty crumbled.

'Everyone believes,' she said. 'Even if they say they don't, there's always that idea inside them. Maybe they're wrong. Well, maybe I'm wrong. So I want to do it here.'

'Enough,' he said, taking a step forward. 'This won't work on me. Not any more.'

'I know how to do it,' she said.

She raised her hands, and for the first time he saw that she held a belt between them. His belt, the one from the waist of his cassock. Two inches in breadth, thick coarse material, a plain metal buckle at one end. She had fashioned the other end into a noose.

'It shouldn't hurt too much if I do it right,' she said, a strange calm to her voice now. 'I just put the buckle over a door and close it. Put this end around my neck and sit down. Simple as that.'

'You won't,' he said, feeling his anger fade. 'And you certainly won't do it here.'

She moved towards the top of the aisle. 'All you have to do is walk out. You don't have to have any part in it. I can manage by myself.'

McKay knew his rage should have burned bright, he knew he should have dragged her by the arm, thrown her out of the church. But instead of anger, he felt something else, something familiar yet strange to him.

Compassion, if he had to put a name to it.

She's right, he thought. Deep down, everyone believes. And I believe.

The urge to weep came upon him once more, but he resisted it. The urge to pray surged in its place. He stepped towards her.

'You're confused,' he said. 'You're angry. You're afraid. I know how that feels.'

She shook her head. 'You don't know how I feel.'

'Maybe not.' He came close, close enough to see the glittering in her eyes. 'But God knows. Why don't you pray with me?'

She turned away, but he stepped around her, wouldn't let her avoid his gaze. Her mouth opened and closed, her eyelids flickered.

'Yes,' she said. 'I'd like that.'

McKay lowered himself to his knees. 'Then let's do it.'

She nodded and said, 'All right.'

Then he saw the movement of her hands, felt the coarse cloth slip across his nose and cheeks and lips, felt the belt settle around his neck.

Quick, so quick he couldn't get his fingers between the belt and his throat, she yanked the noose tight. As he grabbed at the belt, she slipped behind him, pulled hard, taking him off his knees. His heels kicked at the floor, the back of his head cracked on the tile. Pressure inside his skull, in his ears, his temples.

She hauled him across the smooth tiles, crying out at the effort. His jacket whispered on the sheen of the floor as he opened and closed his mouth, trying to vent a scream that could not escape his chest. As she grunted and dragged him across the threshold of the vestry, in the dim light of the lamp, he caught a glimpse of her hands and saw she wore the same surgical gloves as he had the night he killed her husband.

Amid the crushing pressure in his head, through the clamour of his fear, a thought speared into his mind: scratch her. Get some trace of her under his nails. Get it for the police to find. He reached back over his head, but she kept her hands out of his reach.

She stopped inside the vestry, kicked the door over. Then she planted both her feet firm on the floor, tightened her grip on the belt, and hoisted him up by his neck. Somewhere through the storm behind his eyes, he heard her growl. Pain as the fabric cut into his skin, constricted his throat. He scrambled to get to his feet, swung his arms in wild arcs, trying to get hold of her, get hold of the belt, anything at all.

She gave an animal roar as she threw herself towards the door, dragging him staggering after. Up and up, she pulled up, he could see her arms stretching up, pushing back. She howled and wrestled, and for a moment his heels left the floor.

Then the door slammed shut behind him, the handle digging into the small of his back, and she stepped away. Feeling the noose loosen a fraction, he lunged forward, but the belt tightened again, yanked him back against the door. He realised she had fed the buckle over the top, closed the door, trapping it in place.

She stared at him, wide-eyed, her face burning red, panting as he tried to dig his fingertips between the belt and his throat. Then she raised the hood over her head, dropped to her knees, and reached for his ankles. The noose tightened, harder than before, as she pulled his feet from under him, held his ankles in front of her. The belt pulled tighter still, and the storm inside his head swelled into a hurricane. He reached behind to the small of his back, his fingers trying for the door handle, but the weight of his body kept the door closed. He grabbed for her, but his fingers swiped at the clear air between them. His legs kicked of their own accord, but she held her grip firm on his ankles.

Roaring, roaring, roaring between his ears. The pressure behind his eyes like a balloon inside his skull. Bursts of black in his vision. He watched her through a shrinking funnel of light, the wildness of her, and she opened her mouth and sparks flew from it and from her eyes and lightning all around her and darkness eating at the edges of everything and all he could think was Maggie, Maggie, forgive me, Maggie . . .

37

Roberta Garrick held on tight to his ankles long after he'd stopped writhing and twitching, even as the foul odour of his body's expulsions made her gag. Each ragged inhalation brought the smell into her lungs, and she coughed each breath out until she grew light-headed and almost fell. But still she held on.

Eventually, she let go. One easy movement, she opened her fingers, and his body dropped, his back thudding into the door. She watched him for a while, as if the blood would return to his brain, the air to his chest. But he was gone. At last, she stood upright. She rotated her shoulders and cried out as a dagger of pain shot into her neck from the right. She brought her left hand to the offended muscle and massaged it as her heart slowed.

It hadn't been so bad. Not really.

The fourth life she had taken, if she counted her husband's, even though she hadn't actually fed him the morphine herself. The first had been long ago. That other life that seemed so far away now, so distant that she sometimes wondered if it had ever been hers at all. She dreamed about it still, that past version of herself, and she awoke unsure of which life she lived now.

Like that morning when she woke to find Peter in the bed beside her and she didn't know who he was, who she was, and how she came to be there in a stranger's bed. So she had shouted and kicked until he fled, and then she remembered she was Roberta Garrick and he was Peter McKay, the man who killed her husband for her.

A sense of peace settled over her, a sense of having addressed the problems at hand. Now she could proceed unburdened by Peter McKay and his needy whining. She had intended to distance herself from him, in fact had begun to do so, but perhaps this was better. A clean break, over and done with.

Roberta surveyed the room, made sure she'd left nothing of herself behind. Satisfied, she exited the vestry through the side door and went to the car she had borrowed from the dealership. A twelve-year-old Citroën, taken from a customer for a couple of hundred pounds as a token part exchange on a newer vehicle, stored at the rear of her dead husband's dealership ready to be taken to a scrapyard. An unremarkable car, one that would draw no attention on the road.

She opened the passenger door, reached inside for the plastic bag she'd stowed in the footwell, sending ripples of pain through her shoulders and back. The bag's contents clinked and rattled as she lifted it and brought it back to the vestry. There, she opened it and set the ceramic pestle and mortar on the desk beneath the lamp. She bundled up the bag and stuffed it into the pocket of the hooded top she had bought in a charity shop in Lisburn.

Roberta closed the vestry's outer door behind her, went to the car, got in, and turned the ignition. The engine whirred and coughed but did not start.

'Shit,' she said.

Again. More whirring and coughing, and a hard grinding.

'Come on,' she said.

One more time, and as the engine rattled, she dabbed the accelerator pedal to feed it a little more petrol. The car juddered around her as the engine finally clattered into life. Morganstown's main street remained as dark and quiet as when she'd arrived here fifteen minutes ago. She eased the Citroën out onto the road, kept the acceleration light, not wishing the engine to grumble too loudly as she left the village. The back roads stretched black and empty ahead. She took the single-track lanes wherever possible, doubling the length of her journey back to Garrick Motors, but the reduced risk of meeting a police car was worth the extra time. Patrol cars had all sorts of technology now, she'd seen it on television; they had computers that could read number plates and trigger an alert if the car lacked insurance or road tax.

A flash of red on the narrow road in front of her, and by instinct her right foot went to the brake pedal, stamped hard. The car shook and hunkered down as it slowed, the spongy brakes gripping as hard as their wear would allow. She hissed through gritted teeth as the wheels skidded, the near-bald tyres barely keeping hold of the tarmac. When the Citroën finally halted, she watched the road to see what had appeared in her path.

A fox sprinted away from the front of the car – she must have been inches from crushing it – and dived into the hedgerow.

A deep laugh erupted from her belly and she covered her mouth with her hand.

I killed a man, she thought, and I saved a fox.

No, not funny. It was good she hadn't hit the animal. Someone at the dealership would have noticed the damage to the car, the blood, the fur. Someone would have asked questions. Someone would suspect the Citroën had been taken from the rear yard. There were no cameras back there, but still, she could not have it known that the car had been used for anything more than gathering rust and waiting for transport to the breakers.

She set off once more. Not far now. Within ten minutes she had pulled up at the back of the dealership property and opened the gate; she had left the padlock undone when she'd swapped cars earlier in the evening. She moved the Citroën inside, reversed it into the space where she'd found it, though turning her head to look through the rear window caused a spasm in the muscles of her right shoulder. The door to the back shed where the scrap car keys were kept was seldom locked; she had done this many times before. She dropped the keys into the Tupperware tub where she'd found them among the half-dozen other sets, pulled the shed door closed, and went to her Mini Cooper.

As she drove away from the locked gates, back towards her house – *her* house now, not her husband's – she began to laugh again. A joyous laugh, like when she was a girl chasing chickens across her grandfather's yard.

It's all done now, she thought. Every detail squared away. Free of them all, every hand that had ever dragged at her heels.

All except Jim Allison. But he knew nothing, and she'd freeze him out soon enough. Take it slower than she had with Peter, let him down easier. She'd learned from that mistake.

And the policewoman. Flanagan could yet cause her more problems, but nothing Roberta couldn't cope with. If the ideas she had planted in Jim's mind took root, the next few days would be difficult for Flanagan.

By the time Roberta had returned home, driven the Mini into the garage and entered the house, that feeling of peace had come back. Deeper than before, more complete. She ran a bath with a generous dose of soothing bubbles, soaked herself until the water cooled and her muscles tingled. Then she went to bed and slept a solid black sleep until the telephone woke her the next morning.

38

Alistair was still asleep in bed when Flanagan left the house. They had made love last night, and it had been good. Relaxed, easy, nothing begrudged, nothing withheld. As she had lain awake in the dark, she had wondered at how within a couple of hours she had gone from feeling sure their marriage was over to a sense that it had a lifetime left to grow.

She had looked in on the children before she left; they both dozed on, oblivious to her watching from their doorways. She had resisted the urge to sneak in and steal a kiss for fear of waking them.

A warm autumn sun hung low over the trees as she approached Morganstown. Early morning shoppers parked their cars in the filling station forecourt to buy the Sunday papers. Flanagan made a mental note to drop in on the way back, buy an *Observer* and a *Times*, maybe the makings of a fried breakfast for everybody. As she neared the church, her mind was more focused on whether or not she had the ingredients for eggs Benedict than on whatever had been so urgent for Reverend McKay to have called last night.

She parked her Volkswagen next to McKay's Ford and got out. A strange quiet about the place, she thought. Even before she knocked on the front door, she was certain no one would answer. After a wait of a minute or so, and a second knock, she looked across to the church. Maybe he was in there, getting ready for the morning's service. The front doors had been closed as she entered the car park, but perhaps he didn't open them until he was ready for the congregation.

Flanagan walked towards the side door, and as she came close she noticed the lamplight through the small window. She knocked on the door, listened for a response. When none came, she tried the handle. The door opened inward.

She saw the bright red ceramic pestle and mortar by the lamp first of all, had only a moment to wonder why such things were sitting there before she looked towards the door leading to the church. Then the smell hit her.

'Oh Christ,' she said, her hand reflexively going to her mouth and nose.

She saw McKay there, his head at an unnatural angle, legs splayed in front of him, arms loose at his sides, torso suspended above the floor.

'Oh no,' she said.

Flanagan grabbed her phone from her bag and dialled.

DSI Purdy arrived last, pushing his way through the crowd that had gathered at the church gates. A pair of uniformed constables stayed between the people and the church, but the crowd seemed content to watch, concern on their faces. Members of the congregation, most of them, arriving for their Sunday service to find a police line they could not cross. Flanagan recognised some of the faces, saw tears on many.

'Dr Barr here yet?' Purdy asked as he approached.

'He's in there now,' Flanagan said, nodding towards the vestry. Flashes of light burst from inside as the photographer recorded the scene.

Light drops of rain spotted Flanagan's skin, but she still had to shield her eyes against the sun. A rainbow arced above the buildings opposite.

'Tell me what you know so far,' Purdy said.

She looked to the ground, felt it drag her down, felt like she wanted to lie there and let the tarmac swallow her whole.

'I found him hanged just after eight-thirty,' Flanagan said. 'A black belt over the door. There's a belt missing from the cassock that's hanging up in the closet, so that must be it. No immediate sign of anyone else having been here. Everything points to a suicide.'

'Just like last week,' Purdy said.

'Yes, on the face of it. But there's something else.' She indicated the window, the lamp still glowing beyond the glass. 'There's a pestle and mortar sitting there, beneath that light.'

'A pestle and mortar?'

'I haven't touched it – no one has – but I could see a residue of white powder in the bowl.'

'Morphine,' Purdy said.

'I'm guessing so,' Flanagan said. 'Tests will confirm.'

'Jesus. So it was him killed Garrick. He couldn't hack it, so he leaves the evidence out and does himself in. Is that how you see it?'

'I'd say that's how I'm *supposed* to see it,' she said.

Purdy kept his gaze hard on Flanagan. 'Go on.'

'It's too neat,' she said. 'Too easy. A week I've been chasing after this, and all of a sudden it's handed to me on a plate. I don't buy it.'

234

Purdy looked back to the crowd at the gate. He sucked his teeth, tapped his foot, then turned back to Flanagan. 'Well, maybe you *should* buy it.'

She squinted at him, the sun bright behind him. 'Sir?'

'You've had an answer handed to you,' he said, his voice lowered. 'Maybe it's time you just took it and moved on.'

'Sir, no, I—'

'Let me finish,' he said, raising his hands to quiet her. 'You've been grabbing at threads through this whole case, trying to find something other than what was staring you in the face. I'm not saying your suspicions were wrong, we may never know what the truth is, but just think about how much harder you want to push at this. Look at it this way: you suspected this was murder from the start and it looks like you've been proven right. You didn't get the person you wanted for it, I understand that, but maybe you should accept this as a break and have it over and done with.'

Flanagan felt heat in her eyes, shook her head.

'No,' she said. 'I can't. I just can't. I know this is a set-up, and you know it too.'

'I don't know any such—'

'Sir, with respect, you haven't been talking with Reverend McKay or Mrs Garrick. You haven't looked into their eyes like I have. And there's something else.'

'What?'

Flanagan hesitated, then said, 'He called me last night.'

Purdy raised his eyebrows, pointed his thumb towards the vestry.

'Yes,' she said. 'Around nine. He asked me to come over, he needed to talk to me. I said I couldn't. He offered to come to me, and I refused.'

Purdy sighed. 'I know where you're going with this, and you're wrong.'

She kept her voice low, but anger pushed the words out – anger at herself, jagged and bitter. 'I'm not wrong. If I'd gone to him, if I'd let him come to me, he'd still be alive. Whether he killed himself, or somebody else did it, it wouldn't have happened if I'd listened to whatever it was he needed to tell me.'

'Stop it,' Purdy said, pointing a finger at her, inches from her face. 'Fucking stop it. It's bad enough you're looking for someone else to blame for that man's death, let alone yourself. Whatever brought McKay to suicide had nothing to do with you, and I don't want to hear another word on that. Clear?'

Flanagan didn't answer. Cloud obscured the sun, and the rain thickened. Drops gathered on Purdy's glasses.

'Now, I need you to be careful,' he said. 'Something's brewing elsewhere.'

'Sir?'

'I got collared by a journalist on the way in, something about allegations made by Jim Allison. Whether it's to do with what happened yesterday, I don't know, but he's been shooting his mouth off to the press. Watch your step.'

'Yes, sir.'

He pointed to her car, still parked by McKay's house. 'Now go on, get out of the rain.'

Flanagan nodded and turned towards the Volkswagen. She walked with her head down, hearing the murmurs of the crowd.

'Why couldn't you have left them alone?' a voice called.

She stopped, turned her head to the gates. An elderly woman called again. 'Why did you hound them like that? Now look what you've done.'

Flanagan stared for a moment, confused, then resumed the short walk to her car. Inside, rain sounding on the roof, she put her head in her hands and prayed.

39

Roberta Garrick watched the local news bulletin on the small flat screen television in her kitchen, the sound muted, the coffee machine gurgling and hissing. A long shot of the church, taken from the village side, with the rear of Peter's house closer to the camera. Police officers milling around, some wearing forensic overalls. Then a photograph of her and her husband at a Christmas get-together.

She reached for the remote control and turned the volume up. The reporter spoke in voiceover as the photograph zoomed in to fill the screen.

'. . . local MLA Jim Allison, a close friend of both the deceased men, had this to say about the police investigation so far.'

And there was Jim, the church further in the background, the hubbub going on behind him, sunshine making him squint. He wore his Sunday suit and a serious face.

'I have been in touch with the Assistant Chief Constable and expressed my disgust at the treatment meted out to both Mrs Garrick and Reverend Peter McKay over the last week.'

Strange how his voice became nasal and pinched when he spoke in public, not like when he whispered and moaned into her ear in the back of his Range Rover.

'Specifically, Detective Chief Inspector Serena Flanagan has subjected both of my good friends to a week of abuse since

Mr Garrick took his own life. Mrs Garrick has suffered enough tragedy over the last few years without being hounded by a police officer, particularly when the coroner has unequivocally ruled Mr Garrick's death a suicide. Likewise, Reverend McKay, having just lost a very dear friend, has been constantly intimidated by DCI Flanagan.'

Cut to a shot, zoomed in from some distance, of Flanagan outside the church, a taller man leaning over her, a heated discussion, the man's finger in her face.

Cut back to Jim Allison, nodding to emphasise each point.

'I have absolutely no doubt that this police harassment has played at least some part in driving Reverend McKay to an apparent suicide. The Assistant Chief Constable has assured me he will look into this matter, and believe me, I will hold him to that promise.'

Cut to the reporter, an earnest young man with shaving rash on his neck, hunched against a shower of rain.

'Detectives have not as yet confirmed the sudden death of Reverend Peter McKay as a suicide, though that is the view of most of the people I've spoken to this morning. As for Jim Allison's allegations of harassment, the PSNI have declined to comment, saying to do so would be unhelpful at this stage of the investigation.'

Back to the studio, and the news bulletin switched to a story about a factory closure. Roberta turned the television off and waited for the coffee machine to finish. She winced at the pain between her neck and shoulders. Stabbing spasms had been nagging her since she woke, and the muscles of her upper back felt stretched and quivery. She was in excellent shape, made good use of the gym upstairs, but still, dragging Peter across the church floor had been a strain.

No mention of the pestle and mortar. The police hadn't let that detail slip yet; Jim Allison still believed her husband's death to be suicide. Let him go on thinking it, and everyone else, until the police made it known. His railing against Flanagan and the PSNI would come back to haunt him when he was proven wrong, but the short-term damage to Flanagan was more than worth it.

It had been a week of terrors and triumphs. Certain one moment that she had let one small thread slip her grasp, enough to unravel everything; the next moment, confident the way ahead had cleared. And in between those moments a giddy shrieking inside her mind, a feeling of being adrift and lost. The sense that she would never regain control. But those moments passed too, only to return again and again as her thoughts cycled between the best and worst of all things.

She knew what she needed now: stability and peace. The space to calm down, to find her balance. Then she could get on with enjoying the life she had worked so long and hard at crafting for herself. All she had to do was get through these next few days and all would be as she desired.

Patience and a steady hand, that was all.

Roberta went to the coffee machine, lifted the cup from beneath the spout, and the other from the worktop. She carried both, steam and dark aroma rising from the frothy liquid, out of the kitchen and up the stairs to the open door of her bedroom.

Jim waited there, sitting on the edge of the bed, hands clasped together in front of his mouth. He had put his trousers back on, the belt still hanging loose, the flab of his belly spilling onto his lap.

He didn't look at her, even as she held a cup in front of his eyes. He took it, but did not drink. She sat on the chair in the corner, the one where Harry had draped his clothes every night, back when he had been able to dress himself.

'What?' she asked.

Jim stared at the carpet, his toes curling and gripping the deep pile. 'We shouldn't have done that,' he said.

'Of course we should,' she said.

'Harry's only just in his grave, now Peter. And we're . . .'

He turned his head, looked at the scattered sheets.

'Fucking,' Roberta said.

Jim looked at her now, shocked at the word he'd been too afraid to speak for himself. But he dropped his gaze almost as soon as it met hers.

'It's not right,' he said. 'It's too soon.'

'Nonsense,' she said. She blew on her coffee, felt the heat on her lips. Tasted him. 'It's been more than a year. You think it was all right to fuck your friend's wife while he was still alive, but not once he's dead? What's the difference? Apart from being able to do it in a bed instead of the back of your car.'

'It's not right,' he said again. 'It's just not.'

Roberta set her cup on the floor, stood, crossed to the bed. She took the cup from his hand, set it on the bedside locker. Then she put her hand on his bare chest, eased him back onto the mattress. She climbed onto him, straddled him, and with her hands she pinned his wrists down behind his head. She leaned down, her mouth to his ear.

'It's not right,' she said. 'And it's not wrong. It just is. Life becomes so much easier when you let go of right and wrong.'

The tip of her tongue traced the shape of his ear. He moaned as his hips rose to her.

'Believe me,' she said. 'I know.'

40

DSI Purdy had sent Flanagan home half an hour after he'd arrived at the scene. No explanation, only that he would call by and see her later. Regret had been clear on his face, and she knew the order had come from above.

She turned on the radio as she drove the short distance to her house, tuned it to BBC Radio Ulster. The news started as she pulled her car into the driveway. She drove around to the rear of the house, shut off the engine, but kept the key in the ignition so she could listen.

Reverend McKay's death was the lead item, but no mention of the pestle and mortar. A straightforward suicide, according to sources. Flanagan knew the 'sources' were members of the congregation who had gathered outside the church and that they knew nothing of what had occurred inside.

Alistair appeared at the kitchen window, waved to her. She returned the gesture, then raised a finger, mouthed the words, 'One minute.'

He nodded and disappeared from view.

She listened to the rest of the report, unsurprised by any of it until Jim Allison said his piece. Harassment, he said, intimidated. Flanagan flinched at the words, balled her hands into fists. She thumped the power button on the radio with the heel of her hand.

'Arsehole,' she said. 'Fucking arsehole.'

She stayed there in the driver's seat until the anger had ebbed enough for her to speak without a tremor in her voice. No need for the kids to see the rage on her, not with how stretched and thin everything had become in recent days.

Alistair opened the back door as she got out of the car. He put an arm around her waist, kissed her cheek as she crossed the threshold, gave her a look that said she didn't need to explain. She loved him then as much as she ever had, and she entered into the warm scents of the meal he'd been preparing.

'Where are they?' she asked, looking towards the hall.

'Eli's on his PlayStation,' Alistair said, 'Ruth's up in her room reading.'

'So we've got a minute to ourselves,' Flanagan said.

Alistair smiled and took her in his arms. They stayed like that, holding each other until she said, 'A good man died last night.'

'A friend?' he asked.

Flanagan thought about it for a moment before saying, 'Yes. Yes, he was.'

The bubbling and hissing of a pot boiling over pulled Alistair away. She watched as he lowered the heat under the pot, stirred another, peered inside the oven.

'Are we going to be all right?' she asked.

He closed the oven door and turned back to her. 'I don't know,' he said. 'I hope so.'

Two hours later, the children cleared their bowls of dessert and Flanagan gathered up the rest of the dishes. It had been a good meal, no brittle borders between them at the table. Just a family enjoying a Sunday lunch, and Flanagan wished she could drown out the whispering worry that lingered in her mind, along with the pangs of sorrow for Peter McKay.

The doorbell rang as she closed the dishwasher. She looked to Alistair, and he said, 'Go on, I'll clear up.'

DSI Purdy stood on the doorstep with his hands in his pockets, a frown on his face. Without a word, she showed him into the small downstairs office. Booms, thuds and shrieks from whatever game Eli was playing in the next room. Flanagan sat at the desk beneath the window while Purdy squeezed his bulk into the old wicker chair in the corner.

'You know what I'm going to tell you,' Purdy said.

Flanagan nodded. 'Who's taking over?' she asked.

'DCI Conn,' he said.

Flanagan gave a hard laugh. 'Christ, he'll love that. He'll take every chance he can to shit all over me after the Walker case.'

A year ago she had humiliated Conn by pulling a case from under him, proving he had it all wrong. They hadn't spoken since.

'It wasn't my choice,' Purdy said. 'The ACC chose him. Either way, you knew it'd be taken from you.'

'I know,' she said. 'But him.'

'Listen, whatever Conn does with it from here on, the ACC knows you were right all along about it not being a simple suicide. If it wasn't for you, this would've been wrapped up four days ago and the truth would never have come out. I'll be reminding Conn of that, and the ACC.'

'But the truth hasn't come out,' Flanagan said. 'Not all of it. He didn't act on his own. Roberta Garrick has to be interrogated.'

'That'll be Conn's decision to make,' Purdy said.

'Can I offer to assist?' Flanagan asked.

Now Purdy laughed. 'Do you think Conn will have that?'

She shook her head. 'No, I suppose not.'

'Well, then. First thing tomorrow morning, pack up everything you have on the case and give it to me to pass on. After that's done, why don't you take a couple of days off?'

She considered it for a moment. 'No, moping around here won't do me any good. Give me some grunt work to do, anything to keep me occupied.'

'There's always plenty of that lying around.' He smiled, and she returned the gesture, albeit with no feeling behind it.

'You know,' Purdy said, 'it's all for the best. I'll be glad for this to be wrapped up. I don't want to leave any loose ends when I go at the end of the week.'

'But you'll know that woman got away with it,' Flanagan said.

'I don't know any such thing,' Purdy said, his voice hardening. 'Besides, remember where we are. This is Northern Ireland. How many killers have we got on our streets – people you and I know have blood on their hands – that are walking around free, knowing they'll never see the inside of a cell? Even if I thought Roberta Garrick had got away with murder, she'd be at the end of a very long list.'

Flanagan had no comeback for that. She offered him a tea or a coffee, but he declined, said he was needed back at the scene.

'I'll see myself out,' he said, getting up. He stopped in the doorway and said, 'Don't dwell on this. You'll drive yourself crazy.'

'I'll try,' she said, knowing he didn't believe her.

'Take care.'

He closed the door behind him. From her seat by the window she heard his car door open and close, his engine starting, the tyres on the driveway.

'Shit,' she said.

A knock on the door, then Alistair entered. He carried a fizzing glass of gin and tonic, a wedge of lime trapped among the ice, and a pale ale for himself. She gratefully took the glass from his hand, had a sip, savoured the juniper and lime taste, the hard crisp cold of it. He'd made it strong, and she was glad.

'Thank you,' she said.

Alistair took her mobile phone from his pocket; she'd left it on the kitchen table. 'Sounds like there was a text for you,' he said, handing it to her.

Flanagan entered her passcode and saw Miriam McCreesh's name. She cursed herself for neglecting yet again to reply to Friday's message. The text read: *I see from the news that you've got your hands full. Might see you tomorrow. Catch up then.*

But Flanagan wouldn't see Dr McCreesh tomorrow. DCI Brian Conn would stand watch as the pathologist cut Peter McKay open on the cold steel table. That thought, the relief of not having to endure the post-mortem clashing with the regret at not seeing McCreesh, dissuaded her from replying now. She tossed her phone onto the desk and took another deep swallow from her glass.

Alistair perched on the edge of the desk, swigged his ale. She had discussed little of the case with him, given how seldom they'd talked at all in recent weeks, but he knew enough to understand things weren't good if Purdy had called to the house.

'End of the world?' he asked.

'Probably not,' Flanagan said. 'Just feels like it.'

He put a hand on her shoulder, squeezed, took it away.

They sat and drank together without speaking. She thought of the turmoil of the last couple of months, how much her job had cost her, what it cost her family. And yet it came to this. No one saved, no justice served. Another dead man and a hollow feeling in her gut.

Flanagan leaned into Alistair, her head resting against his side, and he put his arm around her.

'Let's get drunk,' she said.

'We've both got work tomorrow,' he said.

'So? Wouldn't be the first time either of us went in with a hangover.'

'What about the kids?'

'They can fend for themselves. He's got his games, she's got her books. I'll throw a ham sandwich at them at some point.'

He smiled and said, 'All right.'

41

Roberta Garrick was not surprised when the police officers called at her home that evening, only that it had taken so long. She recognised the male as she watched him approach through her living room window. He had been with Flanagan, seemed to be an assistant of some kind, but she couldn't recall his name. A younger policewoman followed him, a uniformed officer, sturdy, broad at the hips, but pretty enough in her own way. Roberta Garrick always noticed these things.

'Answer the door, would you?' she said.

Jim had been dozing on the couch, had not heard the police car pull up to the house.

'Hm?' He blinked at her like a slow child asked to solve an equation.

'Get the door,' she said. 'Please.'

Jim looked out to the hall, confusion still lingering on his face. Then the doorbell rang, and he said, 'Oh.'

He got to his feet, tucked his shirt into his trousers, smoothed and straightened himself as he went to the hall. Roberta listened to the murmur of voices, then Jim returned, the two young officers following.

'Roberta,' Jim said, 'Detective Sergeant Murray needs a word.'

'What can I do for you, Sergeant?' she asked.

Murray clasped his hands together as he spoke, an act of supplication. 'There's been a significant development in the case of your husband's death,' he said.

'Oh?' She raised her eyebrows, felt the worry on her face like she'd slipped on a mask.

Murray indicated the couch. 'Maybe you should take a seat.'

She went to the couch, sat down, reached a hand out towards Jim. 'Can Jim stay?'

'Of course,' Murray said.

Jim took her hand and sat down next to her, a good family friend offering comfort and support. Murray sat in the armchair opposite, where DCI Flanagan had sat almost a week before. The uniformed policewoman remained standing near the door. Murray hadn't bothered to introduce her.

The sergeant sat forward, his hands clasped together once more, as if praying. 'Mrs Garrick, I have to warn you, what I'm about to tell you will be upsetting.'

She blinked, searched for that feeling inside, the one she used to summon tears. There, there it was. She blinked again, felt the warm wetness in her eyes. Jim squeezed her fingers between his.

'Go on,' she said.

'Mrs Garrick, we have reason to believe your husband's death was not a suicide.'

She opened her mouth, inhaled, held her breath. Just long enough. 'What do you mean?' she asked in a very small voice.

'We have reason to believe that Mr Garrick was murdered,' Murray said. 'More than that, we believe that Reverend McKay might have killed him.'

Jim looked from the sergeant to Roberta and back again. 'What?'

'No,' Roberta said. 'That can't be true.'

'We have evidence to suggest that's the case,' Murray said. 'It's early days in the investigation, but right now we're not looking for anyone else in connection with this.'

Roberta shook her head. 'There must be a mistake.'

'Mrs Garrick, is it possible that Reverend McKay might have been able to take some sachets of morphine granules out of this house?'

'I don't know,' she said. 'I suppose it's possible. When he came round, he often fed Harry his yogurt with the morphine in it. We kept the sachets by the bed.'

Murray wrote something on his notepad. 'As you're aware, Reverend McKay committed suicide at some time last night. He used a belt to hang himself from the vestry door.'

She pushed the tears out, fished a tissue from her sleeve, dabbed at her cheeks.

'We found a pestle and mortar on the desk in the vestry. It's yet to be confirmed, but there were traces of powder in the mortar that we believe to be crushed morphine granules. We believe that Reverend McKay took some sachets from your home, crushed the contents with the pestle and mortar, then when he came back to your house, he mixed them in with your husband's nightly yogurt.'

Roberta began to shake, more tears. 'No, no, no,' she said. 'It can't be true, it can't be.'

Murray shuffled forward on his seat. 'Where we're struggling, Mrs Garrick, is the reason. Why would Reverend McKay do this?'

She became still and quiet, staring into space. She felt their gaze on her, their waiting breath, their anticipation. Let them wait.

'Mrs Garrick?'

What was the threat she'd made to Peter before he left yesterday? What had she said she'd tell the police? Oh, yes. She slowly came back to herself, shaking her head as she did so. 'No,' she whispered. 'That can't be it.'

'Anything at all you think of, Mrs Garrick.'

She tilted her head as she spoke, knitted her brow. 'There *is* something, but it seems so unlikely.'

Murray's voice took on a pleading tone. 'Anything at all.'

Roberta exhaled, a defeated sigh. 'Peter had feelings for me.'

She felt a twitch in Jim's fingers and had to suppress a smile.

'Feelings?' Murray echoed.

'I always dismissed it,' she said. 'He was lonely. I never knew his wife, she died before I became a member of the church, but I know he missed her constantly, even to this day. And he was all on his own, alone in that big house, the rectory. He was always a good friend of ours, but after Harry's accident we became very close. We talked a lot, just me and Peter. I suppose he hadn't had anyone to talk to like that for a long time. And I suppose it became more for him.'

Murray asked, 'Did he ever make any . . . approaches to you?'

'You mean, physically?'

'Yes.'

'No, at least not at first. It started with him telling me how close he felt he'd come to me over those few months. How he wished he could meet someone like me, someone to keep him

252

company. So I tried to talk him into getting out there, meet people outside the congregation, but it didn't seem to do any good. You know, I didn't think much of it at the time, but he would always hold my hands when we prayed. It seemed to be a very intimate thing for him.'

Dare she push the lie a little further? Murray and the young policewoman seemed so rapt in her words. One more tiny detail to reel them in.

'Then once,' she said, 'he tried to kiss me.'

Jim let go of her hands.

'And what happened?' Murray asked.

'We were praying, like we always did, and he had my hands held to his chest. I remember I could feel his breath on my skin. Then, as we finished, I opened my eyes, and he was so close. He leaned in and kissed me. I was so shocked, I didn't pull away immediately, but when I realised what was happening, I pushed him back.'

'How did he react?'

'I remember his face,' Roberta said, warming to the tale, the picture she painted for them. 'At first, for a moment, he looked shocked, then angry, then sad. He kept apologising, over and over, and I kept telling him not to worry about it, I understood, he was lonely, and so on. Perhaps I led him on. Maybe I shouldn't have let our relationship get so close.'

'How was he after that?' Murray asked. 'Did things get back to normal?'

'Yes and no,' she said. 'He was bashful, timid around me for a week or two, then things seemed to be fine. He still came round to see Harry, to pray with me. Just like before. But there was always this look in his eyes, like there was something going on behind them. And sometimes in church, he seemed to be looking at me in a way he didn't look at the other women. I told myself it was my imagination, but now I'm not so sure. Does any of this help?'

'It helps a lot,' Murray said, closing his notebook. 'Would you be prepared to repeat this in a full statement?'

'Yes, if you think it's necessary.'

'Good,' he said, opening his notebook again. 'One thing, though.'

An alarm sounded in Roberta's mind. She had made a mistake. But what?

'Given what happened between Reverend McKay and you,' he said, 'why did you agree to stay at his house after your husband's death?'

She sat quite still, staring into the empty air between the two officers. Think of something. Think.

There. Imperfect, but it would have to do. She let her features harden.

She turned her gaze on Murray. 'I had just discovered my husband's dead body,' she said. 'Forgive me if I wasn't in the most rational state of mind.'

Murray looked away. 'Of course,' he said, a red flush creeping up past his shirt collar. 'I think that's all for now.'

He stood. Roberta and Jim did the same.

As Murray turned to the door, Roberta said, 'Can you please do me a favour?'

'Of course,' Murray said.

'Please pass on my apologies and thanks to DCI Flanagan. I was harsh with her. I realise now that she suspected something and was just doing her job. If she hadn't pushed so hard, then the truth might not have come to light. I'm grateful to her. Please tell her that.'

Murray nodded. 'I will. I'll be in touch over the next day or two.'

Jim saw them out while Roberta waited in the living room. She watched them get into the car and pull away. As the car passed through the gate at the end of the drive, she felt a warm satisfaction in her breast. She turned away from the window as Jim returned to the living room.

Without looking at her, he said, 'I should go.'

'You should,' Roberta said. 'Your wife will be wondering where you've got to.'

'You should have mentioned Peter to them earlier, after Harry died. How he felt about you.'

'Should I?'

He still did not meet her gaze. 'Maybe if they'd questioned him about it, he might have confessed. He might not have taken his own life.'

'Maybe,' she said. 'Might. I suppose we'll never know.'

'If I'd known, I wouldn't have said what I did about DCI Flanagan on the news. I wouldn't have made a fool of myself like that.'

'For God's sake, get your head out of your arse, Jim,' she said, unable to keep the sneer from her voice.

Now he looked at her. 'What?'

She speared him with her gaze, let him have the full force of it. 'No one cares what you said. Now go on home, there's a good boy. Don't keep Mrs Allison waiting.'

He left without saying another word.

42

Flanagan sat at her desk in Lisburn station, the lamp on so she could read the local newspaper. Always dark in here, the tiny window that didn't open more than a crack. On a warm day the air grew thick and heavy with heat. Today was cool, but that was about all she had to be glad of.

CLERGYMAN'S SUICIDE LINKED TO MURDER.

A shriek of a headline above a story that relished the details of the case, scant as they were. DCI Conn had given a press conference the previous night; she had watched it on the news that morning as she had an early breakfast. Conn at a desk, flanked by DSI Purdy and DS Murray, PSNI insignia behind them.

A suicide, Conn said, believed to be linked to the death of Henry Garrick six days before. Reverend Peter McKay had been very close to the dead man and his wife. They were seeking no one else in their inquiries. A few shouted questions from the journalists, most of them dismissed with pat answers, then one about the relationship between the minister and the widow. A flicker on Conn's face was enough.

The story Flanagan now read had taken those points, extrapolated, made insinuations far beyond anything that was in the public domain. 'Sources close to the investigation' suggested that there was an abnormally close tie between Reverend McKay and Mrs Garrick, and that formed a central pillar of police inquiries.

Purdy had told Flanagan what Mrs Garrick had said to Murray the previous evening, but she felt certain that Murray would not have spilled to a reporter. More likely, whoever had written the piece had grasped a thread and woven his story from that, citing sources that simply didn't exist.

A brief paragraph stated that local MLA Jim Allison had been publicly critical of her handling of the case. No mention of Flanagan's suspicions of murder being proven correct, or of the statement Allison had issued that morning to apologise for his stance. In fairness, that would have been too late for this edition of the paper, but she doubted that any of the news outlets would bother carrying the apology.

When she'd called into Purdy's office this morning, Flanagan had once again offered to assist Conn through the remainder of the investigation.

'I told you no already,' Purdy had said.

She had tried to argue. 'But I could save him so much digging, all the work I've already—'

'No,' Purdy said, his voice higher and harder. 'DCI Conn is going to wrap this thing up, do all the box-ticking. You should be thankful he's saving you from a mountain of paperwork.'

She knew then that Purdy just wanted it over and done with, off his desk before his retirement on Friday. The explanation of events that had been presented to him was good enough. She couldn't blame him. There was no evidence of Roberta Garrick's having had a hand in either death. Her suspicions and instincts did not outweigh what was in front of Purdy's nose.

'All I need you to do,' Purdy said, 'is make sure you have everything gathered and ready to hand over to Conn. And I'd better not get any complaints from him about you sticking your nose in. Understood?'

'Yes, sir,' she said.

Now all her work sat in three file boxes against the far wall while she studied the newspaper piece as if it contained some secret, some new scent for her to track. Nothing but speculation dressed as reportage. As crappy a piece of journalism as she'd ever seen. Salacious and puerile. There, a boxed-out image of Roberta Garrick at her husband's funeral. Flanagan would have been angered at the paper's intrusiveness had it been any other widow at the front of any other funeral procession.

She studied the woman's face, the blankness of it.

Who are you?

The question Flanagan could not escape. She'd been asking it for a week now and had yet to come up with a satisfactory answer. Who is this beautiful woman who appeared in this community seven years ago seeming never to have left a trace elsewhere?

Who are you?

Flanagan set the newspaper aside and once again opened the web browser on her computer. Facebook again. That profile again. This nothing life, this existence of Bible verses and flower arrangements and coffee mornings.

Who are you?

A knock on the door startled her, and she clicked the mouse to close the browser before calling, 'Come.'

DS Murray entered carrying a manila folder. 'Ma'am, these are the bank records. Where do you want them?'

She pointed to the stack of file boxes. 'Stick them in there.'

Murray crossed to them, lifted the lid of the top box, was about to shove the folder inside.

'Hang on,' Flanagan said.

Murray paused, looked at her.

'That's both Mr and Mrs Garrick's personal accounts, yes?'

'Yes, ma'am,' Murray said. 'I went through them like you said, but nothing stood out.'

As a matter of course, DSI Purdy had sought authorisation for a RIPA request for access to two years' records of the deceased's and the widow's current and savings accounts. The Regulation of Investigatory Powers Act meant that any such request had to be made by an officer of his rank or higher, but not one directly involved in the case. Signs of financial distress would reinforce the assumption of suicide, but Murray had found they seemed to be comfortably solvent, to say the least.

'Let me have a look,' Flanagan said, holding out her hand.

Murray brought the folder over. She took it from him and dropped it onto the desk with a thud.

'There was nothing untoward,' Murray repeated. 'Not as far as I could see, anyway.'

'That's fine,' Flanagan said. 'I just want to satisfy my curiosity.'

She pointedly looked to the door and thanked him. Murray took the hint and left. Alone, she opened the folder, slid out the slab of printed paper.

A current account in each of the Garricks' names, an ISA each, a reserve account for tax, as well as a general savings account belonging to Henry Garrick.

Flanagan hesitated for a moment, wondering what she was doing. What did she hope to find? She put her head in her hands and said, 'Give it up.' She had nothing to gain from digging a deeper hole for herself. Even so, she turned over a page and began.

She started with the tax-free Individual Savings Accounts. Only a few transactions a year. Into each account had been deposited the maximum annual allowance on the 6th of April for the last two years, and Flanagan assumed every year before that. A string of small monthly additions as the miserable interest accrued. Nothing she didn't expect to see. Next Flanagan looked at Henry Garrick's own savings account. Again, a series of deposits, no withdrawals. A better rate of interest, presumably in return for not touching the balance.

Now the current accounts. Flanagan started with Henry Garrick's, tracing the tip of her pen down the columns of debits and credits.

A modest monthly amount from Garrick Motors Ltd; his salary from the limited company. Flanagan took a highlighter from the penholder on her desk, coloured each deposit a bright yellow. Then she ran a quick tally in her head; as she expected, the rough total came out well below the individual tax-free allowance. Henry Garrick would pay nothing on this money, and any more that was paid as a dividend would be charged at a lower rate. Plus it avoided National Insurance. She took an orange highlighter, found the additional payments into the account from Garrick Motors Ltd. A couple of thousand here, five thousand there. In every case, a dividend would be paid a few days before a larger outlay. A holiday company in one case, a jeweller in another.

Flanagan marvelled at the sums moving back and forth, the thousands of pounds passed around like loose change, felt the sour envy in her belly she'd felt standing in Roberta Garrick's walk-in wardrobe a week ago. She banished the feeling just as she had seven days before.

Despite the apparent excess of Henry Garrick's finances, they had a solid foundation. For every dividend taken, a percentage was also moved to the tax reserve to be paid when Her Majesty's Revenue and Customs came calling for their due. All very sensible and responsible. Taking whatever steps were necessary to minimise the tax obligation, and ensuring there was always enough to cover what couldn't be avoided. Murray had been quite right: no sign of financial distress. Quite the opposite, in fact. Even the monthly tithe to the church was generous, somewhat above the ten per cent convention demanded.

But something caught Flanagan's eye as she ran her finger down the series of orange highlighted dividend payments, turning pages as she went: beginning five months ago – one month after Henry Garrick's car accident – a string of dividend credits followed by payments to another company.

Manx-Hibernian Investments Ltd.

Flanagan made another tally in her head. Not far off one hundred thousand bouncing through the account over less than half a year, even allowing for the percentage that had been set aside for tax. She highlighted the outgoing money in green then turned to Roberta Garrick's current account.

Not dissimilar to her husband's. She took the same salary from the car dealership – she probably had a token title of secretary or treasurer, and probably took over as director after the accident – and the same kinds of dividends. A similar amount to her husband's paid out in tithe to the church. Flanagan took her time, not leaping ahead to the discovery she sought, highlighting the same transactions in the same colours. Then she moved back five months to a substantial dividend payment, £17,500. Two days later the same amount, minus a percentage moved to the tax reserve, paid out to another company.

Manx-Hibernian Investments Ltd.

Flanagan made another total. Just over a hundred thousand. She checked the total she'd scribbled in the top corner of Henry Garrick's account. Almost exactly two hundred thousand going to what appeared to be an account on the Isle of Man.

She lifted the telephone handset and dialled Purdy's extension.

43

Roberta snapped awake, sprawled on top of the sheets. Falling, still falling, she grabbed the edge of the bed to quell the sensation. Her chest heaving, terror ripping through her.

'Oh God,' she said. 'Oh God.'

She did not remember coming upstairs or lying down. She'd watched the news while she ate breakfast and drank coffee. After that? She recalled feeling weary, but not the decision to climb the stairs and sleep.

And what had woken her?

The thin glimmer of a dream remained in her mind. Peter's hands on her, touching her, kneading at her body while his eyes bulged and his face turned purple. The smell of his dying while he still clung to her. Perhaps the dream had scared her awake. She hoped it was that and not the other.

But then she heard it.

The high keening cry. The calling, Mummy, Mummy, Mummy.

Roberta pulled a pillow over her head, pressed it to her ears, tried to block out the cries. But they cut through, pierced her brain, so high, so loud, always, always, always crying. Never peace, never quiet.

'Stop,' she said, her lips pressed against the mattress. 'Please stop.'

But it did not stop. Calling for her, Mummy, Mummy, Mummy, the name she hated more than any other. Like needles in her skin, burning hot until she screamed into the bed, the pillow still wrapped tight around her head.

Finally, she said, 'All right.'

She threw the pillow aside and sat upright on the bed. The crying did not abate as she got to her feet, it only intensified, little gasps between each shriek. Roberta went to the double bedroom doors, paused there, knowing the cries would be louder still when she opened them. And they were, so fierce that she had to clasp her hands over her ears.

Out on the landing, the cries echoed through the hallway. She knew the source: the bedroom next to hers, the child's room, where her cot had been, the colourful painted walls, the toys, the drawers and wardrobe full of pretty clothes. The squealing, the Mummy, Mummy, Mummy came from in there.

'All right,' Roberta said, unable to hear her own voice above the crying. 'All right!'

She threw open the bedroom door, let it swing back and slam against the chest of drawers. No cot, no colourful painted walls, no pretty clothes. The room had long since been redecorated, but no amount of paint or carpeting would quiet the child who still lived here.

'All right, I'll do it,' she said.

The crying ceased, and she felt the pressure in her head ease. She took her hands away from her ears.

'I'll do it,' she said.

She turned, left the bedroom, and went back to her own. The antique chest, the clean rectangle of wallpaper above it. Roberta went to the chest, opened the top drawer, reached inside. The picture frame cold and hard in her hands. She lifted it up, back to the wall, found the hook, guided the string onto it.

The child stared down at her, that sweet smile on its face, the baby teeth showing. Dimples and blonde curls. The loveliest girl, everyone said, such a wee angel. But they didn't have to listen to it scream, tend to it day and night, feel it bound to her, tying her up, keeping her captive, promising to do so for years to come.

Roberta went to the bed, sat on its edge, keeping her eyes on the photograph. Always watching, it was, always knowing. Even when it was closed in the drawer, it could see.

She closed her eyes, remembered the sensation of thrashing, struggling beneath her hand, and cold, the water up to her chin. Then stillness, a rushing in her ears, then under, tasting salt, then up, screaming help, help me, help my baby . . .

Roberta shivered, opened her eyes, got to her feet. Quiet now. Her bare feet padded across the carpet, out onto the wooden boards of the stairs, down to the kitchen.

Lunch, she thought. What will I have?

44

'Look,' Flanagan said, spreading the printed bank records across Purdy's desk.

'What?' Purdy said.

He sat in his chair, Flanagan standing at his side, leaning over the sheets of paper.

'This,' she said, pointing to the first orange highlighted debit, then the green highlighted credit above it. 'And this.'

'Money going in and out,' Purdy said. 'So what? They had plenty of it to throw around, didn't they?'

'But look,' Flanagan said, pointing at another credit, another debit. 'These start three weeks after Henry Garrick has his car accident. Dividends from the company coming in then going straight out again. I make it two hundred grand in total over a space of five months. All going to this Isle of Man investment fund.'

'So?' Purdy asked. 'It's a tax dodge. All these rich bastards are at it. It's a shitty move, but there's nothing illegal about it.'

'But don't you see?' She stabbed at more debits. 'The tax has already been set aside. There's nothing to be dodged. I checked with HMRC, and the percentage due on these dividends matches what was moved to the reserve account. Why would you set up a tax dodge when you've already put aside the tax to be paid?'

Purdy was silent for a few moments, then said, 'Maybe it's just some savings being put away.'

'There are plenty of savings accounts they could use without going to the Isle of Man. Look, they've got three or four already. Why have this?'

Purdy shook his head. 'I still don't see what you're getting at. Why would Roberta Garrick need to spirit away two hundred grand? She's got ten times that in assets as it stands, plus the money the dealership brings in, and the stock they're holding. There's no need for her to move money away; she's already set up for life.'

'That's right,' Flanagan said. 'She's got all the money she could ever need, and the lifestyle to go with it. But what if she needs to run? What if she was planning all this five months ago, what if she needed enough put away in case something went wrong?'

'An escape fund?' Purdy said.

'Exactly. Two hundred thousand would be enough for her to make a start somewhere else if she couldn't stay here. Maybe she thinks having this money in the Isle of Man gives her some protection. Particularly if it's been bouncing from there to some-where else. If we can see where the money goes from there, we might be able to figure out what she was planning.'

Purdy sat silent for a moment as he thought, then he shook his head. 'No,' he said. 'I don't buy it.'

'Get a RIPA order, sir, get access to the Isle of Man account. Then we'll know for sure.'

'I can't get the order, I'm still involved in the case. It has to come from a superintendent who's not attached to the investigation.'

'McFadden,' Flanagan said. 'He can do it. I can put the request in today.'

'No you can't,' Purdy said. 'It's not your case.'

'Then you ask him.'

'He'll want to know on whose behalf. When I tell him it's for you, he'll refuse it. And he'll bloody well be right, too. This is none of your concern. If Conn wants to make the request, that'll be up to him.'

'For fuck's sake.' Flanagan slapped the desk, walked around it. 'I know there's something there, and you know it too.'

'Flanagan—'

She paced a circle around the office. 'You just can't be bothered with it, can you? It's one more headache you can do without in your last week, isn't that right?'

'Flanagan—'

'You've got an easy answer, and you're going to let Conn tidy it all up, just so you—'

Purdy shot to his feet. 'DCI Flanagan, shut your mouth!'

The ferocity of his voice stopped her pacing. She froze, staring at him.

'Just who the fuck do you think you're talking to?'

'Sir, I—'

'Don't you dare talk to me like that,' Purdy said, his cheeks florid. 'A week from now, when I'm out of this shitty job, you can talk to me however you want. But this week, now, you will address me with respect. Do I make myself clear?'

Flanagan looked to the floor. 'Yes, sir. I apologise, sir.'

He nodded and said, 'Get out.'

She approached the desk, went to gather up the sheets of bank records.

'Leave them,' Purdy said. 'I'll let Conn go through it all. If he thinks it's worth following up on, he can. I won't say you've been chasing it. He'll not bother his arse if your name comes into it.'

'Thank you, sir,' she said.

'All right,' he said. 'Go and do something useful.'

Flanagan waited in the reception area of the General of Register Office.

Something useful, Purdy had said. She had gone back to her office and tried to apply herself to the reports being readied for the Public Prosecution Service, but her mind would not leave Roberta Garrick and the dead she had left in her wake. The Manx-Hibernian account still nagged at her. She wasted more time googling the investment firm, scouring social media, none of it leading anywhere.

There was still one thing, though.

So Flanagan had driven to Belfast city centre, parked, walked to the General of Register Office, and presented her warrant card. She had given Roberta Garrick's full name, place and date of birth, then taken a seat to wait.

Less than ten minutes passed before the clerk came back with a C4-sized envelope. Flanagan thanked him and left the building, walked the five minutes back to her car, behind the Central Library. Huddles of red-brick buildings hemming in narrow streets, once bustling with industry, now mostly abandoned, some in redevelopment.

Once in the driver's seat, she checked the rear-view mirror.

Two young men, baseball caps, hoodies, tracksuit bottoms.

She locked the doors. Hijackings had become commonplace in the city, young thugs taking cars – usually from women – simply to race them around the estates before burning them out on some patch of waste ground.

Flanagan turned her attention back to the envelope and slid out the A4 sheet of pink and purple within. She studied the birth certificate. All was in order. Born Roberta Bailey in Magherafelt Hospital, 15th July 1980. The mother, Maisie Bailey, née Russell, the father Derek Bailey. Nothing untoward.

She glanced back to the rear-view mirror. The two young men separated, each approaching at either side of the row of parked cars behind her. She looked in her side mirrors, made eye contact with one of them. He didn't look away.

Flanagan set the envelope and the birth certificate on the passenger seat. Her right hand unclipped her holster, the other took her mobile phone from her bag. She dialled DS Murray's number, brought the phone to her ear.

The young men reached the car, and they each tried the door handles. The one at the driver's side tapped the window with the blade of a knife. Flanagan drew her Glock 17, let him see it. She smiled as he sprinted away towards the city centre, his friend still at the other side of the car, staring after him. He looked down into the car, saw the pistol, and followed the other, the soles of his trainers blurring as he ran.

Murray answered, and Flanagan holstered her weapon.

'Are you at your desk?' she asked.

'Give me a second, ma'am.' A few seconds of rustling and fumbling. 'I am now. What do you need?'

'Call up the electoral register,' she said.

She listened to a minute's worth of mouse-clicking and key-tapping, along with a few muttered curses, before Murray said, 'Right, got it.'

'Bailey, Derek,' she said, 'and Bailey, Maisie. Magherafelt area.'

More key-tapping, then a pause. 'Bailey,' Murray said. 'That's Roberta Garrick's maiden name.'

'That's right,' Flanagan said.

'This is DCI Conn's case,' Murray said. 'I'm not sure I should be doing this for you, ma'am.'

'I won't tell if you don't,' Flanagan said.

Another pause, then the key-tapping resumed. 'All right,' he said, 'I've got an address in Moneymore. Are you ready?'

Flanagan pulled the notepad and pen from her bag, juggled them and the phone as she got the cap off the pen and found a new page to write on. 'Go ahead,' she said, and wrote down the house number, the road, the postcode.

When she thanked him, Murray asked, 'What's going on, ma'am?'

'Nothing for you to worry about,' Flanagan said as she started her engine.

45

The police arrived at Roberta Garrick's home at five in the afternoon. A small group of them led by a middle-aged man who introduced himself as DCI Brian Conn.

'Where's DCI Flanagan?' Roberta had asked.

'She's no longer working on this case,' Conn had said, and she could see that he suppressed a smirk. In truth, she had to do the same.

The scene of her husband's death had to be reopened, Conn told her, and a cursory search undertaken. He hoped she would understand, and apologised for the intrusion. She had graciously offered to make tea for Conn and the three other officers, and they accepted.

Murray was not among them, she noted. A pity, she thought. Murray was much easier on the eye than the group Conn brought with him.

Now they worked in the rear reception room where the hospital bed remained. She heard grumbling about the futility of the search, particularly as she'd had the cleaner in since last week. Surely nothing useful could be found. Look anyway, Conn instructed.

Roberta listened with one ear as she watched the evening news. She had watched a lot of news in recent days; it was becoming a habit, adding punctuation to her routine. The newsreaders had become familiar, their names, their mannerisms, their turns of phrase. On a few occasions she had caught herself mimicking the female presenters, the tilt of their head, the pitch of their voice, the shape of their mouth. An old habit from her childhood, distant as that now seemed, the taking on of others' tics and quirks.

On the television, Peter's house appeared, and the church. Police officers wandering in and out. Just like here, she thought, as she heard two pairs of shoes climb her stairs. Searching the bedroom next. It didn't matter. They would find nothing there. Everything she had worth hiding was nowhere near this house.

The television caught her attention again.

'George,' she said as her brother-in-law filled the screen with his loping frame and country-handsome face. She had spotted him at the funeral, lurking at the back, keeping his head down. She had pretended not to see him. Not that she cared, anyway.

The reporter caught George on the doorstep of some shabby terraced house – his home, presumably, since his wife had kicked him out – and questioned him about his brother's possible murder.

'I don't know what I can say,' George mumbled in that blunt-edged country way of his. 'I don't think we'll ever get to the truth of it. There's more to this than will ever come out, but that'll be up to the police, and them that knows what really happened. And them that does know, I hope their conscience will guide them. If it doesn't, then I pity them.'

He glanced at the camera lens, and Roberta knew he spoke to her.

'They'll have to live with this and everything else that's gone on. I don't think they'll have a peaceful night's sleep as long as they live. And I know I couldn't live too long with that hanging over me. That's all I have to say.'

The report cut back to the studio, and she threw the remote control at the screen, making it flicker.

'Fuck you,' she said. 'Fuck you.'

'Is everything all right, Mrs Garrick?'

She spun to the voice. DCI Conn in the kitchen doorway, concern on his face.

'Fine,' she said, offering a regretful smile. 'It's fine. It's been a difficult time, that's all.'

He nodded and said, 'Of course.'

She went to the door, closed it behind him as he left. Alone now, she rested her forehead against the cool wood. No good. This wouldn't do at all. She was nearly through it, almost out the other side. All she had to do was keep control.

Her hand shot to her mouth, stifling a cry, as her mobile phone trilled and vibrated on the granite worktop. She went to it, saw the number, thumbed the green icon.

'Jim,' she said.

'Roberta,' he said.

Then nothing. She could picture him at the other end, mouth moving like a goldfish as he reached for the words.

'Say what you want to say.'

'I just . . .'

'Come on,' she said, her patience flaking away.

'I don't think we should see each other any more,' he said.

She smiled. 'I think you're probably right.'

'I want you to stay away from me,' he said.

'That won't be a problem.'

'I mean it,' he said. 'Stay away. I've deleted all those photographs. Don't send any more. Don't call me. If you do, I'll . . .'

'You'll what?'

Call the police, she thought. It was clear he suspected, but he was too much of a coward to do anything about it. A weak man, even weaker than Peter had been, weaker still than her dead husband.

'Nothing,' he said.

'That's right,' she said. 'You'll do nothing. That'd be better for everybody, don't you think?'

'Just keep away from me,' he said, and the phone died.

46

Flanagan followed the satnav's directions, skirting the town of Magherafelt, heading south towards the village of Moneymore. A long steep descent down a hill, pastureland all around, deep greens and cattle and sheep. The smell of the countryside, thick and heavy in the air. She passed a tractor coming the other way, towing a slurry tank, slow on the incline, half a mile of traffic backed up behind it. Drivers with angry faces, impatient for the tractor to pull in and let them past.

A thirty-mile-per-hour limit sign as she entered the village. She slowed the Volkswagen, shifted down to fourth gear, noted the newbuild houses climbing the hillside to her left, older dwellings to her right. A busy filling station that doubled as a supermarket. A sweeping bend and a small roundabout brought her into the heart of Moneymore. A typical Ulster plantation village, lacking the quaint charm of an English equivalent but pleasant in its own way. Austere functional buildings, painted rendering rather than attractive stone-work, bunting and Union flags still lingering from the dying summer's marching season.

She followed the road through a sharp bend, passing an Orange Hall and a Presbyterian church, obeyed the satnav's command to go straight on, the signs guiding her in the direction of Cookstown. A quarter mile outside the village, the satnav told her to take the next right, a narrow lane, its junction barely visible until she was on top of it.

Another quarter mile, and the Baileys' house was up ahead, on the apex of a bend. A large open gate leading to a modest bungalow set in half an acre of well-tended lawns and outbuildings. As she steered onto the short driveway, she saw a chicken pen to the rear of the house. Somewhere at the back, a dog barked at her arrival.

Flanagan shut off the engine and checked her mobile phone. No signal out here. She had intended on texting Alistair to apologise for missing dinner, but that would have to wait.

As she got out of the car, the front door opened, and a white-haired man stared out at her. Mid sixties, she thought, neatly dressed, wearing a tie for no apparent reason in the way that country Protestant men did.

'How're ye,' he said, a wary look on his face.

'Good evening,' Flanagan said with as friendly a smile as she could manage. 'Are you Mr Bailey?'

'Aye,' he said, giving a single nod, his expression impassive.

Flanagan wondered had he been a reservist, a part-time soldier or policeman; many of his generation had been during the Troubles. Not very long ago, a strange car pulling up at a reservist's home meant danger, shots fired through windows, doors broken down, men killed in front of their children. He said nothing more and remained watchful.

She reached into her bag, produced her wallet and the warrant card within, brought it to his doorstep. With quick blue eyes, he read it as she spoke.

'I'm sorry to disturb you, Mr Bailey,' she said. 'I'm Detective Chief Inspector Serena Flanagan, based at Lisburn. You can call to verify, if you'd like.'

She hoped he wouldn't. No one knew she had come here, and Purdy would rip her to shreds if he found out.

'That's all right,' he said, looking from the card to her face, a flicker of worry in his eyes now. 'Is there something wrong?'

'Nothing for you to be concerned about,' she said. 'I wanted to have a word with you and Mrs Bailey about your daughter, Roberta.'

'Roberta?' he asked, his brow creased.

'Yes, if you can spare a few minutes.'

He stepped back, opened the door fully. 'You'd better come in.'

'Thank you,' Flanagan said as she entered.

Mr Bailey reached behind the open door, lifted the double-barrelled shotgun he had propped there and put it into a closet. 'I've got a licence for it,' he said. 'There's still some bad boys about the country. Maisie's just doing the dishes. Go on in the living room and I'll get her.'

Flanagan heard water running, the clatter of cutlery. The house smelled of beef and potatoes and boiled vegetables, warm homey scents that sparked a memory of her grandmother, even though she barely remembered what Granny Jane looked like.

She thanked Mr Bailey once more and walked through the open door into the living room where a log burned red and grey in the hearth. A plush three-piece suite, small bookcases, a china cabinet, figurines, brassware. A carved wooden elephant on a sideboard.

On the mantelpiece above the fire, a framed photograph of a young girl, fiery red hair, pretty, someday beautiful. A school portrait, and Flanagan imagined the young Roberta Bailey, the first flush of puberty about her, sitting for a photographer in an echoing assembly hall while a line of children waited their turn.

She turned a circle, looking for more pictures. There were a few, all of her as a youngster, smiling. A little girl who was loved.

What happened to you? Flanagan thought. What went wrong?

Mr Bailey entered, followed by his wife, a sturdy woman showing little sign of going grey, still more copper in her hair than silver. A redhead like her daughter. High cheekbones like Roberta's, but the face rounded with age. She dried her hands on a towel and tucked it into the pocket on the front of her apron.

'Hello,' Mrs Bailey said. 'Would you take a cup of tea?'

'No, thank you,' Flanagan said. 'I don't want to use up any more of your time than I have to. Do you mind if I sit down?'

'Not at all,' Mrs Bailey said. 'Go ahead.'

Flanagan took the armchair, and the Baileys sat on the couch, both watching her with a mix of curiosity and worry. She readied her notebook and pen.

'As I said, I wanted to ask you about your daughter, if you don't mind.'

The Baileys looked at each other, then back to Flanagan.

'Ask away,' Mr Bailey said, that knot of caution still on his brow.

'She was a pretty girl,' Flanagan said, indicating the picture over the fireplace.

'Aye, she was,' Mrs Bailey said, a sadness in her voice. 'She was gorgeous.'

'How was she as a girl?' Flanagan asked. 'Was she well-behaved or did she give you any trouble? Was she sociable? Was she shy?'

'She was a good girl,' Mrs Bailey said. 'She was a wee bit shy, I suppose, but she had plenty of friends. The teachers always liked her at school. She loved school, so she did.'

'So never any problems,' Flanagan said.

'No, never.'

'I'm curious, then, what happened later on? Why did she become estranged from you?'

Mr and Mrs Bailey looked at each other again, then back to Flanagan.

'What do you mean?' Mr Bailey asked.

'I know there was a falling out when she was older,' Flanagan said. 'That she got into some trouble later on. Can you tell me about that?'

They stared at her. Tears welled in Mrs Bailey's eyes.

'I'm sorry,' Mr Bailey said. 'You've made a mistake.'

'I don't understand,' Flanagan said.

'Our Roberta's dead,' he said, a waver in his voice. 'She died in March 1993. Meningitis. Two other children at her school died around the same time.'

Flanagan's skin prickled. Her mouth dried.

'I'm very sorry to hear that,' she said. 'You're right. I must have made a mistake. I'm sorry to have bothered you.'

She reached for her mobile phone, saw there was still no signal.

'If it's not too much trouble,' she said, 'do you think I could use your landline?'

47

'This is good coffee,' DCI Conn said, raising his cup to her.

Roberta smiled and said, 'I can't take credit. The machine did the work.'

'Still, it's very good,' Conn said. 'Thank you.'

He took a sip and set the cup on the black granite. She sat opposite, on the other side of the island, nursing her own cup. Conn looked tired, stubble darkening his jawline. The other police officers had left more than an hour ago, but he had remained, going through the wardrobe and drawers in the back room, looking for God knows what.

He was a tall man, not bad looking, though he had a meanness about him. The kind of man who enjoyed petty victories, held on to anger at every small defeat. She could read men that way, always had done, a talent she'd developed when she was barely a teenager. How easy it had been to manipulate the boys with their crude and simple impulses. And they never grew out of it. They never learned to let their brains do their thinking. Even the smartest of them. When everything was stripped away, they were all the same, from the highest to the lowest, animals whose sole drive was to rut with her.

And here she was, alone with this man. He wore a wedding band, but she had noted how he toyed with it, sliding it from knuckle to knuckle. And how he glanced at her body, thinking himself sly and unnoticed. It would be so easy to take him, just move closer, fingertips, delicate butterfly touches, let him feel the heat of her.

'Is something wrong?' he asked.

She snapped back into the moment. 'I'm sorry?'

'You were smiling,' he said.

'Was I?' She let the smile spread, felt it light up her face. He couldn't help but reflect it back to her. 'I was just thinking about something,' she said.

'What?'

'Oh, nothing. Just a memory.'

He nodded, smiled once more, and took another sip of coffee.

'You've been very kind,' she said. 'I hardly knew you were here today. Very professional. Not like that Flanagan woman.'

Conn cleared his throat. 'Well, she has her own way of doing things.'

Roberta saw the way he bristled at the name, the tightening of his jaw. She caught a scent, followed it.

'She was so . . . hard,' she said. 'Do you know what I mean? And rude. What's the word? Abrasive? Yes, abrasive, that's it.'

He gave a shallow smile, looked at her, looked away. 'I can't really comment.'

She saw the angle, honed in on it.

'Call me old-fashioned,' she said, 'but women in jobs like that. They overcompensate, don't you think? They think they have to out-man the men. It makes them bitchy and mean, doesn't it?'

He shrugged, laughed, raised his hands in a motion of surrender. 'If I said that out loud to anyone, they'd have me off on one of those equality awareness courses.'

Got him, she thought.

'I'm glad you've taken over,' she said. 'I feel better having you around, Brian. Can I call you Brian?'

She reached across the worktop, almost let her fingertips brush his.

'I suppose,' he said, his cheeks reddening, his eyes flicking to her and away, over and over.

Like a schoolboy, she thought. So easy.

Reel him in or let him go?

Conn's mobile phone chimed, making the decision for her. What might have been relief broke on his face as he reached for his breast pocket. He looked at the display and said, 'Sorry, I have to take this.'

'Of course,' she said as she drew her hand back to her side of the island.

He brought the phone to his ear and said, 'DCI Conn.'

She heard a metallic voice, words she could not discern.

'Yes, I'm at the Garrick house now.'

His features slackened. He looked at her, eyes blank, then looked away again.

'I understand,' he said. 'Give me twenty minutes, half an hour.'

When he hung up, she asked, 'Is everything all right?'

He lowered himself from the stool, slipped the phone back into his pocket. 'Fine, fine,' he said. 'They need me over at the church is all. There's something they need me to see. Thank you for the coffee. I can let myself out.'

'You're welcome,' she said as he hurried out of the kitchen.

She listened to the front door open and close, the bark and rumble of an engine. As it faded, a cold finger touched her heart.

'No,' she said. 'It's nothing.'

Yet the chill remained. A warm bath would help. Yes, she thought, a soak to wash the day away. She finished her coffee, set the two cups in the sink, and made her way upstairs. In the master bathroom, she plugged the tub, turned on both taps, adjusted until the temperature was just so. Added a generous dose of bubble bath.

She went to her bedroom, into the walk-in wardrobe, and selected a nightdress and gown, brought them out and laid them on the bed. As she set about unbuttoning her blouse, she glanced up at the wall over the antique dresser.

The child stared back down at her.

Roberta crossed the room, took the picture from its hook. She opened the dresser's top drawer, placed the picture inside, and slid it closed again. Her hand against the wood, she held the drawer in place as if the image of the child might try to climb out again.

'Now be quiet,' she said.

48

Flanagan knocked on Purdy's office door and entered without waiting for an invitation. She found Conn pacing the floor, Purdy sitting behind his desk. DS Murray sat in the corner, his arms folded across his chest. They all looked to her as she closed the door behind her.

'When do we bring her in?' Flanagan asked.

Conn and Purdy exchanged a glance.

'Not tonight,' Purdy said.

'Why not?'

'All we have right now is the suspicion – suspicion, mind – of identity theft. The best we could do is some sort of fraud, and even that isn't straightforward.'

Flanagan approached the desk. 'She's been ghosting for years. Surely that's enough to arrest her on.'

'In itself, yes,' Purdy said. 'But is that really all you want her for? Ghosting on its own will be a minor offence. It's what she did with the identity that counts, not just that she's used it.'

'So what do we do?' Flanagan asked.

'We wait,' Purdy said. 'First of all, we need to find out who she really is. Let's hope that Isle of Man account can tell us something. If there's a name attached, we reference that back to the credit reference agency, find any other accounts connected to it. We'll have to go through the Attorney General's Office, but we should have that information some time tomorrow morning, maybe afternoon, and young Murray here will go through it. Then we can look at her history under the fake identity. Any bank account she has in the name Roberta Bailey or Garrick is a financial fraud, even more serious if she's taken out a credit card or a loan.'

'Come on,' Flanagan said, 'we're not taking her for credit card fraud. Two people have died.'

Now Conn spoke, raising himself to his full height. 'Hang on a minute. *We're* not taking her for anything. This is my case. Any involvement you have from here on will be simply as a courtesy for your work up to now.'

'Oh, fuck off,' Flanagan said. 'If I hadn't kept digging, you'd be wrapping it all up now with no idea she wasn't who she said she was.'

'I'd have found out,' Conn said. 'Sooner or later.'

'Bollocks.' She turned back to Purdy. 'Sir, I request that you speak with the Assistant Chief Constable and ask that this case be reassigned to me.'

'No,' Purdy said, shaking his head. 'Not going to happen.'

'Sir, please, I—'

'I said no, and that's final.' He raised a finger before she could protest again. 'But I'm not freezing you out. You will provide any assistance needed to DCI Conn, and I will personally make sure the ACC and the Chief Constable know how much you contributed to the investigation. If that's not good enough for you, then you're welcome to step aside.'

Conn put his hands on his hips, placed his body between Flanagan and Purdy. 'Sir, with respect, I don't need any further assistance from DCI Flanagan. I have all the materials I need, and I feel DCI Flanagan would be more hindrance than help at this stage.'

Purdy gave him a withering stare. 'DCI Conn, Brian, listen very carefully. Are you listening?'

Conn swallowed and said, 'Yes, sir.'

'Don't be a dick. I'm offering a workable compromise. For Christ's sake, show some intelligence and take it.'

Conn took a step back. Flanagan noticed the flush on his cheeks. Murray put a hand over his mouth to hide a smirk.

'Yes, sir,' Conn said.

'Good,' Purdy said, nodding. 'Now, I want the three of you to bugger off home, get some sleep. We'll have the new information by late morning, and I expect you to come up with a plan of action between you. A way to prove she killed those men. Get whatever you can on this woman, whoever she is, and bring her down. I want her in custody by tomorrow evening, the day after, at the latest. With any luck we'll get a confession out of her, but only if you have enough evidence to put in front of her. I want nothing done half-assed, no acting on nothing more than a feeling.' He pointed at Conn and Flanagan in turn on those points. 'Understood? Now piss off, the lot of you.'

Flanagan, Conn and Murray left the office without speaking. Out in the corridor, Purdy's door closed, Flanagan and Murray held back while Conn strode towards the stairs.

'He'll try to freeze me out,' Flanagan said. 'I'll need you to keep me up to speed. Tell me what he won't. Okay?'

'Yes, ma'am,' Murray said.

She put a hand on his arm, squeezed, a gesture of thanks, and left him there.

Flanagan slept poorly that night. The children were in bed by the time she got home, the dinner things cleared away, Alistair once again sitting at the kitchen table working through a stack of essays. She took the plate of food he'd left in the fridge for her, blasted it in the microwave, and ate it opposite him. They said nothing beyond the greetings they'd exchanged when she came in.

His nightmares woke him in the small hours, and she pretended to be asleep as he climbed out of bed and left the room. She rode the waves of the soft burble from the television downstairs, in and out of sleep, dreams and disorientation, spectres and shadows in the darkness. Eventually she gave in and reached for the lamp on the bedside locker.

Still scared of the dark. Strange how the fear grew when she felt under pressure, became less containable. She pulled the duvet up to her chin, closed her eyes, and tried to find the rhythm of the waves once more.

In the morning, Alistair and the kids had only started breakfast when Flanagan left for the station. She arrived a few minutes after eight and went straight to the temporary office that had been allocated to Conn. He and Murray sat there, each hunched over a computer.

'Nothing yet,' Conn said. 'I'll call you when we've got what we need.'

'I can stay,' she said. 'Help go through whatever you get.'

'That won't be necessary. I'll call you when I need you.'

Murray looked up from his computer, met her gaze, then looked away again.

'All right,' Flanagan said. 'I'll be waiting.'

So she waited. Nine o'clock passed, ten, eleven, then twelve. She tried to fill her time by working through the mound of Public Prosecution Service files Purdy had asked her to review, but her concentration lagged. Every time the phone on her desk rang, or her mobile, she grabbed at it, hoping and expecting. Every time she was disappointed.

As the minute hand on her watch dragged close to the six, her mobile rang once more. She looked at the display. DS Murray.

'Yes?' she said.

'Ma'am, can you come to DCI Conn's office right now?'

'Yes,' she said, and hung up without waiting for a reply.

She knocked on Conn's door less than a minute later. Murray opened it, and she looked past him to see he was alone.

'Where's Conn?' she asked.

Murray stepped back to let her enter. 'He went out. That's why I needed you to come now, while he was gone.'

Flanagan noticed the printouts spread across the two desks. 'What's happening?'

'DCI Conn didn't want you to be told anything, but I thought I should let you know. I'm aware I've gone against his instruction.'

'It's all right,' she said, walking to the other side of Conn's desk. 'What've you got?'

Murray came to her side, sorted two pages from the rest. 'The Isle of Man account has money moving out as soon as it goes in, same as both the Garrick accounts. It only goes out to one account.'

He pointed to eight digits that appeared several times, months apart. Then he reached for another set of pages.

'The account belongs to a Hannah Mackenzie. I've got the info from the credit reference company. Date of birth is 29th of April 1978. Two years older than Roberta Garrick. The address is in Ballinroy, an estate off the Airport Road, between Glenavy and Nutt's Corner. She's had that house at least six years, as far back as the credit report will show. I'd guess it's a private rental, not social housing, or maybe she owns it, given the money she has access to. There's another bank account attached to that name, and a credit card. The card hasn't ever been used. I'm waiting for more coming through on the financial side. I checked with the DVA, and there's a driving licence under that name and address, but no insurance. The licence was last renewed five years ago. There's a British passport, renewed three years ago, and I'm waiting to hear about an Irish passport.'

'Okay,' Flanagan said. 'So you reckon this is her?'

'Ma'am, there's more.'

He reached for the computer mouse, moved it to wake up the machine. The monitor flickered and an image of a young woman appeared, red-haired, bright-eyed. A mug shot, the flat lighting, the blank background. But it was her, no question.

'Tell me,' Flanagan said.

'Hannah Mackenzie was convicted in 1997, when she was nineteen, of the manslaughter of another young woman, a friend of hers. She was sentenced to seven years in Hydebank, served five, got out in 2002.'

'Jesus,' Flanagan said. 'And Conn knows all this?'

'Yes, ma'am.'

'That bastard was supposed to let me know as soon as he had anything.'

'Ma'am, can I speak freely?'

'Yes,' Flanagan said.

'DCI Conn is a complete prick,' Murray said. 'I wanted to call you as soon as the Isle of Man account came in, but he wouldn't let me. He'd kill me if knew I'd gone behind his back.'

'You did the right thing.' She put a hand on his shoulder for reassurance. 'Where is he now?'

'He's with DSI Purdy,' Murray said. 'He wants to mount an arrest operation this afternoon, but he doesn't want you involved. I tried to argue, but he wouldn't have it.'

He had barely finished the sentence when Flanagan ran out of the room and into the corridor. One floor up to Purdy's office, she was breathless when she hammered the door with her fist, then shouldered it open.

Purdy and Conn looked up from either side of the desk. Sergeant Beattie from E Department, Special Operations Branch, kitted out in tactical gear, stood over both of them.

'Flanagan,' Purdy began.

She cut him off. 'What's happening?'

'Sit down,' Purdy said.

'I'd rather stand, sir. What's happening?'

'Sit down,' he repeated, his voice hardening.

Flanagan moved the free chair a few inches further away from Conn and did as she was told. 'Sir, please tell me what's going on.'

'I was going to call you when things were a bit more solid,' Purdy said, 'but now you're here, I might as well fill you in. We're planning an arrest operation for this afternoon. Four-thirty, to be exact. DCI Conn and I will make the arrest with the support of Sergeant Beattie's team.'

Fury, fury, white hot inside her. Keep it inside, bury it.

'What about me?' she said.

'You won't be involved.'

'Why not?'

'It's the ACC's shout. He reckons you've been too personally involved in this case, that your judgement is clouded.'

'Bullshit. I'm not—'

'I agree with him,' Purdy said. 'You're out, that's all.'

'Sir, I—'

'I'm not arguing with you, Flanagan. The decision's been made.'

Purdy stared her down, dared her to speak. Instead, she closed her eyes and nodded as she fought to steady her breathing. Grinding pain in her teeth from clenching her jaw. She forced her teeth apart, bit her tongue until the sting pierced her mind, bringing clarity with it.

Purdy's features softened. 'If it makes any odds, I'll person-ally make sure that everyone, right up to the Chief Constable, the press, everyone, knows you drove the case this far, that DCI Conn here only came in to finish the job.'

Conn spoke up. 'That's hardly fair, sir.'

'Tough shit,' Purdy said. 'When it's all over and you're speaking to the press, you'll give DCI Flanagan due credit for her part in the investigation. Understood?'

Conn's lips thinned. 'Yes, sir.'

'Good.' Purdy turned back to Flanagan. 'If you want to make yourself useful, you and Murray head over to this house in Ballinroy. I'll make sure you're cleared to force entry if need be. See if there's anything there to back up the identity fraud. I'll call when I've got the RIPA forms back. Good enough?'

Flanagan exhaled, slumped in the chair. 'No, sir, but it'll have to do.'

'All right. Now go and get Murray, get yourselves ready to roll.'

'Sir,' she said as she stood.

In the corridor, after she'd closed the door between her and the officers, Flanagan bit her knuckle to stifle the anger.

49

Once more, Roberta Garrick was woken from sleep by crying. She sat upright on the bed, the cardigan she'd draped over herself falling away. Her heart thudded heavy in her chest, her breath coming in sharp swallows. While she napped she had dreamed of the child dragging her down with it, its small hands clinging and clawing. Under the salt water, waves washing over both of them, it still cried, the shrieks cutting like blades.

Awake now, she said, 'Shut up.'

But the crying went on.

'Shut up.' Louder this time, the edge of her voice sharpened.

And still it cried.

Cold, suddenly, Roberta reached for her cardigan and slipped off the bed. She walked towards the chest of drawers.

'All right,' she said, 'just be quiet.'

She opened the drawer, lifted the framed photograph out. As she reached up to the hook on the wall, a movement caught her eye, a white flash reflected on the glass. She turned to the window, saw it again, a brilliant white form racing along the lane that flanked her property. Then it was gone behind the small wood that bordered the rear of the garden.

A clamour in her head, like a bell ringing, beware, beware.

Then another white shape moved along the lane, not so quick, and this time she knew what it was: a police Land Rover, painted white with garish blue and yellow stripes on its side. Again, she lost it behind the trees, but she could see that it had been slowing.

The baby had ceased its wailing. Now there was only the hammering of her heart, the thunder of blood in her ears.

Roberta slipped out of her bedroom, the photograph still in her hand, and crossed the landing to the guest room with a window overlooking the front lawn. She kept to the wall as she moved to the glass, the voile curtain misting everything beyond. The sheer material brushed her cheeks. She parted the curtains with one finger, nothing more than a sliver for her eye to peer through.

Nothing. She could see nothing.

Look, look, look. Are they coming?

Are they coming for me?

There. Adrenalin hit her system the moment she saw it. The bright white and yellow and blue of another marked police Land Rover, this one not moving. Flashes of paintwork visible through the hedgerow. Barely a glimpse, but it was there.

Yes, they have come for me.

Now the baby's wailing cut through the noise in her head and she threw the photograph against the far wall, glass shattering, and then silence.

Run, she thought. Run now.

Her bare feet slapped on the floor as she sprinted to the master bedroom, dug in the drawers for socks, then in the wardrobe for trainers. She had minutes at most, maybe seconds. She pulled a sliver of glass from her heel, ignored the sting. The socks on, then the shoes. Out of the room, down the stairs, to the kitchen. Harry's old coat hung in the utility room, dark green, a hood. She grabbed it, pulled it on, put her hand in the pocket, felt the padlock keys she kept there. Unlocked the back door, threw the house keys to the floor, she'd never need them again.

Fast across the landscaped garden to the cluster of trees that bordered it and the fields beyond. In the shadows of the balding branches, the chest-high fence that marked the edge of the property. Up and over, she fell on the other side, landed hard on her shoulder. In a crouching run, she went to the far edge of the small wood, looked up, over to the lane that cut down to the far side of the house. Through the hedgerow and branches she saw another Land Rover, saw its passenger door open.

The gate into the next field only ten yards away, to her left. Up on her feet, another crouching run, and she was over it. Cows watched as she moved along the line of trees and barbed wire, peering through the gaps as four – no, five – policemen entered the other field and trudged towards the trees at the rear of her house. She paused and watched them enter the wood she had left moments before.

What had happened? What had they discovered? It didn't matter now. All she could do was run. She got moving, keeping to the treeline, towards the church steeple in the distance.

Roberta arrived at the rear of the dealership half an hour later, her feet heavy with mud, scratches on her cheeks from the low branches and thorns. She looked both ways as she crossed the narrow lane to the gate. Reaching inside the hole in the gate, she found the padlock undone, as she'd expected. She pulled back the bar and pushed the gate open, latched it to the wall.

Young Tommy McCready stood at the door of the back shed, watching her, his hands in the pockets of his oil-stained overalls. Concern sharpened his features.

'You all right, Mrs Garrick?' he called.

She marched towards him. 'I'm fine. I need one of the cars.' She scanned the line of vehicles. The Citroën she'd taken two nights ago still sat closest to the gate. 'That one,' she said, pointing.

Tommy stepped aside as she reached the shed, allowed her to enter.

'I don't know if you can just take it,' he said. 'You don't have trade insurance, do you?'

'Doesn't matter,' she said.

'If the peelers stop you, you'll get points,' he said.

'Doesn't matter,' she said as she lifted the plastic tub of loose car keys and emptied them onto the desk. She spread them out with her fingers, looking for the Citroën logo.

Tommy shifted his weight from foot to foot, scratching at his head with oily fingers.

'Here, I'll go and get John-Joe.'

John-Joe Malone, the grubby workshop manager who picked his nose with oily fingers while he eyed her up every time she visited the dealership.

'You don't need to,' she said. 'Where's the key to the fucking Citroën?'

'It's going to be scrapped tomorrow,' Tommy said. 'Look, hang on, I'm going to get John-Joe.'

He turned to go, but she grabbed his arm with her left hand. 'Just tell me where the key to the Citroën is.'

'It's there,' he said, pointing to the wall, a row of hooks with the words FOR SCRAP in a childish hand above them. There, on its own, the key.

He pulled his arm from her grasp, said, 'I'm getting John-Joe.'

'Yes, go and get him,' she said. 'Go now.'

He kept her in sight as he backed towards the workshop door.

She heard him calling his boss as she grabbed the key. She saw John-Joe and Tommy in the rear-view mirror as she pulled out of the yard, staring after her.

50

As Murray steered his 1-Series BMW around the Moira round-about, Flanagan noted the distance from there to the Ballinroy estate. Roberta Garrick – Hannah Mackenzie – lived only a few minutes from the junction, and another twenty would bring her to Ballinroy. Fifteen from Ballinroy to the International Airport.

'Perfect,' Flanagan said.

'Ma'am?' Murray asked as he exited the roundabout onto the Glenavy Road, the filling station and café of Glenavy Services half a mile ahead.

'Ballinroy,' she said. 'It's perfect for her. She can get there in less than half an hour when she has to pick up mail or whatever, and it's only a few miles more to the airport if she needs to get out in a hurry.'

'It's a rough estate,' Murray said. 'Old Housing Executive houses, most of them bought up by investors and rented out to migrant workers. After the property crash, a lot of them were left to rot. There's been problems with over-occupation, the land-lords shoving in as many people as can sleep in shifts.'

Flanagan had heard and seen similar around the country. Young men and women from all over Europe, and further afield, desperate for a better existence, exploited by landlords and gangmasters.

'One part of the estate – the side furthest from the airport road – is still local people, loyalists, and they don't like the new arrivals. I spoke to an old mate of mine who's stationed near there. He's been called out more times than he can remember. One side always fighting with the other or between themselves.'

'She doesn't have to live there,' Flanagan said. 'If there are a lot of people coming and going, that'd suit her better. Easier to slip in and out without anyone paying attention.'

The road stretched ahead, long straights, sweeping bends, few roadside houses. Twice they were caught behind tractors, unable to pass until the tractor pulled off into a side road. Before long, Flanagan saw a cluster of homes to the left, a quarter mile ahead. She had driven past this estate dozens of times on her way to the airport but had never given a thought to the condition of the houses or who lived here.

Murray flicked the indicator stalk and slowed the car as he approached the turn. He pulled in, reducing the speed to a walking pace, and glanced at the map on the BMW's touch-screen. An arrow showed their direction of travel, a chequered flag their destination.

'Just up here and around to the right,' he said.

The houses stood in semi-detached pairs, each block of two separated from the next by an alley, or in terraces of half a dozen. Made with dull beige brick, wooden boards beneath the windows, wire fences suspended between concrete posts to mark out the gardens. None of the houses had garages, and cars were parked bumper to bumper on the pavements leaving barely enough room for Murray to steer his way through. The rags of a Union flag fluttered on a lamp post. The gable wall of one terrace bore the words NO FOREIGNERS NO TAIGS in two-foot-high red painted letters. This place rang with the kind of hatred that only poverty fosters.

'Here,' Murray said as they neared the end of a row of semi-detached homes. 'Number thirty-six.'

With no room to park in front of the house, he pulled around the corner, put two wheels on the patch of stubbly grass and shut off the engine. Flanagan cursed as she stepped out onto the soft ground, narrowly avoiding a mound of dog excrement. Murray thumbed the key to lock the car. He loved the little BMW in the way a child loves a puppy. Cute in a child, slightly pathetic in a grown man. She let him lead her around to the front of the house, a small crowbar in his hand. Single-glazed, paint peeling from the door and window frames, the small patch of garden knee-high with grass and weeds, the chain-link fence long gone.

'This isn't the kind of living Mrs Garrick is accustomed to,' Murray said.

'Mrs Garrick isn't real,' Flanagan said. 'Hannah Mackenzie lives here.'

A rusted iron gate hung between two concrete posts, serving no purpose that Flanagan could see. She stepped around it onto the cement path and walked towards the house. A step up to the door, and the alley beside it. She cupped her eyes with her hands and peered through the frosted glass by the door into the hall. Nothing to see, only vague shapes and shadows. Her footsteps echoed in between the walls as she walked through the alley, avoiding the puddle from a blocked drain, towards a pair of wooden gates to the rear, each leading to the backyards on either side.

Somewhere to the rear, a dog objected to their presence, its barks high with alarm.

The gate belonging to number thirty-six hung loose on its hinges, the wood rotten and crumbling. It dragged on the cement as Flanagan pushed it inward, leaving fragments and a smear of algae and dirt. A paved yard beyond, grass growing in the cracks, a row of bins against the back wall. Green clung in flakes to the bare wood of the back door, two panes of mesh safety glass. A small square kitchen inside, decades-old fittings, a freestanding electric cooker. A space where a fridge had once been.

Murray picked at the door with his thumbnail, the wood splitting and splintering.

'Rotten,' he said.

'Go ahead,' Flanagan said.

He wedged the crowbar's blade between the door and its frame, rocked it back and forth, applying more weight as it burrowed in, until Flanagan heard a dull crack.

'Almost there,' Murray said.

Flanagan startled at the sound of a bolt sliding. She spun on her heels and saw the gate on the other side of the alley ease open. A small man with black hair peered out at them. Flanagan reached into her bag, showed her warrant card. The gate slammed shut, the bolt slid back. None of his concern. A perfect place to hide in plain sight.

Murray grunted with effort, another crack, sharper this time, and the door swung inward. Musty odours drifted out to them. The stale smells of a house that had not been a home for many years. Dust everywhere. Spiderwebs in the corners, the carcasses of flies tangled in them, or lying loose on the surfaces. Just inside the doorway, a space where a washing machine had once stood, the hoses hanging from the pipes to the rear, the withered remains of a mouse curled on the floor.

'Lovely,' Murray said.

Flanagan stepped past him, her shoes clicking on the worn linoleum. Murray pushed the door to behind him, followed her into the hall. A concrete floor, patches of carpet liner still stubbornly glued to it. A cupboard under the stairs.

She put her fingertips against the door to the living room, pushed it open.

'Fuck me,' Murray said.

Flanagan said nothing.

Thin curtains drawn across the window coloured everything in dim oranges and reds. Dozens, perhaps hundreds of photographs lined the far wall, some framed pictures perched on the mantelpiece above the tiled fireplace. Boys and girls, men and women, all of them with a familiar figure, holding her, smiling with her, dancing with her. Roberta Garrick, Hannah Mackenzie, whoever she really was, young and pretty and bright-eyed. Among the photographs were printed pages, letters and forms. From her place on the threshold, Flanagan recognised one of them as an exam certificate. She stepped forward to look at it, a list of eight GCSE results, As and Bs. Another certificate showing three A-level passes.

A letter of offer from a university. A birthday card to Hannah, with all my love, Granny, a ten-pound note still clipped inside. Boxes all around the floor full of books, letters in envelopes, old cassettes and VHS tapes, ornaments, the kind of worthless bric-a-brac that meant the world to a young woman.

Flanagan turned in a circle, seeing Hannah Mackenzie's life crammed into this room, her entire existence stowed away for safe keeping. A shrine to the girl left behind. She stopped when she saw the writing scrawled on the wall facing the window. Rows and rows of neat script, arranged in columns, broken up by slashes through the letters, sentences crossed out, words obliterated.

She reached for the light switch, ignited the bare bulb above their heads, then stepped closer to the wall until she could make out the writing. Flanagan took in snatches of it, lucid phrases and rambling ideas colliding against the faded flowers of the wallpaper.

I know she hated me so I that's why I pushed her …

It's broken I broke it never put it back together now …

Can't stop the crying even when I put her back on the wall again …

'What is this?' Murray asked, his voice low.

'It's where she keeps her madness,' Flanagan said.

They stood in silence, turning in circles, the ghosts of Hannah Mackenzie glaring at them from the walls. Eventually, Murray spoke.

'Ma'am, we should call DSI Purdy. Get a proper team up here.'

Flanagan nodded. 'You're right. Let's clear out. We'll wait in the car.'

Murray was on his way back to the kitchen before she finished speaking. She switched off the light and followed him out into the yard, through the gate and into the alley. A thought occurred to her, and she stopped.

'Go on,' she said. 'I'll be out in a minute. I just want to check something.'

He turned and looked at her, then to the house, before saying, 'Okay.'

Flanagan watched him leave the alley and pick his way through the overgrown grass before she went back to the rear of the house and pushed the door open once more. That musty smell again, and something else, something she hadn't noticed before. Something low and bitter.

She walked through the kitchen and into the hall, where she stopped at the cupboard beneath the stairs. A small door, waist-high, with a plain plastic handle. She crouched down and pulled it open. Inside, an old-fashioned safe with a dial combination lock. She brushed the scarred surface with her fingertips, felt the cold steel, reached inside, tried to move it. Too heavy.

'What are you hiding?' Flanagan asked the air, knowing full well the answer.

Everything in the other room was a memento, a story of a past life. But in here was the proof. In here was whatever Roberta Garrick needed to become Hannah Mackenzie once more.

'Got you,' Flanagan said.

She gasped at the sound of the iron gate opening outside, the metallic clank as it closed again. Murray? What had he come back for? The place gave him the creeps, obviously, and he had been glad to leave. She stood upright and looked towards the frosted glass of the door.

A form grew and solidified as it approached. Hooded and dark. Then hands reached up and pulled the hood away.

Red hair blazing through the glass, Roberta Garrick come to take back her true name.

51

Roberta Garrick turned the key in the lock, pushed the door open. As Hannah Mackenzie, she had rented a house on the same street, and kept it after she had changed and married Harry. Then this place came up for sale, priced at a pittance due to the property crash and its poor condition, so she had paid cash and said nothing to her new husband.

She breathed in the air, the stale smell she had grown to love.

Except it wasn't stale.

Not as stale as it should be. The air had a cool freshness about it, she could taste it, as if a window had been left open. She paused in the doorway, holding her breath, listening.

If they had come for her, could they also have found this place? Did they know about Hannah Mackenzie? Had they come looking for the woman who lived in this house?

'Stop it,' she said aloud.

Panic had been threatening to break free ever since she had fled across the fields, and she had kept it in check all this time. She would not let it take her now. Paranoia crept alongside the panic, but it was more slippery, harder to hold. It now whispered in her mind, told her to turn around, get back in the car and go.

Go where?

Without the contents of the safe, she could go nowhere. Fear be damned, there was no choice. She stepped inside, closed the front door behind her. Her shoes, still muddy from the fields, left dark prints on the concrete floor as she moved along the hall.

The living room door stood open, the kitchen door closed over. Had she left them that way? She dredged her memory; it had been only three days since she had been here to retrieve the pestle and mortar. She seldom left long between visits.

Over the month leading up to Harry's death, she had come to this house more frequently, sometimes spending the night. She had waited for his dose of morphine to shut him down, then she drove to the dealership, took one of the scrap cars, and drove to Ballinroy. Here, the dreadful effort of being Roberta Garrick was left outside. Here, she slept soundly on the mattress upstairs. She always woke in time to drive back to Morganstown, swap cars, and get home to serve Harry's breakfast.

Sometimes, but not often, she woke in the night, sprawled on the mattress, cold and frightened. She lay in the dark, quiet as the dead, and listened. Sometimes she heard Roberta Garrick outside, trying to get in. Scratching at the doors and windows, seeking entry so that she could eat Hannah Mackenzie whole.

But not often.

The living room open, the kitchen closed. Had it been so the last time? Didn't matter. She needed to empty the safe, that was all.

Roberta got to her knees in front of the cupboard, opened it, revealing the safe she had found on a second-hand goods website. She remembered the man who delivered it here six years ago, how he struggled to move it with the hand truck, how he grumbled when she asked him to bring it inside and put it in the cupboard.

The dial clicked as she turned it, listening to the tumblers fall into place. Then the door wheezed open half an inch, and she pulled it the rest of the way. Inside, on the top shelf, one thousand pounds in sterling, another two thousand in euros, and passports in the name of Hannah Mackenzie, one British, one Irish. On the lower shelf, a birth certificate, an envelope full of bank statements, one debit and one credit card.

Everything Hannah Mackenzie needed to get out, get away, start again. Maybe even find another dead girl whose life was lying around waiting to be picked up and used again.

Twelve years ago, Hannah Mackenzie had been shocked at how simple it was to become Roberta Bailey. Death and birth records were easily searchable, and not cross-referenced. She had gone to the library and checked old editions of local newspapers to find any deaths of young girls around a decade or so before. It didn't take long to find the headlines about a meningitis outbreak in the Magherafelt area. One of the victims a twelve-year-old girl, an only child, taken so tragically young. Red hair, just like hers. Pretty, just like her. Hannah Mackenzie simply paid for a copy of Roberta Bailey's birth certificate, and the rest was easy.

The new life she had manufactured for herself had, for a time, been glorious. Harry had not been hard to find. The dating website was full of lonely men with money to spend, and she had gone on several dates. But Harry was the best of them all; not only the wealthiest, but the most willing to be drawn in by her. The religion part had been easy, seeing as her mother had made her go to church and Sunday school every weekend, just to get her out of the house. She bluffed what she couldn't remember, and Harry was swept away by her, this young attractive Christian woman.

That life only began to crack when the child took root in her belly.

She didn't want to think about that. Instead, she concentrated on gathering up what she needed, stuffing rolls of cash into her coat pockets, slipping passports and documents into the envelope with the bank statements.

Not far to Antrim from here, and the outlet mall, a complex of shops selling discounted brands. Buy a few changes of cheap clothes and a small carry-on bag, along with a prepaid mobile phone. Call an airline, get a ticket to anywhere so long as it was out of this country. She could find a guesthouse for tonight if need be. This time tomorrow, she would be somewhere far away, somewhere warm where no one knew what Hannah Mackenzie or Roberta Garrick had done, those wicked sisters with their poisonous sins.

She pushed the safe door closed and spun the dial. Done. Time to go.

As she withdrew her hand, she felt air move across the back of it, cool on her skin. She turned her head towards the kitchen door. Again, a draught.

A strange calm settled on her then. The panic should have torn itself loose, crashing through her mind. She should have sprinted for the front door, out to the car, and away. Instead, she got to her feet and reached for the kitchen door handle.

52

Flanagan stood wedged into the space between the door and the end of the row of high- and low-level cupboards, the edge of the tiled worktop digging into her hip. Perhaps she should have made for the back door, but she could not do so in silence. Roberta, Hannah, whoever the hell she was, would have heard the door creak open and would have either attacked or fled.

But what to do?

She had listened to the woman on the other side of the door, heard the clicks of the combination lock, the rustling of paper, then the clank as the safe closed once more. Then deep silence. Why didn't Roberta go? Just turn around, go back out and drive away? Flanagan and Murray could find her, follow her. It was almost certain she would head north towards the airport. But she did not go. Flanagan pictured her on the other side of the door, listening as Flanagan listened.

Slowly, Flanagan let her fingers creep towards the holster attached to her waistband. She undid the catch, eased her Glock 17 from the leather, brought it up to her other hand. No round in the chamber. She could not risk racking the slide, the snick-click sounding like a thunderclap in the quiet.

The door handle moved, the springs of its mechanism creaking. Flanagan held her breath, pressed herself deeper into the space. The handle depressed, the door opened, cracking from its hinges. She felt the door against her shoulder. In the window, her faint reflection, and that of Roberta Garrick, separated by a barrier of white-painted wood.

53

Roberta looked into the kitchen, saw the source of the breeze: the back door open, its frame split at the lock. Cool air on her face.

Who had been here? And when?

Perhaps a burglary, some intruder hoping for an easy haul. They would have been disappointed, the only thing here a safe they couldn't open and would have struggled to move.

But no. Too great a coincidence.

It had been the police. Had to be. So they had traced Hannah Mackenzie to this house. How? The only thing that linked Roberta to Hannah was a payment bounced through the Isle of Man account, and the accountant had assured her that it was in a separate jurisdiction, one that was known for its financial discretion, and no UK authority could touch it. What if he had been wrong? Freddie Boland had been her husband's accountant for years, and she had always had a low opinion of him, but surely he couldn't get something like that wrong?

She would have cursed him, but it didn't matter now. The police had been here, and the passports and documents were now useless to her. The only remaining option was to head for the border, use the cash to buy some time until she could figure out what to do next.

She was about to close the door, head for the car and get out of here, when she noticed her reflection in the window, silhouetted by the light from the hall. Hannah Mackenzie's reflection. Roberta Garrick's reflection. The lives of both of those women had now ended, and she felt a pang of mourning for them both.

Move, she thought. Get out. Find a new woman to be.

Then she noticed the other reflection, faint next to hers.

A woman on the other side of the door.

For a wild moment, she thought it was another her, Roberta and Hannah separated, standing side by side. As panic flared in her breast, she stared, forced her eyes to focus on the faint form.

Then she knew, and the panic turned to scorching rage.

54

Flanagan stared at the ghosts on the glass, met Roberta's reflected eyes, thought: She sees me.

They both stood still and quiet, not a breath between them, watching, watching, watching.

Slowly, so slowly, Flanagan raised her left hand up to the pistol held in her right, gripped the slide assembly, silently counted to three, then pulled it back, released it.

She didn't see Roberta move, only felt her weight on the other side of the door as she slammed her body against it and into Flanagan. The door drove Flanagan's hip into the edge of the worktop, and the side of her head into the upper cabinet. Hot and heavy pain burst behind her eyes, she saw the room turn as if upended. A warm trickle over her ear. Her knees gave way, but she caught herself with an arm on the worktop.

A moment to swallow a breath, then Roberta screamed and rammed the door into her once more, the weight of it now trapping Flanagan's chest between the wood, crushing all air from her lungs. She fell, her right hand striking the linoleum first, the pistol clattering from her grasp, then her chest and chin, sending more black stars to dance in her vision.

The pistol, get the pistol.

She tried to get to her hands and knees, but her lungs shrieked for air, her diaphragm flexed and spasmed. The Glock remained three feet beyond her reach, and she crawled on her belly towards it, but Roberta fell on her back, put a knee between her shoulders. Flanagan croaked, a string of spit flowing from her mouth.

Air, air, please God, I need air.

Roberta drove her fist into the side of Flanagan's head, and Flanagan heard a crunch and a cry of pain before everything went grey for a moment. Another cry, and Flanagan knew something had broken in Roberta's hand. She turned her head, tried to shift her weight, but Roberta's forearm dropped onto her cheek, slammed her head against the floor, and once more she lost the edge of her consciousness to the grey.

Then the weight left her back, and she felt she could float there an inch from the floor, and she saw Roberta scramble to the pistol, grab it with her left hand, heard the bark of its discharge as her finger found the trigger, sending a bullet into the wall. Roberta gasped and dropped it again, the empty cartridge jangling across the floor. Flanagan squirmed towards the pistol, her ears ringing with the shot, but Roberta retrieved it, crawled to the other side of the kitchen.

Blood pooled on the linoleum beneath Flanagan's chin. Her mouth filled with hot pennies. A stream of it around her ear. She tried to inhale, choked on it, coughed a spray across the floor. Then she vomited, her gut convulsing, the grey flooding in, and now she wanted to sleep. Roll away from the foulness she lay in, close her eyes, let the darkness take her.

Concussion, I've got concussion. Stay awake.

Flanagan forced her gaze upwards and saw Roberta hunkered against the wall, cradling her right hand in her lap, the pistol held loose in her left. Roberta raised the Glock, her hand trembling. She pushed up with her legs, her back sliding on the tiled wall. The Glock's muzzle twitched in Flanagan's vision. Roberta brought up her right hand, already swelling around the break, and steadied her left wrist against her forearm.

'Don't,' Flanagan said.

She saw the muzzle flash, felt the pressure in her ears, and linoleum and concrete exploded inches from her face. Somehow she found the strength to roll to the side, her back hitting the cupboards as another boom hit her ears, another burst of concrete.

Stop, she wanted to shout, stop, let me see my children again.

She opened her mouth, found a gasp of air, heard the crashing of wood through the high whine, saw the gate through the back door, saw it slam against the wall, teetering loose from its hinges. Murray there, his weapon up and ready, peering into the dimness of the kitchen.

Roberta saw him too, swung her left hand around, pulled the trigger once, twice, three times, the glass spidering, fragments hanging from the wire mesh, spent cartridges falling to the floor. Flanagan saw Murray duck back into the alley, his head down. Roberta sank back into the corner where the worktop met the wall. Her back against the cupboard doors, Flanagan smelled cordite and vomit, and her stomach threatened to revolt again.

Murray edged back to the door, then dipped away again as two more shots cracked and boomed. Flanagan got to her knees, but Roberta turned her jittering aim back to her, and Flanagan raised her hands, knew beyond all certainty that Roberta would not miss this time.

Another shot, but from outside, and the cupboard door closest to Roberta's head splintered. She turned back, fired again and again, hitting nothing but glass and air, Murray taking shelter once more.

Flanagan crawled back towards the kitchen door, keeping her eyes on Roberta. She threw herself through, catching a glimpse of Roberta turning back to her, heard an animal scream, a shot, felt wood splinters scatter above her head. She got to her hands and knees again and crawled into the living room, turned on her back, kicked the door closed, put her feet against it.

'Bitch!' The voice high and fractured on the other side of the door. 'Fucking bitch!'

The door pushed against Flanagan's feet, and she pushed back.

Crack, crack, crack, three splintered holes in the door, three explosions of plaster dust, photographs falling from the wall. Then another shot from further back, Murray, coming after her. And running footsteps, the front door opening, slamming closed again.

Flanagan got up on her knees, grabbed the door handle, hauled herself to her feet, opened it as Murray emerged from the kitchen, his pistol smoking.

'After . . .' Not enough air to finish the command, Flanagan pointed at the front door.

Murray sprinted for it, open, through, out onto the street. Flanagan heard the spinning tyres, a metallic thud as Roberta's car hit another, then the engine roaring and fading. She staggered to the front of the house, tried to tell Murray to get his car, but her lungs would not allow it. He understood anyway, ran to the side of the house where he had parked.

Flanagan lurched along the path, stopped to throw up once more, wiped blood and vomit on her sleeve. She followed Murray to the corner, and he reversed to meet her. He spoke as she collapsed into the passenger seat, but she couldn't hear him above the whine in her ears and the roar in her skull.

The car launched forward as she closed the door, and through the chaos in her mind she wondered why Murray drove this way. Seconds later she understood as he followed a curving lane that looped back to the main road. They rounded the bend in time to see a wreck of a Citroën pull out of the junction, causing another car to swerve.

The Citroën went right, not left. 'Not . . . going for the . . . the airport,' Flanagan said, squeezing the words between shallow gasps.

'She's heading back to Moira,' Murray said. 'The airport's no good to her now. She's going to try for the border.'

He flicked on the car's hazard lights. His own personal vehicle, the BMW was not equipped with blues or a siren. He accelerated out of the junction, two cars between them and Roberta.

Flanagan slumped back in the seat, fighting nausea. 'Just . . . keep her in sight. Not a . . . pursuit.'

Roberta's Citroën edged to the centre of the road as she searched for a gap to overtake the car in front of her.

'Get Pu . . . Purdy on the phone. Tell him . . . she's coming back their way. Head her off.'

Murray kept one hand on the wheel as he fished his mobile phone from his pocket, the call connecting over the car's

Bluetooth system. Flanagan wound the window down, let the rush of cold air blast the fog from her mind, willed herself not to throw up over Murray's upholstery.

Ahead, Roberta Garrick, Hannah Mackenzie, the animal, veered between cars, nothing but death in front of her.

'I won't let her die,' Flanagan said.

Murray glanced at her. 'What?'

Purdy's voice barked over the car's speakers before Flanagan could say it again.

55

Roberta Garrick glanced in the rear-view mirror.

Yes, Roberta Garrick. Hannah Mackenzie remained back in that house, a ghost to haunt it for as long as it stood. Hannah Mackenzie was gone, and Roberta Garrick was here, looking in this mirror. She craned her neck, saw her own eyes, wild and wide. Then the road behind her.

The white BMW still there, but hanging back. She hadn't seen them get into that car, but it had followed her out of the junction. It had to be them. So why didn't they chase her?

The gun lay on the passenger seat, a faint pale ribbon of smoke still coming from the muzzle, filling the car with its acrid smell. She didn't know how many bullets it held, how many were left. She kept her left hand on the wheel, her right forearm holding it steady when she needed to change gear.

The end of the world, she thought.

This morning it seemed as if everything was on track, her future secured. And then, in less than two hours, it had all burned to the ground. She would die today, there was no doubt of that. It was only a matter of how and when. How much pain could she endure in the act? All the pain in world. She could take every burning drop of it.

The car drifted to the centre of the road, forcing the oncoming traffic to move to the hard shoulder. Horns blared, but she could barely hear them. One jerk of the wheel, and she could meet one of the cars head on. Or she could lift the gun from the passenger seat, put it to her temple, or into her mouth.

'Not yet,' she said.

Roberta Garrick – and that was her name, she was almost certain – began to cry. A desperate keening. She wished to take it all back, to start again. The same way she'd felt when that other her, Hannah, after that drunken night at the Students' Union bar when she had pushed her housemate down the stairs, after she'd stood and watched the girl bounce down the steps, arms flailing, and the snap of her neck as she hit the floor. Back then, Hannah, sober in a cell, had cried and begged God to take today, wipe it out, and make it yesterday.

She wanted that now. The past hours to be erased, the clock to be reset to midnight. And that could not be, so tears were all she had. Had her rational mind been in control, she might have been conscious that she wept not out of remorse for her sins, but out of fear for herself. She did not want death, but it wanted her, and it would have its due.

Another pealing of car horns as she drifted once more, her vision blurred, the road ahead a streak of grey cutting through green. She wiped her eyes on her right sleeve, blinked them clear. She saw the BMW in the mirror, still keeping its distance. How long had she been driving? And where to? She knew she was headed back to the Moira roundabout. There was no chance she would make the border, and even if she could, it wouldn't help.

Home, she thought. I'm going home. To my beautiful house and the beautiful gardens and all the beautiful things that I worked so hard for. The home in which my beloved husband took his own life after months of suffering. I'm going home, and I'm going to lie down on my bed, and I'm going to put the muzzle of this gun to my temple and squeeze the trigger.

The decision made, she felt better. She pressed the accelerator with her foot and passed another two cars, thinking of that fiery bloom inside her skull, the comet trail of the bullet through her head.

56

'Stay back,' Purdy said, his voice crackling through the speakers. 'Don't make her panic and hurt anyone else. We'll close everything but the Glenavy side of the roundabout, so if she enters it, she won't get out of it again.'

'She might not go that far,' Flanagan said.

'Maybe, but it's the best guess right now. A pursuit car is heading your way, but I don't know if it'll reach you in time. Stay on the line, I'm going to patch in Command.'

Flanagan's head had cleared a little, but the movement of the car, the sway as it pulled out and past other vehicles, churned her stomach. She watched road signs as she listened to the dial tone.

A young woman's voice said, 'This is Command, go ahead.'

'Glenavy Road,' Flanagan said. 'A26, we're just coming up to Hammonds Road, heading south, speed seventy miles per hour. Target is approximately one hundred yards ahead, two cars between us. Will update.'

'Pursuit car and support should join you at Glenavy Services. Helicopter in the air in five minutes.'

'Understood,' Flanagan said.

A road sign said one mile to the roundabout. If Roberta intended to get off the main road, she'd need to do it soon. Only a few more turn-offs before the roundabout. They reached the brow of a hill and the long incline on the other side. Glenavy Services at the bottom of the dip, the railway bridge beyond. The Enterprise train crossed it on its way to Belfast.

Flanagan strained her eyes, looking for the marked cars that should have been waiting at the service exit. There, she could make out the bright blues and yellows. She nudged Murray's arm.

'Get moving,' she said.

'Yes, ma'am,' Murray said, shifting down a gear and stepping on the accelerator.

He hit the button to activate his hazard lights and eased out into the centre of the road. Flanagan felt the BMW's engine thrum as the acceleration pushed her back into the seat. Only a small number of oncoming drivers, who hit their horns and flashed their lights as they had to swerve onto the hard shoulder. No more ahead. Flanagan understood the traffic had now been stopped at the roundabout, no more coming this way. They passed the first car between them and the Citroën, got an angry look from the driver. Flanagan held her warrant card up to the window, but it didn't seem to placate him. The second car edged over to the hard shoulder to make room, and Flanagan waved thanks on the way past.

'Now slow down,' Flanagan said. 'Leave space for the pursuit car to get in.'

Murray eased off the accelerator. Flanagan saw smoke plume from the Citroën's exhaust; Roberta had seen them close the gap and was speeding up.

Up ahead, the pursuit car, a Skoda Octavia VRS, nosed out of the junction. The Citroën wavered as Roberta saw it. She braked for a moment, then accelerated again. The Skoda shot out of the Services exit as she passed, building speed so fast she couldn't create a gap between them. The support car went to follow, but Murray leaned on his horn, and the driver held back to let them take the place behind the pursuit car.

'We're behind the pursuit car now,' Flanagan said.

'Understood,' came the voice from Command.

Once the support car had slotted in behind Murray's BMW, it slowed to a crawl, forcing the traffic behind to keep back. As the trees in the roundabout's centre island came into view, so did a string of slow-moving cars at the entrance to the roundabout. Flanagan saw a pair of uniformed officers in fluorescent jackets pointing them in the direction of the motorway exit. They intended to close the exit before Roberta's car got there, trap her like a fly in a jar.

The evening sky dimmed, cloud thick and grey above.

Let them take you, Flanagan thought. Don't fight.

But she knew there would be no easy end to this.

57

Roberta wept when she saw the police car edging its way out of the junction. Adrenalin had been raging through her system ever since she found Flanagan in the house, and now it needed its release.

This is it, she thought. This is the end.

Not yet. She could still fight.

She stood on the Citroën's accelerator, and its engine moaned under the pressure. The speedometer needle crawled higher, the little car already running at its limits. Wisps of smoke trickled from the sides of the bonnet, whipped away by the wind.

Up ahead, a line of traffic queuing to enter the roundabout. Nothing coming from the other way. Then she understood: they had closed the entries and exits.

'Fuck,' she said, her face wet with tears. 'Fuck, fuck.'

Roberta jerked the steering wheel to the right, onto the other side of the road, heading the wrong way to the roundabout's exit, keeping her foot planted. She glanced in the mirror, saw the police car and the BMW had followed her move. So had the other police; they'd left this exit open, anticipating that she'd come this way. A marked Land Rover waited by the exit, reversed in to block it as soon as she and the two cars in pursuit had passed through.

She did not slow as the Citroën's tyres scrabbled for grip, the car leaning as she steered the wrong way around the curve, then onto the elevated straight section that led to the Moira exit. She glimpsed the line of cars on the ramp leading off the motorway's northbound lane, held back by another Land Rover. Uniformed officers everywhere.

'Fuck,' she said.

The marked car accelerated past her on the inside, its engine roaring, then pulled in front of her. She jerked her steering wheel left and right, but there was nowhere to go. The white BMW pulled up close behind her, and the convoy slowed as it rounded the eastern end of the roundabout, then onto the straight leading back to the western end.

Two Land Rovers blocked the road ahead completely. Trapped. She was trapped.

One thing left to do.

Roberta closed her eyes. Slammed her foot hard on the accelerator pedal. Hauled the steering wheel to the right. Readied herself for the impact and the fall.

The crash came, and she was thrown against the steering wheel, feeling it punch her chest. No airbag, her torso took the full force of it. But no fall. She had expected the car to plough through the fence and plummet to the motorway below, but it had merely buckled the metal.

She pushed herself off the steering wheel, howled at the pain, then groaned as she realised she had broken something inside. Her vision cleared, and through the smoke and steam she saw that the BMW and the marked car had stopped twenty yards ahead, in front of the Land Rovers that blocked the road. A few blurred figures emerged from the cars.

Roberta reached for the pistol on the passenger seat, found it wasn't there. She blinked smoke out of her eyes, coughed, screamed at the pain. Her hand explored the seat, under it, down the sides. The gun had slid off in the impact, bounced away somewhere in the recesses. It didn't matter now. What good would it do her?

She tried the driver's door handle, but the door wouldn't budge, jammed in place. Despite the pain, she leaned over to the passenger side, pulled the handle, let the door swing open. She hauled herself across, pausing to cry out at the grinding of whatever had fractured in her chest, her broken right hand clutched to her belly. The ground slammed into her left shoulder as she fell out, and she lay for a few seconds, glorying in the pain and the sudden clarity it brought.

'Don't move!'

She craned her neck to see who had shouted at her. A woman's voice. She could barely hear it above the whine and clamour inside her head. Flanagan, maybe? There she was, behind the BMW, along with a line of other officers. Weapons pointed at her.

'Put the weapon down!'

'I don't . . . I . . .'

She didn't have the breath to push the words out. Somehow, she got her knees under her, and her left hand, then her feet. Upright, she raised her good hand, showed them it was empty, her right still held tight to her stomach.

'Drop the weapon!'

She tried to lift her right hand, but a sun burned there, too heavy for her to lift.

'I don't have it,' she said, but she heard her own voice as a rumble inside her head and throat. 'Don't have it,' she said again.

Pretend you do, she thought. Pretend you're going to shoot them, and they'll shoot you. And then it'll be over.

She smiled and pointed her left hand at them, made the fingers into a gun, moved her thumb to mime the hammer fall. Then she laughed at the foolishness of it, and howled at the pain it brought.

Flanagan moved from behind the BMW. Someone, that nice young policeman whose name Roberta could not recall, tried to stop her, but Flanagan shook him off and kept coming.

Roberta looked to her right, saw the traffic backed up on the slip road down to the motorway beneath, the cars slow on the inside lane, quicker on the outside, all heading away towards the city to the north-east. The idea presented itself clear and simple to her. So she acted on it.

She walked the few steps to the metal railing covered in blistered blue paint. One hand useless, the other grasping, she pulled herself up on it, screamed at the fresh surge of pain from her chest.

I don't have the strength, she thought.

Yes you do.

She hauled her left leg over, then her right.

Somewhere very far away she heard Serena Flanagan shout, no, no, no, but she ignored the frantic voice as she found the concrete ledge with her toes. Her chest to the railing, her back to the wind, she saw Flanagan coming in a lopsided, limping run, Murray sprinting behind her, more officers following.

Roberta's eyes met Flanagan's, and she gave her a smile.

Then she let go.

58

Flanagan ignored the pain, the nausea, the drifting of the world on its axis, and threw herself towards the railing, her hands outstretched. The fingers of her left hand snatched at the fabric of the coat, took hold, her other hand reaching further. Then Roberta's weight jerked her forward, and her body slammed into the railing, her shoulder shrieking at the strain. As her feet left the ground, she got her right hand under Roberta's arm, pulled with everything she had.

Her legs kicked at the air as her chest slid over the top of the railing. Roberta writhed in her grasp. Flanagan pushed her foot through the gap in the railing, hooked it there, tried to stop the steady slide over the top.

'Let me go,' Roberta screamed, her mouth inches from Flanagan's ear.

'No,' Flanagan hissed. 'You don't get to die.'

Roberta wedged the soles of her feet against the concrete ledge, pushed, pulled Flanagan until the top of the railing dug into her stomach. She screamed, hooked her other foot into a gap.

'Then you can come with me,' Roberta said, and she jerked her body from one side to the other.

Footsteps behind. Flanagan turned her head, saw Murray and two uniforms, shouted at them to help. She closed her eyes as her feet began to slip, her own weight beginning to carry her forward, out over the edge.

'You don't get to die,' she said again.

Then strong arms around and over her, hauling her back.

'Don't let her fall!' she shouted, her hands digging into the fabric of Roberta's coat, her fingernails bending and tearing.

More footsteps, more arms and hands.

'Get her, don't let her fall!'

The fabric slipped from Flanagan's fingers and she was weightless, tumbling back, the road hitting her shoulders hard. She heard a scream, waited for the shrieking of tyres, the sound of a car hitting flesh and bone.

But it never came.

Instead, Flanagan heard another body hit the ground beside hers, followed by a cry of pain and despair and anger. She turned her head, saw Roberta Garrick, Hannah Mackenzie, face down, staring back at her, pure fiery hate in her eyes.

'You don't get to die,' Flanagan said.

59

They kept her in a side ward, away from the good people. Four beds in this room, all empty. A laminated sign taped to the door said ORTHOPAEDIC CLINIC. Bustle beyond the door, voices and footsteps. Somewhere out there an old man shouted incoherent rants between cries of pain.

Roberta had not cried out when the doctor set her hand. Instead, she bit down hard until the muscles either side of her jaw ached with the effort. The young doctor had inserted a needle between her third and fourth fingers, and again in her wrist, and a vague numbness followed. But not enough to blank out the pain as he realigned the bones.

She had cracked a rib, he said, looking at the X-ray clipped to a light box. He had been nervous in the company of the police officers, unable to look her in the eye. Afraid of her. She had smiled for him, parted her lips, let him see the tip of her tongue. But the fear did not leave him, because he knew what she was. They all did.

Now the nice policeman, Detective Sergeant Murray, dozed in a chair in the corner of the side ward while two uniformed officers sat in silence by the door. Pale dawn light through the windows. The cast felt clumsy and heavy on her hand, the skin beneath itching. Strapping around her chest made it impossible to take more than shallow breaths.

The anaesthetic in her hand had long since worn off, but she could endure the pain. It wouldn't be for long, anyway. She'd be left alone sooner or later, and she had no intention of going back to prison. A belt, a length of material, a sharp edge. She had studied these things, the methods, over many months. All she needed was the opportunity.

A little after seven in the morning, going by the clock on the wall, DCI Serena Flanagan entered the ward. Swelling on her lip, a gauze pad on her temple. Murray jerked awake, cleared his throat, sat upright. Flanagan came to the bed beside Roberta's, sat on its edge.

She pointed to the side of her head, said, 'Three stitches, in case you're wondering.'

'I wasn't,' Roberta said.

'We'll be leaving soon,' Flanagan said. 'The Serious Crime Suite in Antrim. We'll make sure it's a ligature-free cell. We won't give you the chance.'

Roberta smiled at Flanagan's perceptiveness. 'I'll find a way. I tend to get what I want.'

'I know you'll try,' Flanagan said. 'You'll be in DCI Conn's custody for the journey. This is still his case. But I wanted to ask you something before you go.'

Roberta waited, still smiling.

'Did you kill your daughter?'

She felt the smile leave her mouth like dust blown from glass. Closed her eyes, opened them again, stared at the fluorescent light above her.

'Yes, I did,' she said.

A crackle went through the room, a lightning arc between the men, but not between Flanagan and Roberta. There were no

333

secrets between them; perhaps there had never been, right from the start.

'Tell me,' Flanagan said.

'Do you really want to know?'

'No, I don't. Tell me anyway.'

Roberta took a breath, turned her eyes to Flanagan, and began.

'The pregnancy was unplanned. I never wanted a child. I had everything I wanted. What did I need a baby for? Harry knew I was pregnant before I did. He said I'd changed, something was different. My period was late, but I didn't think it was that, not a baby. I ignored him, and another week went by with no period, then another. Then he brought home one of those testing sticks. And there it was, a little blue cross.

'If I could have, I would have got rid of it. Flown to England, if I had to. But there was no way to get past Harry. He was so happy. He'd told everyone almost as soon as the test was done, so there was no getting out of it, unless I had some sort of accident. And I did try. All I did was make myself sick.

'Then the baby came – I had a Caesarean – and everyone around us was so delighted and all I wanted to do was throw it out of a window. But I played my part. I fed it, I looked after it, and it grew. I suppose I liked it well enough, but what about me? It was constant, not a second to breathe. My life had gone. Harry was no use, he thought it was a woman's job to look after it. He just played with it now and again. And his brother and that horrible little wife of his, always hanging around. I hadn't worked so hard for this life to lose it to a baby. I stood it for almost two years, two years of my life soaked up by this little creature that wasn't even really mine.'

334

Flanagan cocked her head to the side. 'Not yours?'

'Who gave birth to it? Was it really me? It never felt like it came from my body, even after they cut it out of me. Anyway, I persuaded Harry to take a week off work and take us to Barcelona. We rented an apartment in Poblenou. Do you know Barcelona?'

Flanagan shook her head.

'It's beautiful in Poblenou, not so many tourists. Our apartment was on the Rambla there, just a stone's throw from the beach. Every evening when Harry went to sleep, and the baby, I went and sat out on the balcony and just watched people pass by. It was lovely.

'Then one day the three of us went to the beach. Harry didn't want to go in the water, so I left the baby with him and went swimming by myself. I'm a good swimmer, did you know? I always have been. When I came out, Harry asked me, why don't you take the baby in for a while? It had one of those special nappies on, the ones for swimming. So I carried it out, up to my waist, then a bit further.

'I remember it was shivering, saying cold, cold. So I walked out a bit further, till the water was up to my chest. That lovely feeling when the waves lift you off your feet. Then a bit further again, and I felt the drop beneath my feet. Not much, but enough that I couldn't stand with my head above water.

'You know, I didn't plan anything. It's not like I set out to do it. I remember suddenly seeing it, all those years stretched out in front of me, raising it, sending it to school, all the times it would get sick, and I'd have to clean it up, years and years before I could get my life back. So I knew what to do.'

335

A pause, then in a very small voice, Flanagan asked, 'What did you do?'

'I held it under. One hand on the back of its neck, paddling with the other, kicking with my feet. It was hard to do. Physically, I mean. I struggled to keep my mouth and nose out of the water. I started to get a little afraid, especially when it started thrashing around. Then it stopped, and I let go.'

Roberta remembered the sensation of floating in the water, lifted and dropped by the waves, her right hand beneath the surface, so terribly empty. A few seconds of elation.

'And then I realised what I'd done,' she said. 'I realised I shouldn't have. I wanted to take it back. I thought maybe I could save it. I suppose I panicked a little. So I dived under with my eyes open – you can keep your eyes open in seawater, it doesn't hurt – and I could just make it out, drifting near the bottom. I swam down and tried to get hold of it, but I needed air, so I had to go back up. That was when I called for help. I went under again, but it had drifted further away, and I had to stay under longer. I breathed water. It hurt. Everything went black. Next thing I remember is lying in the sand, vomiting salt water. And that's all.'

Quiet for a long time, not even the sound of breathing. Roberta wondered if she should have felt some sort of relief from telling it all, but there was none. Same as before. A hollow place where she supposed her guilt should have been.

Eventually, Flanagan slid off the bed, stood upright, and said, 'Okay, let's go. Get up.'

Roberta reached out her left hand. 'Please.'

Flanagan took her hand, helped her sit upright. Then Roberta lowered her feet to the floor, straightened, and faced the policewoman. It hadn't occurred to her before now, but she stood a good couple of inches taller than Flanagan. The policewoman seemed so small now, so tired.

When Roberta opened her mouth to say she hoped Flanagan would get some rest, the fist shot up, caught the underside of her jaw, and the floor tilted beneath her feet. She fell back on the bed, her mouth filling with blood from the bite in her tongue. Then Flanagan's hand was on her throat, the policewoman's weight on her chest, and the pain, oh the pain.

'It was a she,' Flanagan said, her teeth flashing. 'Her name was Erin.'

Roberta wanted to scream, but she couldn't draw breath, and pressure swelled in her head as the fingers tightened beneath her jaw. Flanagan's nose inches from hers, Roberta saw her mouth work, the lips part, then felt the hot saliva as Flanagan spat in her face.

Murray grabbed Flanagan by the shoulders, pulled her away, the hand slipping from Roberta's throat.

60

Alistair slipped a hand around Flanagan's waist, and they leaned into each other as the waiter led them to the restaurant's back room. Deep and rich aromas drifted through the place, turmeric, cardamom, garlic, fresh baked bread. Diners ate tandoori chicken, bhunas, saags. The sights and smells made Flanagan's stomach growl, the first real appetite she had felt in almost two weeks.

She had called Miriam McCreesh that morning, and they'd had a long talk. Flanagan had apologised at least three times for not being in touch, but McCreesh had brushed it off each time. She knew the demands of this life. After the call, Flanagan had locked her office door and kneeled beneath the window. She prayed thanks for her blessings, for her family, for her own health, and for Reverend Peter McKay's soul. A female minister from the north-east coast had given a statement, said she'd met McKay on the beach at Cushendun. They'd talked about faith and prayer, and Flanagan hoped it had done McKay some good.

Flanagan took a half day, went home at two o'clock, and luxuriated in the rituals of getting ready to go out. It seemed an age since she and Alistair had gone anywhere as a couple, so long a time that she didn't dare count the months.

They arrived early, and DSI Purdy and his wife were the only ones waiting in the private room. Purdy already had an empty bottle of Cobra beer in front of him, and was working on the second, his arm draped around his wife's shoulder.

He stood as Flanagan and Alistair entered. He shook Alistair's hand, then wrapped his arms around Flanagan, tight, squeezing the air out of her.

'Thanks for coming, love,' he said before planting a kiss on her cheek.

'Love?' Flanagan said, leaning back.

He grinned. 'As of five o'clock this evening, I am no longer your boss, and I can call you love if I want. And I can give you a kiss if I want, so here's another one.'

She giggled and accepted the gesture, smelled the booze on him. 'Jesus, when did you start?'

'One minute past five,' he said, his smile beaming. Flanagan couldn't help but reflect it back to him.

They took their seats, Purdy insisting that Flanagan sit beside him. His wife didn't seem to mind; she was every bit as merry as her husband.

'She's confessed everything,' he said.

Flanagan didn't need to ask whom he meant. 'Her husband? And Reverend McKay?'

'That's right,' Purdy said. 'She started an affair with McKay not long after the husband had the car accident. He was weak, and she knew she could manipulate him. She convinced him to slip Mr Garrick the overdose, thinking she could break it off with him after and he'd be too scared to say anything. But you messed it up for her, talking to McKay the way you did. He was ready to tell you everything, so she did him in.'

Flanagan pictured the last time she'd seen McKay, watching her drive away from the church, the look of a lost and desperate man. A man who would still be alive if she'd only gone to him when he asked.

'I know what you're thinking,' Purdy said. 'Stop it. You'd no way of knowing what was going to happen. Roberta Gar— sorry, Hannah Mackenzie killed that man. It was nobody's fault but hers. If you keep thinking different, you'll tear yourself to pieces.'

Flanagan shook her head. 'I know, but I—'

'Stop it,' Purdy said. 'That's an order.'

She allowed him a hint of a smile. 'I thought you weren't my boss any more.'

'I came out of retirement, there, just for a minute.'

The room began to fill, and Purdy's attention turned to the other guests. Alistair wrapped his fingers around Flanagan's. With his free hand, he adjusted her hair, hid the cluster of stitches and the coin-sized shaved patch. She kissed him for the kindness of the gesture.

Food came and went, beer and wine, stories told and retold.

Amid the chatter, Flanagan put her arm around her husband, brought her lips to his ear and said, 'We're going to be all right, aren't we?'

Alistair kissed her neck, sending sparks down her spine. His breath warm on her ear as he said, 'Yes, we are.'

Acknowledgements

I am indebted to all who have helped me get this story out of my head and onto the page:

My agents Nat Sobel and Judith Weber who help me navigate these often-turbulent waters, and all at Sobel Weber Associates. And also Caspian Dennis, who listens to me moan more than anyone should have to, and all at Abner Stein.

My editors Geoff Mulligan, Alison Hennessey and Juliet Grames, who help turn my sow's ears into something resembling silk purses. And all at Vintage Books and Soho Press, especially Bronwen Hruska and Paul Oliver.

A special thank you to Canon John McKegney. This novel began life as a short story written for radio, and John's kind words about that piece helped encourage me to expand it into a book. Later on, John kindly provided me with tremendous insights into the workings of a church and the life of a clergyman. Any inaccuracies in the depiction are entirely mine.

I am deeply grateful to my local libraries for providing a quiet haven in which to write, and to all the bookstores who continue to fight the good fight. And to my friends in all corners of the crime fiction community.

Thanks to my friends and wider family for the constant support; it's always appreciated.

Finally, and most of all, I owe this book and my remaining sanity to my family: Issy and Ezra, and especially Jo, who has given me so much time and space and support, even when I least deserved it, and also proved an invaluable sounding board.